I could not come

I am a realist. I don't believe in fantasies, reincarnation, or even fortune telling, none of that mystic or voodoo stuff. Therefore, it was very difficult for me to comprehend what was going on. In order for me to believe, I would have to throw out all my preconceived ideas about life and death. I always thought that a person is born; he lives; he dies. Once his body is buried in the ground, or he is cremated and scattered where his relatives decide to dispose of him, then that is the end of him. Kaput. Nil. Zilch. That is my dilemma. I would have to throw these beliefs aside to make room for an altogether different mindset, one that placed Avery Archer and me somewhere near the same physical location but separated from each other by sixty-seven years, yet being able to communicate with one another. Not only were we separated by time, but also Avery was dead and I was alive. How is that for a mind-boggling exercise? Would anyone blame me for being doubtful? I was simply not quite ready to give up my reality.

TO PAM,

Your grandma loves you,

Let Freedom Ring

by

June Summers
and
Wendelin Saunders

Let Freedom Ring

Cover Art by *Kristian Norris*

The Wild Rose Press, Inc.
PO Box 708
Adams Basin, NY 14410-0708
Visit us at www.thewildrosepress.com

Publishing History
First Mainstream Historical Edition, 2016
Print ISBN 978-1-5092-0834-0
Digital ISBN 978-1-5092-0835-7

Published in the United States of America

Dedications

In memory of Wendy.
No other footprints on this earth will ever match yours.
~*~
To Greg, my very first reader.
~*~
To Ron, thanks for the help.

Chapter One

Thursday, June 25, 1998

I'm a lousy cook. I'm hoping Beth is better than I am. Most of the time, I rely on such culinary delights as Stouffers frozen dinners to keep me healthy. They're quick, quasi-nutritious, and best of all, easy to prepare. I just pop them in the microwave for five minutes, and I have a healthy, well-balanced meal. I won't mention their salt and fat content.

I was putting one such succulent meal into the microwave that evening about seven-thirty when the telephone rang. I picked up the phone, expecting to hear Beth's melodic voice. Instead, I heard a faint, muffled voice that sounded like someone with a mouth full of marbles or a kid trying to disguise the way he talked.

"Daddy? Is that you? Please, Daddy, come and get me! Oh! They're coming!"

Click. Abruptly, the caller hung up the telephone.

Kids! They always have to be doing something mischievous. I continued with my cooking skills by taking my delicious chicken dinner out of the microwave, thinking nothing more of the telephone call.

After dinner, I relaxed on the couch with my shoes off and feet propped up, watching television with my dog, Spree, beside me.

Spree is a dark brown Labrador mix that followed me home from the Seven-Eleven a few months ago. She came up to me while I was on Shell Lane, and I stopped to pet her. That's my normal gesture when a friendly dog approaches me. What a mistake it was to pet this Lab! I later learned the sheriff evicted her former owners from their home. They decided not to take Spree with them when they skipped out in the middle of the night. When Eddie, my older brother, and I were kids, we always had a dog. So how could I look into this sad-eyed dog's face and refuse to take her home with me? She's a good dog. Most of the time.

Beth is not sure how she will handle Spree, and I have misgivings about how Spree will handle Beth. I envision these two brunettes in my life in competition for my affection. I guess I'm a lucky guy.

I was about to call Beth when the telephone rang again. It was the same kid or person as before.

"Daddy, is that you? I'm really scared!"

"Who is this?" I asked, not recognizing the voice.

"Please come get me, Daddy. I want to come home." The voice sounded as if the person was crying softly.

"Who are you?" I was rather irritated by then.

Click.

This person's childish game was annoying me. Didn't he have anything better to do than to harass tired, working people who liked to relax in the evening? I reminded myself that I had been a kid once and had played similar pranks on the telephone. I fleetingly thought about what the kid had said, and although I didn't appreciate his type of humor, I chalked it up to some kid prank when the phone rang a third time. This time it was Beth calling from Chicago.

"Guy, whatcha up to?" she asked in that sweet, lilting voice of hers.

"Watching a rerun of *Home Improvement*. I need to hone up on my skills from Tim Taylor."

"Oh, yeah," chided Beth. "He *is* your hero."

"Yep. Not only can he fix anything that's broken, but he is such an understanding husband."

"I think you meant to say 'break anything that's fixed', didn't you? And as far as being understanding, Jill Taylor gets more understanding from a book than from Tim."

I retorted as if I were offended, "You can be really hard on a guy. Do I have this to look forward to for the rest of my life?"

"Suit yourself."

Beth then inquired, "What's on the agenda for the evening? Do you have a hot date or a wild party to go to?"

My name is Kenneth Patrick Driscoll. Dad had insisted on naming me after the patron saint of Ireland, but Mom refused to give me "Patrick" as a first name, claiming there were too many Irish Patrick's in the United States. Beth usually calls me "guy." Actually, I think it's cute and affectionate, thus she gets no objections from me. I don't really have any pet name for her, other than the usual, like "sweetheart" or "honey." She hates when I call her "babe." It reminds her of a mobster from the Prohibition Era calling his girlfriend his moll or his chippie. So unless I want to tease her and take the punishment resulting from that teasing, I avoid the "babe" term of endearment.

"Right." I responded to her hot date/party question.

"As if I don't have enough problems with you and Spree that I would inflict more pain on myself by becoming involved with another female."

We often banter back and forth like that on the telephone. Otherwise, we would be so melancholy about our situation that one of us would probably end up crying. It would definitely be Beth, since *real* men don't cry. I haven't seen Beth since coming to Florida in March.

"I spent most of my lunch hour on the phone trying to get a D.J.," she said. "It seems D.J. Dave won't be available for the wedding reception. He accepted a job in Los Angeles. Fine time to let me know."

"Did you have any luck finding someone else?"

"I think I'll be able to book this D.J. called Rockin' Robin. There's only one problem. He is a *she*. You won't have any issues with that, mister male chauvinist, will you?"

"Hey, I'm no sexist." I countered as if I were offended.

She always accuses me of being a little chauvinistic. I don't understand why. I just have a few distinctive ideas. For instance, a male should always drive the car when in the company of one or more females. In addition, he should never sit in the back seat if females are in the group. Or he should never do dishes if a female is available for that task. Now, would you call that being chauvinistic, men?

"Right. Haven't I heard that before?" I heard a chuckle in her voice.

Then she turned serious again. "Really, guy, would a female D.J. be a problem for you?"

"Listen, sweetheart, I won't care who is playing the

4

music. I have other plans for you during and after the reception, and it doesn't involve music at all."

"Ken! You're making me blush."

I knew I'd get a rise out of her with that remark. "Oh, yeah! Are you covering your beguiling, blue eyes in that cute, adorable way that you do? Damn! I wish I could see you."

Beth is actually beautiful. She has chestnut brown, shiny, shoulder length hair that cascades flawlessly around her high cheekbones, framing her perfectly oval face in a gorgeous manner. Her light, powder blue eyes twinkle like iridescent moonbeams. She also has a petite, yet voluptuous figure that most females envy (as well as males when they see me with her). Her figure comes naturally. She doesn't work out much, maybe walking a few times a week, but nothing strenuous.

"I sure miss you. You did get three weeks off for the wedding, didn't you?" she asked.

"Yep. Kincaid signed my vacation slip last week. We got a new client this week, and my job is to organize their paperwork. They also need last year's tax return done, but all that should be completed by October. Besides, Kincaid told me to take as much time as I needed. His words were, 'You only get married once.' So, young lady, looks like you'll be stuck with me from October to forever."

Of course, I didn't tell Beth that Kincaid was currently on his third marriage.

"I don't consider that much of a punishment. You might even say I'm looking forward to it just a little."

Abruptly, Beth changed the subject. "Oh, I forgot. Rachel called me last night. She's pregnant. Isn't that great? She can still be in the wedding because she isn't due until January. I'm so happy for her."

Rachel is Beth's older sister by two years. They are and always have been very close.

"When you talk to Rachel, wish her luck for me. I don't care if she is as big as a house; she has to be your maid of honor."

"Oh, oh, gotta go," she said suddenly. "Mom is calling. Talk to you later. Love ya."

"Bye, sweetheart," I said as she hung up.

I really don't know why Beth fell in love with me. They say that people are first attracted to one another because of looks, which was the case for me. However, I truly don't know what Beth saw in me. Don't get me wrong. I don't look like Freddie Krueger, but I'm no Tom Cruise either. Beth tells me I'm a cross between Kevin Bacon and a young Robert DeNiro, rugged like DeNiro, but boyish like Bacon. My skin tone has that typical, ruddy, Irish complexion that inevitably burns just by thinking of the sun. My hair is muddy, reddish brown, and very uncontrollable. I keep it exceptionally short so I don't have to try taming it against its will. Beth wants me to grow it longer for the wedding. I keep telling her that if I did, I'd probably scare our entire wedding guests out of the church.

After talking to Beth, I'm always sorry I moved to Florida without her. We had hoped that we could've moved together, but things didn't work out that way. When Beth and I decided we wanted to settle in Florida, I had flown down to find an accounting position. Kincaid & Company hired me after my first interview. They wanted me to start work the next week, which didn't allow much time for planning a move together. After several discussions, we decided that I'd be settled, and she'd join me after the wedding.

Beth has already given her notice at the insurance company where she works in Chicago. We bought a three bedroom/two bathroom house in Nawinah, Florida, outside of Orlando. It's not a big place, but plenty of space for us. And Spree, of course. I needed somewhere to crash while I was here waiting for her arrival. Since we were already making wedding plans, we decided it would be prudent to find a place for both of us.

I usually get to bed after the ten o'clock news. I like to get into the office before everyone else to relax with a cup of coffee and a bagel before I start looking at any client's work. Being the newest employee, I'm still learning how the firm operates. So some of the time is spent getting used to new procedures and protocol.

After the news, I let Spree outside to do her business and then took a quick shower. It was about eleven o'clock by then. As I was turning down my bedspread, the telephone rang again.

"Daddy, why aren't you coming to get me? I don't want to be here. Ohh…"

Again, the caller abruptly hung up.

I was getting very irritated. Was this creep going to keep me awake all night? I crawled into bed and was asleep almost immediately.

Chapter Two

Friday, June 26, 1998

I was having this fabulous dream about lying with Beth on a sandy beach late at night under a full moon and a sky filled with brilliant stars. The glow of the moon reflected in the droplets of water on her face, glistening like diamonds. She was snuggled up against me so close that a sheet of paper couldn't fit between us.

Around her neck, she wore the gold necklace I'd bought for her birthday. It's made up of a string of very tiny, gold bells. When I pulled her close, the little bells softly tinkled. I thought those little bells were tinkling when it was actually the telephone ringing on my nightstand.

I turned over, grabbed the phone, and answered incoherently. "Aagghh, hullo."

Again, it was the voice of that kid. He talked in such a hushed tone I had to listen very closely to hear him, which is extremely difficult when rudely awakened from a dream-filled, deep sleep.

"Daddy? Where are you? It's really dark. I'm so hungry. They won't give me anything to eat. Please, please come and get me."

I looked at the clock and scowled. "Do you know it's two in the morning? What's wrong with you? Leave me alone."

This was nonsense. Let him play his stupid games on someone else, so I hung up. It was my turn to be rude. I had to go to work in the morning. I only hoped that I could fall back to sleep again.

Just as I was about to drift off to sleep, the phone rang again.

"Please, Daddy, don't be mad. I'm sorry I went into the woods. I'll never do it again."

I was getting very exasperated.

"Who the hell are you? Who are you trying to call? I'm not your dad. Now, can you please bother somebody else?"

There was hesitation on the other end. I heard what sounded like sighs, or maybe they were sobs. It was hard to tell.

Finally, he said, "Where is my dad?"

"How the hell do I know where your dad is? I don't even know *who* your dad is."

The kid timidly responded so quietly that I could barely hear him, still sighing or sobbing. "He's Samuel Archer."

"Well, there's nobody here by that name. What number are you trying to call?" I calmed down somewhat.

"790R"

"What? 790R? What kind of number is that? I asked you for the telephone number, not the apartment number."

"That *is* the telephone number." The kid sounded confused.

"Listen, kid, you said, '790R.' That's an impossible telephone number."

"I…I…don't understand. Th…That is my father's telephone number."

I grabbed a pencil and paper from the nightstand. "Okay, tell me the number again."

"790R."

I wrote down the number as he said it. "Kid, like I said, that's three numbers and a letter. What are the other numbers? There should be seven numbers, no letters."

"But I don't understand what you're saying, mister." It sounded as if he were on the verge of breaking into a heavy crying jag.

Then abruptly he hung up again.

I tossed and turned for the rest of the night. I kept hearing his pleading voice and having second thoughts about my original evaluation of the calls. Were they really prank calls? Or could the kid be in some serious trouble? Just maybe the calls were legit. Eventually, though, I drifted back to the beach with Beth, a much more pleasant experience.

When the phone rang the next morning, Beth had disappeared, and I was just in my private sleep world. This time I thought it was the alarm clock. I even reached over to turn it off before I realized it was the phone. I looked at the clock; it was five-forty-five. When I finally picked up the phone, I heard the same kid's whinny voice again.

"Please! Please! Get my dad! Please!"

My voice was very stern, but I needed answers. "Okay, kid, you keep waking me up. Tell me again. Who is your dad? What is your name?"

"My name is Avery Archer, and my dad is Samuel Archer. My mom is Esther Archer. I am eleven years old. We live at 1201 Scruffsdale Road in Winter Park, Florida. My telephone number is 790R." He spoke as if he were somberly reciting the Pledge of Allegiance, yet with firm conviction.

"Okay, Avery, so you live on Scruffsdale Road. Once again, this phone number thing. It's weird. You have to have seven numbers in your phone number."

"No, mister! There's only three numbers. I don't know any seven numbers. It's 790R!" He was becoming very emotional and defensive.

"All right, Avery, if that's really your name. If we can't make any headway with your dad's telephone number, from what number are you calling?"

"I...I...don't know. They just brought me here yesterday. Mister, will you please find my dad? I don't know what to do."

The kid's voice had some quality that made me think he might actually be telling the truth. I decided to hear him out.

"Okay, calm down. I'll try to help you. Do you know where you are? Who brought you there?"

"Nooo, I don't know where I am. They blindfolded me in the woods. Then they dragged me to a truck and threw me in the back of it. One of them held me down in the back while the other one drove. It was very bumpy, and the man kept pushing my face down on the truck. My cheek is scraped and sore. Mister, it's very dark here. Oh! Oh! They're coming. I have to hang up."

Click.

Nervously, I thought about the calls. Suppose this kid was in real danger. If it were a prank, he was carrying it way too far; but something in his voice made me think it was real. What could I do? I couldn't make any sense out of his telephone number. So how could I call 911 and get him any help?

Then I had a brilliant idea. I pressed *69, which would bring up the number of the most recent call made to me. As the phone was ringing, I thought to myself, "You smart bastard! You missed your calling. You should have been a detective."

As all this was going through my mind, someone answered on the other end.

"Hullo," said a very sleepy voice.

"Beth? Is that you?" I was so surprised that I almost dropped the phone.

"Of course, it's me. What time is it? Oh, Ken! It's five in the morning. (Chicago is on Central Daylight Time.) Why are you calling me so early?"

What was going on? I was bewildered! "Beth, did you just call me?"

"No, stupid! You called me!"

She hadn't a clue what I was talking about, and at five in the morning I didn't feel it was the appropriate time to explain the situation in detail. So I shortened the version.

"I'm really sorry I woke you. Some kid has been calling me and hanging up. I'm not sure if they are prank calls or if he is serious."

"Huh?" Obviously, she was still half-asleep. Maybe she was dreaming about being on the beach with me.

"Anyhow, I'll be brief. I know you're not fully awake yet. After the last time this kid called, I pressed *69, and the phone dialed your number. I know it sounds crazy, and I know you aren't coherent enough to assist me, so I'll talk to you tonight. Sorry, I didn't mean to wake you. Love ya,"

"Mmm, ditto." She hung up.

When she finally did wake up, she'd be thoroughly confused. She probably would wonder if my phone call had all been a dream. She's really a sound sleeper.

Beth and I first met six years ago at Northwestern University. The rain was pouring down, and the wind was very blustery. My next class was halfway across the campus. As I ventured out into the weather, Beth stood directly in front of me, struggling to open this gigantic, red umbrella.

"Here, let me help you with that." I approached from behind and took her umbrella, opening it, and snuggling beneath it next to her. At first, she didn't say anything, simply glancing over her shoulder, giving me a weird look as we both swiftly walked on through the heavy downpour.

I asked, "What's your name? Where's your next class?"

Looking straight ahead, she said, "Beth Nelson. Beasley Hall."

"Great, Beth Nelson. That's where I'm headed too."

Each time she turned to look at me, I got a better look at her and realized she was a real beauty. However, there was something else—something about her. I knew in that instant she'd be very special to me.

When we reached Beasley Hall, I gently grabbed her arm. "Wait! Will you go out with me Friday night?"

She hesitated then said, "Yes."

That was it. Since we met, neither of us have had any desire to be with anybody else of the opposite sex, or for that matter, the same sex. We saw each other exclusively from that first rainy meeting to this very day.

Now we are planning our wedding for October 15 in Chicago. I feel a little guilty leaving her to do most of the wedding plans while I'm here in Florida. I'm thankful her mother and sister are able to help.

After Beth hung up, I thought about the calls I was getting from this kid. Deep down, I hoped they were prank calls. I didn't need to get involved in somebody else's problems. I was too busy with my own—the new job, my new house, and getting ready for our wedding. But this kid would not get out of my mind.

I couldn't get back to sleep, so I shut off the alarm before it rang. I detest the sound of that clock ringing. I hope Beth will do the honors of awakening me in the morning. That's a female thing too, though it is unlikely she will be the one to awaken quite readily, as was demonstrated from our most recent telephone conversation.

My ritual used to be to take a shower, brush the teeth, shave, and get out the door. Since moving in, Spree has made other plans for me. The house has a small, fenced back yard. The rest of the back yard butts up to Lake Ripple with a gate in the fence leading to the shoreline of the lake. A huge, willow tree takes up most of my yard within the fence close to the lake. Spree is not happy about leaving her morning excrement in this fenced area. For that matter, I don't like piles of shit building up like cow paddies either. And I'm not adept with using the pooper-scooper, by choice, of course. I guess that's another job for Beth.

Actually, Spree and I both prefer to walk along the lake in the back of the subdivision. It's a picturesque lake, not very big, but a great place for Spree to run without fear of going into the street. The other homes on the lake have fences to keep her out of their yards also. The subdivision is on one side of the lake, perhaps twenty homes or so. That allows plenty of room for her to romp and play.

On the other side of the lake is a grand, old home currently under renovation. I'm not much into architectural styles, but on both sides of this house are magnificent, cylindrical, silo-like towers capped with large, cone shaped roofs. I read an article in the local paper about the house's restoration. It stated that Vladimir Kouprianov, a landowner who emigrated with his family from Russia, originally built the house in 1890. His family had owned it for many years. However, back in the 1950s, the grandson, who was the last Kouprianov to live in the house, moved to California and gave the house to the village of Nawinah. They used it as a community center for several years but never did much in the way of repairs on the old place. The article had stated the new board of commissioners decided to restore the house and eventually open it as a museum. The workers have been steadily refurbishing it since I moved in my house. I bet it was one of the finest homes in the area when it was first built.

In the back of this majestic home is a gazebo at the end of the dock jutting into the lake. Spree and I are planning to walk over to the other side of the lake someday to get a better look at the house and the gazebo.

Spree usually takes a short swim in the lake water. That's the Lab in her. She tries to swim after the ducks and geese, but they always manage to evade her reach. She comes out of the water dripping wet. Obviously, I've learned to take her on these walks *before* my shower.

That Friday morning while I was walking her along Lake Ripple, I couldn't get the phone calls from the kid out of my mind. I didn't once think about problems at work or problems with the wedding plans. I hate to admit this, but I didn't even think about Beth. I kept hearing the kid's voice, pleading for help.

Spree did her usual doggie things, and we made our way back to my house where I fed her, gave her fresh water, and took my shower.

Spree had not been a good dog when she had followed me home a few months ago. That first night she behaved well because she was so hungry and tired. Four hot dogs had been the extent of the food in the house, which she ate without taking time to breathe. Then she slept throughout the entire night, snuggled up against the wall in the hallway outside my bedroom. No accidents. No barking. No chewing. No problems. Good dog.

All that changed the next day and night. I'd planned to search for her owner after work, not knowing of her abandonment at that time. Meanwhile, I'd left her in the house when I'd gone to work. I hadn't trusted her in the backyard, the fence being only four feet high and no place for shelter from the Florida sun. I guess I was so naïve that I thought she'd behave herself as she'd done the night before. All the dogs that Eddie and I had as kids, Mom did the dirty work of house training them.

When I arrived home from work that evening, I

couldn't believe the damage this one dog had done. Dog shit and piss occupied every room of the house. She also chewed everything she could find, from my Italian sandals I had left under the bed to the nightlight plugged into a living room outlet. When it was time for bed, she would bark incessantly. If I put her outside, she not only would bark but also would howl as if I were torturing her. I was a little afraid my neighbors might call the police or the humane society.

This went on for several days and nights, but pushover that I am for gorgeous females with dark brown hair, I persevered. After a week of this craziness, I took her to discipline classes. Finally, after six hundred dollars and countless hours of "heal, sit, down, stay, and come," she has some resemblance to a civilized dog.

Was it worth it? Well, she's been my companion in a strange town with no human, dark-brown-haired female to keep me company. Besides, when she looks at me with those big, brown eyes, she knows she's here to stay.

I accomplished my shower that morning as quickly as possible. It is lucky my hair is so short, for I completely forgot about combing it. With my thoughts going in so many different directions, I was actually about ten minutes late leaving the house.

I live in Nawinah, a town to the west of Orlando, and I work in Longwood on the north side of Orlando. I encounter the intersection of Routes 434 and 436 on my way to and from work. I have waited at that intersection through five changes of the traffic light. Once the traffic was backed up for four miles.

On that Friday, I didn't notice how many times the

light changed at the intersection, nor how much of a backup there was. My mind was on that Avery kid. I usually listen to a soft rock station on the radio while I accompany the tunes with my fabulous singing voice. I could hear neither the music nor the D.J. chatter that morning. And I didn't drown out the radio with my singing. I could only hear the sound of that kid pleading for my help. As many times as I played it back in my head, I could not decide if he was playing a prank or in serious trouble.

The accounting firm of Kincaid & Company occupies the ground floor of the building where I work. Three separate suites occupy the second floor—a consulting service, an insurance agent, and a sales representative. Usually the first person from the accounting office that arrives opens up the front lobby. I got to work at seven forty-five. Eric Ferguson had arrived before me and had unlocked the building.

"Hey Eric, what brings you in before eight this morning?"

Eric is usually late for work. Mister Kincaid is not aware of this since he comes in after Eric. Eric does a hell of a job, and it's none of my business what time he gets to work.

"Would you believe I'm turning over a new leaf?" Eric answered.

"No, I would not believe. Did your girlfriend kick you out of your apartment again?"

"Ye are a very astute young man, Kenneth Driscoll."

"What did you say to her this time? Last time you complimented her by telling her that her breath smelled like Pine Sol. Some compliment," I advised.

"Well, I meant that it smelled fresh. Shit! How was I to know she'd be offended?"

"Eric, you've got to learn to be a little more diplomatic," I scolded.

"Yeah, you're right."

"Sooo? What happened this time?" I asked.

"I just told her that she should wear her hair different to hide her ears. Jeez, she's so sensitive. Guess I'll have to pick up some flowers again on my way home tonight. I seem to be keeping that florist in business." Eric shook his head in disappointment.

"That's a wise decision. An apology wouldn't hurt either, but be careful how you apologize. You have a tendency to put your foot in your mouth too often, even with apologies," I said as if I were an authority on giving advice.

"These relationships are very difficult for me. How do you and Beth handle it?"

"I don't know. It just comes naturally." I'm sure Beth would agree.

"Someday maybe I'll be so lucky," he brooded.

"I doubt it."

We then both went to our individual offices. I contemplated telling Eric about the phone calls from Avery, but I changed my mind. He seemed to have enough to deal with that morning.

Eric and I have become good buddies in the few months I've been at Kincaid & Company. We often stop for a beer after work. He has told me all about his girlfriend, Melanie. I haven't met her yet, but I'm sure once Beth got down here, we'd hang out with them.

I knew I wouldn't be able to concentrate on work until I first made an attempt at finding out about the telephone number that the boy had given me. My plan was to call the telephone company and tell them about the *69 incident. I hoped they could tell me why I got Beth instead of the boy when I dialed the *69. I punched in the telephone company's number on my phone and got a recorded message that I had to wade through.

"If you have a touch-tone phone, press one now. If you wish to hear the message in English, press two."

After several other choices, I then pressed nine to talk to a service representative.

"Good morning. This is Tanisha. How can I direct your call?"

"Oh!" I responded, a little bewildered. "I thought I was going to talk to you."

"Sir, I can connect you to your party. What is the extension?"

"I don't know the extension?" How was I supposed to know this?

"Sir, to whom do you wish to speak?"

"I don't know." I didn't know who worked at the telephone company. That was her job.

"Sir, what is the nature of your call?"

"I'd like to talk to someone about a problem I am having."

"Sir, what is the nature of your problem?"

"Well, that is what I wanted to talk to someone about." What kind of a game was she trying to play?

"Sir, if you will tell me to whom you wish to speak, I will connect you."

"I don't know to whom I wish to speak. I'd just like to talk to someone about my problem."

"Sir, what is the nature of your problem?"

I was getting frustrated.

"*69."

"Sir, did you say *69?"

"Yes, I did."

"Sir, you dial that code on your telephone if you wish to determine the last party from whom you received a call. There is a seventy-five cent charge for the service each time you use it."

"I know all that. My *69 is not working correctly." I tried to explain.

"Sir, that is impossible. That code works throughout the telephone system over the entire country. It has nothing to do with your individual phone set."

"Well, it may work throughout the entire country, but it is not working on my telephone."

"Let me connect you to a service representative."

"Good! That's exactly what I wanted five minutes ago," I said in a very frustrated voice.

I waited on the line for about two minutes, listening to some wordless music. Then another recording came on the line.

"All of our representatives are busy at this time. Your call is very important to us. Please stay on the line, and the next available representative will assist you as soon as possible. Your approximate wait time is two minutes."

Again, the wordless music channeled into my eardrum.

Thirty seconds later.

"Your approximate wait time is two minutes."

It seemed like every thirty seconds I heard the same message. "Your approximate wait time is two minutes."

Two more minutes went by.

"All of our representatives are busy. Your call is very important to us. Please stay on the line, and the next available representative will assist you as soon as possible."

If this is how they treat "important phone calls," I wonder what occurs when a call is unimportant.

Finally, a live person came on the line.

"This is Linda. How can I help you?"

"It's nice to hear your voice, Linda. I've been waiting quite a long time to hear it."

"I am sorry, sir, but we are very busy. I hope you were not inconvenienced."

"I'll get over it if you can help me with a problem I'm having on my home telephone. Not that I want to tell you about my love life, but my girlfriend called me from Chicago last night around seven-thirty. We talked for about twenty minutes. Shortly after I hung up, I received several telephone calls of a strange nature from a person I don't know. After these calls, I dialed *69 to determine the source of the calls. To my surprise I got my girlfriend in Chicago."

Linda asked, "Did you ask her if she had called you?"

"Yes, I did, but I knew she didn't call. First, I would recognize her voice. Second, it was five in the morning Chicago time. There is no way she would call me at that time."

"Could someone else have called from her residence?"

I was a little indignant with that suggestion and snapped a little too hastily. "That is very unlikely. She lives alone, and we are engaged to be married."

"I don't mean to pry into your affairs, sir, but *69 will inform you of the immediately preceding telephone call before you dialed *69."

"I know that. That's exactly what I'm telling you. Her call was at seven-thirty last night. I had at least three calls after that one from this stranger."

"Are you sure no one else in her house would be making the calls?"

"She lives alone. She'd better be alone at five in the morning!"

"Then I'm afraid I can't help you. The system is such that only the preceding number will be connected upon dialing *69. I've never heard of any incident contrary to this. The only thing I can suggest is to send you a printout of all the telephone calls to your number on that particular day. You can then verify what calls you had received."

This was crazy! What good is modern technology?

"Okay, Linda," I said with resignation. "Could you give me a printout of all calls on Thursday, June 25, and this morning, June 26, up till now?"

"Yes, that is possible. What is your name and the telephone number on which you would like me to run the query?"

I gave her my name, address, telephone number, and the last four digits of my social security number.

"Thank you, sir. I'm sorry we couldn't be of more assistance. I'll put this in the mail today. You should receive it by Monday. Is there anything else we can do for you? Perhaps you'd like to order Caller ID on your telephone as a permanent feature. The cost is only seven dollars and fifty cents per month. If you order today, you'll get a free Caller ID Display Unit valued at forty-nine ninety-five, plus free activation. I'd be glad to take care of that for you at this time."

Quickly, I answered, "No, you've done enough. I have a feeling it wouldn't work either. Thank you for your *help* (said a bit sarcastically). I'll be looking forward to receiving that printout."

"If you change your mind, Mister Driscoll, you can call 1-800-CALLNOW from eight in the morning to nine at night to sign up."

"Thank you. I'll keep that in mind."

What an unproductive effort that was. I hoped the printout would provide some answers.

It was then almost eight-thirty. I had just enough time to try another possible solution. The kid had said he lived on Scruffsdale Road in Winter Park. When I looked up Samuel Archer in the telephone book, I found no such name in the book. However, there was an S. Archer listed not on Scruffsdale Road as the boy mentioned but on Gralla Parkway in Orlando. And the telephone number definitely was not 790R. I tried calling the listed number anyhow. The phone rang several times. I was about to hang up when someone answered.

"Hello," said a fragile, frail voice.

"May I speak to Samuel Archer, please?"

"Did you say Samuel Archer?" asked the feeble voice.

"Yes, Samuel."

"I'm sorry, but there is no Samuel Archer at this number."

"Do you know a Samuel Archer, ma'am?"

"No, sonny, I don't. This is the residence of

Stephen and Mary Archer. I'm Gertrude Perkins, Mary's mother. I'm sorry, but Stephen has no relatives by the name of Samuel that I know. He has a brother, Duane, and a brother they call Snowy. I believe his given name is Clarence, but they both live in Maryland. Are you sure that you dialed the correct number? What number were you trying to call?"

"Well, I was trying to call your number, 555-4618, hoping it would be the home of Samuel Archer. I'm very sorry to have bothered you."

"Oh, that's all right, sonny. No bother at all. Good luck in your search. I'm very sorry I couldn't help you. If you call back after six tonight, Stephen will be home. Perhaps he could help you a little more than I could."

"Perhaps I'll do that. Thank you for your assistance."

I was at an impasse. The telephone book didn't help out, and I hadn't received any satisfaction from the telephone company either. The only thing left to do was to go to the address physically. I'd have to postpone that task until tomorrow.

Work was routine except I had a difficult time keeping my mind focused. At quitting time, Eric came into my office. "Care to stop for a beer tonight, Ken?"

"I'll pass, Eric. I've got something on my mind that I have to resolve."

"Oh, oh," he chided. "Maybe this relationship with Beth is not so perfect after all."

"No, no," I quickly answered. "Actually, this has nothing to do with Beth."

"Ah ha. Is there another love interest in the Orlando area? You, with the perfect love life?" teased Eric.

"No, this has nothing to do with any female," I swiftly retorted.

I debated with myself. Should I tell Eric about the phone calls? After all, he opened the door, didn't he?

I confessed, "It concerns a young kid."

"A young kid? Is something going on that you failed to tell me about?"

"No, there is nothing going on. Last night before and after I talked to Beth about seven-thirty, I got several phone calls from a kid who said his name was Avery Archer. First, he thought I was his father, and then he pleaded with me to get in touch with his father. He wanted his father to rescue him. He told me some men had kidnapped him. Most of the time the kid would hang up before I could get any more information out of him. He kept saying that 'they were coming.' When I asked him who 'they' were, he said he didn't know."

"Sounds to me like somebody is messing with you. You probably told them what a fool you were with that destructive dog of yours, so they thought you were a prime target for some serious ribbing," Eric advised.

"That's what I thought at first too, but you didn't hear the way this kid sounded. He was genuinely frightened. I don't believe he was just acting. The weirdest thing of all was that after his last phone call, I dialed *69 to determine where the call originated. Can you believe I got Beth in Chicago? I woke her up at five in the morning Chicago time."

Eric seemed perplexed. "Hmmm, that *is* strange. Uhh...I hate to ask this, but are you sure the calls weren't coming from her house?"

"Of course, I'm sure." I probably raised my voice a

little too loudly. "And that's not the end of it either. When I called the telephone company, the representative assured me that *69 works every time. She agreed to send a printout of my incoming calls for yesterday and this morning. Hopefully, it'll clear up the mystery."

"I don't know what to say. This is puzzling," agreed Eric.

"There's more. I also looked in the telephone book under his father's name, Samuel Archer, but the only Archer in the book with a first name beginning with 'S' was Stephen Archer. When I called him, a woman told me Stephen had no relative named Samuel. Maybe the kid's number could be unlisted. I'm completely baffled."

"Did the boy mention where he lived?"

"Yeah, he said he lived on Scruffsdale Road in Winter Park. I'm not sure where that is, but I plan to hunt for it tomorrow."

"It's somewhere off Lakemont around one of those lakes," suggested Eric. "Lots of big houses are in that area."

I cleared off my desk at a quarter until six. I said goodnight to Nancy, the receptionist, and told her to have a good weekend.

The office building is on Route 434. It's a challenge to get out of the parking lot, especially on Friday evenings. I need to make a left hand turn, but most of the time I turn right and make a U-turn at the next intersection. Traffic was extremely heavy that Friday. I pulled my Hyundai into the rush-hour flow, thinking I had plenty of leeway. Suddenly, I heard tires screeching and a horn blasting behind me. I quickly glanced in my rear view mirror and saw a mammoth, black, monster truck inches from my bumper with the driver mouthing some obscenities at me. He must have been travelling seventy miles an hour in a forty-five mile per hour zone to catch up with me so quickly. I had to get into the left hand lane in order to make my U-turn at the intersection, but this moron would not permit me to change lanes. He had moved into the left lane and had stayed abreast with me. Rolling his passenger window down, he glared at me while making some choice hand gestures in my direction. I was not in the mood for a confrontation. Besides, I consider myself more mature than to allow a traffic incident to cause me to react like this maniac was acting.

No way he was allowing me to change lanes. Instead, at the light, I acquiesced and turned right to avoid having to look at his ugly face any more. He went straight on Route 434, blaring his horn while I turned around in the shopping plaza in order to head south.

It wasn't over yet. Apparently, an accident had occurred at my favorite intersection, Routes 434 and 436, and traffic was at a standstill. I cut over Wekiva Springs Road, which took me out of my way somewhat but was well worth the extra miles. Traffic was slow, but at least it was moving.

By the time I reached Nawinah, I was in a foul mood. I simply wanted to relax and not deal with this Avery thing. As I unlocked the door, the telephone was ringing. When I picked up the phone, the party on the other end had hung up. Since my answer machine picks up after four rings, the phone must have rung three times or less.

"I'm sure they'll call back. I can try my fabulous,

never failing, *69 to determine who it was," I thought sarcastically.

After dinner and taking care of Spree, I called Beth. "Hi, honey, are you awake yet?"

She bombarded me with questions. "What was all that about this morning? When I finally woke up, I thought it had been a dream. The more I thought about it, I realized you really did call me at five this morning. Don't you know that's grounds for a divorce before the wedding?"

"I'm really sorry, but something very strange is going on, hon. Before and after I talked to you last night, I received several calls from a young boy named Avery Archer."

I described the telephone calls to Beth. Then I said, "The weird part is that after his last phone call, I dialed *69 and woke you up."

"But I talked to you earlier in the evening," Beth said in a bewildered voice. "I was sound asleep when you called *me*."

"That's what I'm trying to tell you. The kid called at least three times after I talked to you, but still the *69 gave me your number." I tried to explain the improbability of the incident.

"That's impossible."

"That's exactly what I thought. I called the telephone company, and they told me the same thing. I did order a printout of all the calls I received yesterday and this morning. I'm hoping it'll make some sense of this enigma."

"Did the boy give you any details whatsoever?"

"Yeah. Besides his name and his parents' names, he told me he was eleven years old. He even told me where he lives, but his number is not in the telephone book either. Beth, I'm worried. Suppose he was kidnapped, I'm the only one he has contacted, and I've been sitting on my ass with this knowledge. But I don't know what to do next."

"Did you ask him for any other relatives that you could try to reach?"

"That's a good idea. There really wasn't enough time to ask him too much. He kept hanging up on me. If he calls back, I'll try to get more information on his family and friends. Another strange thing, he keeps insisting that his telephone number is 790R."

"790R? What kind of a number is that?"

"That's exactly what I asked him. He didn't know what I was talking about. He was very adamant about that number. The more I tried to force the issue, the more upset he got."

"This is worrying me now. Maybe you should call the police. You can't handle this on your own."

"You're right. Things seem to be getting out of hand. If he calls back, I'll try to get as much detail as I can, and then I'll go to the police or call 911. Right now, I'd feel foolish with just the little information I do have. With or without another phone call, tomorrow I will check out the address he gave me."

"Have they mentioned anything about it on television? I would think something like that would make the nightly news."

"I've been so wrapped up thinking about it that I never even thought to check out the news. I'll do that as soon as I hang up. Maybe they'll give a phone number to call."

"Call me back to update me, no matter what time it

is." I knew she was concerned.

"I'll call you if it's something serious. Otherwise, I'll wait until tomorrow night. I'm really sorry I brought you into this. You have enough on your mind. I'm sure there's a logical explanation for everything. You just get some sleep, okay?"

"Okay, but don't forget, if anything appears out of the ordinary after checking out the address, go to the police right away. Don't get involved in something you can't handle."

"You're right. I will. Love ya, sweetheart. Talk to you later."

"Love ya, too, guy."

After talking to Beth, I turned on the television to find some mention of a kidnapping on the local news. I watched for at least an hour, but there was nothing about any kidnapping or abduction. Perhaps the police didn't want to make the kidnapping public knowledge for some reason. I gave up and tried to get interested in a rerun of *Coach*.

At eight-thirty, the telephone rang. I picked it up after the first ring.

"Mister? Did you find my dad?"

It was Avery. He was speaking in a hushed, frightened voice.

"Avery, I can't find your dad. His telephone number is not in the phone book. I will go tomorrow to your address since the phone number you gave me won't work."

"Why? I don't understand. My phone number is 790R. Is that what you called? He's home. I know he is. He's worried about me. Please try again, mister."

"Avery, believe me. I can't get in touch with your

31

dad by telephone. I've tried. It's impossible."

"Then you have to go to my house, mister. You have to go tonight. Please! I am so scared. They keep me in this dark room all day and night. All they gave me to eat was some dry bread and soup and just a little water to drink, and they won't let me use the toilet. I have to keep holding it and holding it. I'm not going to wet my pants, and I'm not going to cry, but you have to get my dad tonight. I can't stand it much longer."

"Avery, I'm new in town, and it's getting dark. I'll have a hard time finding your address. Tomorrow is Saturday. I'll have more time to look, and it'll be light out. How about if I wait until then?"

"No, mister, please! You have to go tonight. These men are really mean. I'm so frightened. Please, please go tonight."

"Do you know anything about the men who took you? How did all this happen?"

"No, they just grabbed me when I went into the woods near my house. I wasn't supposed to go there, but my baseball went over our fence. Dad would be mad at me if I lost it. All I did was go after it. One of the men grabbed me from behind and put his hand over my mouth and nose. I could hardly breathe, and his hand smelled like cigarettes. They pushed me to the ground and tied my hands with a skinny rope. It cut into my wrists. They're bleeding now. Then they dragged me to their truck."

"Did anybody see them take you? Do you know where you are?"

"Nobody else was around. I don't know where I am now, but the ride was… Oh! They're coming now! Please help me!"

He hung up.

Damn. I had hoped to get more information from him, anything that might give me more insight into what was happening. Maybe find out why it wasn't on the news yet, but he hung up too quickly. I had no choice but to look for his father's house tonight. I couldn't get interested in the reruns, anyhow. I got out my wrinkled and worn map of the Orlando area and plotted out a route.

On my way out the door, a light sprinkle was falling. The streets become very slick, especially when the rain first starts and isn't hard enough to wash all the auto fluids from the roadways.

I might also mention that I am colorblind. I have trouble distinguishing red and green. I've learned to compensate for this problem while driving by memorizing the position of the colors on a stoplight. Under normal circumstances, I have no difficulty, but on a rainy night with lights reflecting from everywhere on the streets and on my windshield, sometimes there is a problem. To make matters worse, my Hyundai is in need of new wiper blades, and the rain was starting to come down heavily.

Such was my predicament as I went in search of Samuel Archer. As I reached Silver Star Road, the rain came down very heavily. Don't get me wrong. With the dry conditions, we were having, I was thankful for the rain, but it didn't help my driving ability. After a few skids and a near miss, I finally made it to Fairbanks Avenue. According to the map, Fairbanks turns into Aloma in Winter Park. Then Lakemont Avenue intersects with Aloma, and Palmer is off Lakemont. Scruffsdale Road is off Dasher Avenue, which is off

Sky Drive, which is off Palmer Avenue. Confused yet? I was.

Without too much difficulty, I found Sky Drive. After several times passing it up and turning around, I finally found Dasher Avenue. The clock in the car read almost ten o'clock. After almost a half-hour of trial and error, I finally came upon Scruffsdale Road. I was about to give up when at last I spotted it. I turned the car so suddenly that I almost went off the road.

Finding the street was easy compared to finding the house. Since I didn't get a chance to ask the kid to describe his house, I wasn't sure what I was looking for. The houses on the street were very stately and imposing. They were set back from the roadway probably by a half of an acre. Towering stone walls surrounded each mansion. Massive iron gates expanded the driveway entrances. In the darkness, the house numbers were almost impossible to see.

I was finally able to ascertain that I was in the 1100 block of Scruffsdale. The number 1201 couldn't be too much further. Then my eyes fell upon the most colossal house I've ever seen. It was ominous yet stunning, glistening from the rain, yet foreboding in the darkness. The haze and the wetness made it difficult to make out much of the detail, but the size of the house was overwhelming. No lights illuminated either the inside or the outside of the house. Across the entrance of the drive was the same type of gate that had blocked the access to all the other homes on the street; but this gate had a yard high, ornate, iron replica of an orange tree in the center of it with gilded, golden oranges on the iridescent green leaves of the tree. On the top of the gate were sharp, sword-like, iron rods sticking up from the frame about a foot. If somebody landed on one of those daggers, it would pierce clear through flesh and bone.

I keep a folded, clear plastic raincoat in the glove compartment of the Hyundai just for occasions such as this. Of course, I knew I'd be investigating the occupancy of a mansion in the rain. After some difficulty with maneuvering the raincoat on my sticky, sweaty body while behind the steering wheel of a minuscule, compact car, I wriggled out of the car. I had been using my flashlight to help find the streets and house numbers while on this sojourn, and I grabbed it upon my disentanglement.

I focused the light all around the gated area and the expansive wall to which it was connected. I searched for some type of bell or electronic device to signal the residents of the house that I wanted their attention. Finally, I found a metal plate about six by six inches also with a similar replica of the orange tree engraved on it. I discovered that upon pressing the tree, a signal went to the mansion. I pressed it several times, but there was no response.

This seemed unusually strange. Surely, Samuel Archer knew of his son's kidnapping. Shouldn't several police cars be at the house? Shouldn't every light in the place be lit? I would think the police would be in the yard checking out the area where Avery had been playing. I would think spotlights would be illuminating the wooded area behind the house trying to find any clues the abductors may have left behind. I would think that the place would be swarming with television news reporters.

None of this was seen. I was standing alone in the

rain before a dark, gigantic, empty house. I was at a loss as far as to what action to take next. Undoubtedly, no one was home. Even if the Archer's were at the police station, wouldn't at least a servant be available to answer the door? I tried again, but to no avail. Eventually, I gave up, got back in my car, and sat there for another five minutes trying to decide what to do next. No way could I get inside that gate. Even if I could, what good would it be if no one was home? With resignation and regret, I struggled out of my raincoat and started back to Nawinah.

I didn't get very far. When I pulled onto Dasher Avenue, the road seemed extremely rough and bumpy. Then I realized that the road was fine, but my tire was creating the rough ride. I had a flat! I pulled the car over as far as possible to the side of the narrow road.

"I really need this tonight!" I actually said aloud to no one.

Back on with the raincoat, twisting and turning in the seat, almost punching the roof out trying to get my sweaty arms back into the wet, sticky plastic. I then got out of the car again into the still pouring rain. I surely hope this rain was putting out some of those brush fires in the area because my temperament and disposition were suffering as a result of it.

The front driver's side tire was flat. Just what I needed!

Compact cars do not have a regular spare tire. They have one of those miniature tires supposedly safe enough to get you to your destination. I extracted the excuse for a spare tire out of the trunk. The tire wrench had to be there somewhere. After a thorough search of the trunk, I remembered I had loaned it to Eric last week and had forgotten to get it back. Great. Now what? I do have Triple A, but with trying to save money, I had never purchased a cellular phone. To add to my predicament, on my way to the house on Scruffsdale, the last business that I'd seen was back on Aloma, a couple of miles away. I looked at my watch. It was now almost eleven o'clock. If that Avery kid was not really in serious trouble, he would be after I got through with him.

I locked the car and walked in the direction from which I'd come. My plan was to see if anybody was home at any of the houses on Dasher Avenue. I'd ask them to call Triple A for me. Yeah, definitely a risky plan. If someone looking like me came to my door at eleven at night, I would probably slam the door in his face. I decided to chance it anyhow. What choice did I have?

The houses on Dasher Avenue were by far not as impressive as those on Scruffsdale Road were. They were not small, cement block bungalows like my house, but they weren't nearly as grandiose and stately as the Scruffsdale residences. Actually, I thought that was more to my favor. They'd be more approachable. No high, sword-like gates to pierce my heart would block the drive, or no stone walls I'd have to climb would surround the property.

I walked for half a block before coming to a house with the lights on.

"I guess this is the lucky place," I uttered aloud.

I must have looked a sight. The clear, plastic raincoat was clinging to my body, making me look blurry and undefined. To keep the rain from dripping on my face, I had the hood over my head partially covering my eyes. My gym shoes made squishy sounds as I walked up the driveway.

As I approached the front door, a motion light on the porch flashed on. From inside the house, I heard deep, gruff barking that sounded like it came from a ten-foot-tall, thousand-pound Doberman. Timidly, I stepped onto the entranceway. I was about to press the lighted door buzzer when I heard a male voice from inside the house intermingled with the bark of the giant Doberman.

"Who's there?" the voice called out loudly. "What do you want?"

"Sir? My name is Ken Driscoll. My car is down the street with a flat tire. I know it's late and I wouldn't blame you if you refused, but could I use your telephone to call Triple A? Maybe you could call them for me and give them the information. I'd sincerely appreciate it."

At first, the voice didn't answer, but the giant dog was still barking. Eventually, the man responded, "Do you have some identification on you?"

I felt my back pocket through the raincoat. Yes! I had my wallet. Something was going right for a change.

"Yes, sir, I do." I reached under the raincoat into the pocket to retrieve it.

"Pass it through the mail slot in the door. What did you say your name is?"

As I was passing my soggy driver's license through the slot, I gave him my statistics. "It's Kenneth Driscoll. My address is 1334 Razzle Road in Nawinah, Florida."

The dog had stopped barking. Several seconds later the man on the other side of the door spoke, "Well,

Mister Driscoll, looks like you are who you say you are."

I heard the bolt turning on the door. "Schmoo, be still. Go lie down."

He gave the command to the dog as he opened the door. What a trusting individual!

He appeared to be in his fifties and was dressed in his T-shirt, blue jeans, and slippers. He probably had been watching television, for muffled voices were coming from another room. The giant Doberman transformed into a sandy colored Cocker Spaniel about a foot high. I am still amazed that such a little dog had such a ferocious bark. Who needs a Doberman with that dog around?

"Come in, Driscoll. Now what seems to be your problem? You're a long way from home, aren't you?"

"Yeah, I guess I am. My car is down the street with a flat tire. I have one of those little spares, but I loaned my tire wrench to a friend last week and failed to get it back. I'd like to call Triple A to change the tire for me."

"I can help you." He reached inside a closet in the foyer to retrieve his raincoat and changed his slippers to a pair of shoes lying in the foyer. "How far down the road is the car?"

"Sir, you don't have to bother. I can call Triple A."

"It's no bother. I was bored with the idiot box anyhow. It's not necessary to call Triple A. Sometimes you have to wait hours for them. With us finally getting a little rain, they're probably responding to lots of calls tonight. We could have the tire changed long before they'd arrive. Let's go."

I followed him out the door and over to the side entrance of his garage. He unlocked the door and went inside while I waited outside. I didn't want to appear too threatening, although he gave me no indication he felt that way. Shortly, I heard him start his vehicle, and the garage door opened. When the truck pulled out of the garage, he called to me. "Hop in. I put my hydraulic jack in the bed of the truck. This will just take us a couple of minutes."

I climbed in the passenger side and directed him to my Hyundai.

At the car site, the man took charge. He must've changed tires dozens of times before, for it appeared effortless to him. I asked him several times what I could do to help, but he insisted he didn't need it. What took him ten minutes tops would have taken me at least forty-five minutes, especially in the rain. He changed the tire, put on my tiny spare, and threw the flat into my hatchback.

"That's it. How about coming back to the house for a cup of coffee and a chance to dry out a bit?" he suggested.

"Oh, I don't know. You've already been so helpful. I hate to impose on you anymore."

"It's not an imposition; it's an invitation. Like I told you earlier, I'm not anxious to get back to the television."

"I guess I could use some coffee. This has been a crazy day for me," I told him after thinking about a nice cup of fresh, hot coffee.

We both got in our vehicles, and I followed him back to his house. He pulled his truck into his garage, and I parked in front of the garage door.

"Let's go in the back door. The wife would not be happy if we tracked water and sand on her clean carpet."

The backyard was well lighted, and a meticulously landscaped yard surrounded the pool area. We entered the screened porch where we both stripped off our rain gear. I also removed my squeaky gym shoes. Schmoo, the Doberman-turned-Cocker Spaniel, started barking at us again, but this time I was prepared for the transformation.

The kitchen was neat and cozy. He began brewing the coffee in the automatic coffeepot, and the smell of the fresh coffee permeated the kitchen, making me thankful I accepted his invitation.

"Sir, I'd like to thank you again for your assistance. You are a life saver."

"No problem. I was glad I could help. By the way, my name is Ben Swisher. I have an auto shop in Winter Park."

"Ah! That explains why you were so handy at changing my tire."

"Yeah, I could probably change a tire in my sleep. I don't mean to be nosy. Can I ask you what brought you out on such a night like this? You mentioned you were having a bad day."

"Actually, maybe you can help me out on another matter. I'm trying to get in touch with a Samuel Archer. I tried contacting him by telephone but was unsuccessful. That's why I ventured out this evening. It's very important that I contact him. I was told he lives on Scruffsdale Road, but the house was completely dark. No one answered the buzzer either. You wouldn't happen to know the Archer family, would you? They have a boy named Avery, who is eleven years old, and the wife's name is Esther."

Ben brought the coffee to me and placed sugar and powdered creamer on the blue and white checkered tablecloth.

"I've lived here twenty-five years. For the past ten years, families come and go so quickly that they hardly move in before they are moving out again. I used to know all the neighbors on this block, but I don't anymore. As far as Scruffsdale Road goes, I know *of* those people, but I do not and never will know them personally. We aren't quite compatible financially with them. For some reason, though, the name, Samuel Archer, sounds familiar, but off hand, I don't know why."

The coffee was just what I needed. Being wet in spite of my trusty raincoat, and with the air conditioning in the house, I had the chills. I took several gulps. "So you don't think you know of the family, then?"

"No, I don't. Now, if Elsie were here…that's my wife." He leaned across the table and furtively looked around before resuming his conversation in a whisper as if someone besides me might hear him. "I only say this when she's not around, but she's the neighborhood busy body. I swear she knows everything that goes on in all Winter Park. She sits home all day and gossips with all the other ladies in the neighborhood. She's out playing cards with her lady friends tonight, being fortified with new gossip. But I'll be sure to ask her about this Archer family when she gets back."

Ben looked at the clock on the wall. I also glanced at it. It was now midnight.

"Come to think of it," said Ben. "She should be back any time now. The rain must have slowed her down."

At that moment, I heard someone opening the screened porch door. A short, plump lady with red hair entered the kitchen. She was dressed in a polyester, pink pantsuit with a hot pink shell underneath it. The surprise at seeing me in her kitchen was very evident on her face.

"Elsie, this is Ken Driscoll. He had a little car trouble, and I helped him out. We came back for coffee to dry out."

"Very nice to meet you, Ken." She grabbed a cup of coffee for herself.

"Elsie, do you know a Samuel and Esther Archer on Scruffsdale? Ken is out on this miserable night looking for them."

She thought for a moment. "Samuel and Esther Archer... No, I don't believe I do."

"Now, Elsie, you just called me a liar. I told Ken you know everyone around here."

"Oh, Ben, that's not true," she corrected as if offended. "However, I do know most of the people in this area, at least their names, but I don't know any Archer family."

I decided it was time for me to leave. I rose from my chair and reached my hand out to shake Ben's. "I really can't thank you enough for getting me out of this predicament. And the coffee was just what I needed."

"Glad I could be of some assistance. You be sure you get that tire fixed tomorrow. Those temporary spares will wear down quickly. You can't go very far on them."

I gathered my wet raincoat from the porch, not putting it on since the rain had slowed down. I didn't bother putting on my shoes but went out in my bare feet.

Chapter Three

Saturday, June 27, 1998

On the drive home, I kept slapping my face to stay awake, finally arriving home about one in the morning, very exhausted. No walks for Spree that night. I let her out in the back yard to do her thing. My only thought was to take a warm shower and go to bed. As I was preparing for the shower, I checked the messages on my machine.

"Hi, guy. Where are you? It's eleven-thirty. I thought you were going to call me tonight. Are you okay? Please call me when you get in. Bye."

Before I took my shower, I called Beth. She answered on the first ring. "Ken, I've been so worried."

"I'm sorry, hon. I didn't mean to get you upset. It has been a terrible night."

"Why, what happened? Are you okay?"

"I'm fine, but I was unable to contact the Archers. Despite all the rain tonight, I managed to find their house. It was completely dark, and no one answered the buzzer. Sure is weird. I thought somebody would be home. So I gave up on reaching them tonight. Then top off the disappointment, I had a flat tire on my way home and no tire wrench to repair it."

"Oh, Ken. How did you get home?"

"Believe it or not, I found a house where someone

was still awake. He actually believed I wasn't a serial killer when I knocked on his door looking like one. Then he even changed the tire for me."

Wearily I said, "Hon, I'm really tired. I hope you don't mind if I cut it short tonight."

"Sure, guy. I was just about to give up on your calling back. What are you going to do tomorrow? Are you going to the police?"

"I'm hoping Avery calls back and I can get more information from him so I have a little more to tell the police."

"Be sure to let me know what happens tomorrow. I'm going over to Mom and Dad's, so if I'm not home, call me there. We're going to pick out the menu for the rehearsal dinner. Do you have any preferences?"

"Oh, Beth, I'm sorry. I've been so wrapped up with this Avery thing that I completely forgot to ask how the plans are going. Whatever you decide will be fine with me."

"That's okay. You have a lot on your mind. I'll choose something delicious. Don't worry about it. Mom and Rachel have been invaluable. We'll get it done. You just be careful."

"Right. I'll talk to you tomorrow. Love ya."

I felt guilty that I wasn't taking part in the wedding plans. However, her mom and sister had gone through all this wedding stuff before. They knew more than I did about napkins, invitations, caterers, and all that crap, but I should be giving Beth more moral support. Fine fiancé I am.

I took a quick shower and went straight to bed.

I had been asleep for only a short while when the telephone rang. When I picked up the receiver, the clock read three o'clock.

"Hullo."

Frantically, Avery answered, "Mister, I've been calling and calling you all night long. Did you find my dad? Is he coming to get me?"

"Avery, slow down. No one was home at your house, at least at the address you gave me. I rang the buzzer several times, but nobody answered."

"No! That's not right! He'd stay close by the telephone waiting for me to call. He'd be so worried about me that he wouldn't leave the house. You must've gone to the wrong house. What did it look like?"

"It was especially dark out tonight, and I had a difficult time seeing the house itself. I do know it was a big house with an iron gate. It had a big orange tree ornament made out of iron on the gate itself."

"That's it. That's my house. That's my gate. But where is my dad?" He was getting very emotional.

"Get hold of yourself, Avery. I'll find him. Tomorrow when it's daylight, I'll have a better chance of seeing just what is going on at your house. And I'm going to the police for help too."

"The police? Oh, no, that's not a good idea! The man told me if my dad calls the police, they'll kill me for sure." I could hear the fear in his voice.

"Take it easy. I'm not your dad. And they don't even know that you've been talking to me, do they?"

"Nooo...I don't think so." He calmed down somewhat.

"Then they won't know anything about it, but I do want you to give me as much information as you can about them and about yourself. The more I know, the more I can tell the police. Anything, just the littlest thing, could be the key to finding where you are and where your dad is. Let's get started before you have to hang up. Do you know the telephone number for the phone from where you are calling?"

"There is a number on this phone. Let's see. 358L. That's what it looks like, I think."

"Look again. Are you positive that's the number?"

"Yes, that's the number, I'm sure, I think."

"I hate to put you through this again, but there has to be seven numbers in a telephone number."

"You keep telling me that, but I don't know what you're talking about? I'm looking at the phone right now, and all it says is 358L. It's scratched, but that's what it says."

"Perhaps some of the numbers have worn off. Is it an old phone?"

"I…I…guess so. Maybe…I don't know." He was getting agitated again.

"Okay, try to stay calm. We'll think of something else."

"Mister, please don't call me here. They can't know I've been talking to you."

"I won't call you. I just wanted a number to give to the police that might help them find you. Let's try something else before you have to hang up. Do you have any brothers or sisters?"

"No, just me. Dad and Mama told me they wished that I had another brother or sister, but I don't. I have a cousin who's twelve, and I play baseball with him sometimes. His name is Gerald Archer, and he has a sister, Margaret. We don't like to play with her 'cause she's a girl. She always wants to play house and school and stuff like that."

His speech was monotone and hurried. It was as if he were trying to oblige me by giving me as many details as possible in as short of time as possible.

"Who are their parents?"

"Uncle Harold and Aunt Sophie. Uncle Harold is my dad's brother."

"That's good," I encouraged him. "Anything else?"

"Let me think. Hmmm. We have five servants in our house. Isabel is the maid; Fritz is the cook; Homer is the butler; Clayton is the chauffeur; and Mrs. Warden is Mama's secretary."

"Do all these servants live at your house?"

"Yes, most of the time. Sometimes one of them is gone, but somebody is always at the house. I don't know where they were tonight. I don't understand."

He was getting anxious again. I had to change the conversation.

"Avery, you've done a great job. You have to be brave for a little longer. Tomorrow I'm sure I'll find your dad, and we'll get you out of that place. If you think of anything else, even if it doesn't seem important, call me. I may not be here when you call. I may still be talking to your dad or the police, so if I'm not here, just leave a message on the machine."

"Machine? What do you mean?" he asked uncertainly.

"Leave a message on the answer machine."

"What is an 'answer machine'? Oh, oh, here they come."

Great. Oh, well, I at least got some information. I lay back down in bed. Thinking back, I wondered why he asked me what an answer machine was. If this kid was eleven years old, he would know what it was. Kids his age are computer whizzes. They know more about electronics and the Internet than most adults know. The situation seemed to be getting more bizarre the more I learned.

I tossed and turned for most of the night. I was getting worried too, but I didn't want Avery to know my concern. I couldn't understand why *somebody* hadn't been at his house. After all, if my only son were missing, I'd be by that phone constantly, day and night, waiting for it to ring. Well, I'd find out more tomorrow. Hopefully. I had to get some sleep.

I finally drifted off to a fitful sleep. I woke about six in the morning to the sound of my next-door neighbor mowing his lawn. Who mows their lawn at six on a Saturday morning? I have a strong feeling this guy is not going to be my best buddy. I should get up anyway. I had a full day ahead of me, and I didn't want to end up being out until one in the morning again.

The mower also awakened Spree. Maybe I should start leaving her outside to bark at three in the morning when Avery calls the next time. I'd see how lawnmower man would like that. There is a slight possibility that perhaps that *is* the reason already that he mows the grass so early. Remember how I said that Spree was not always well behaved? I guess it's best not to have any confrontations with this man. After all, Beth and I have to live here for several years.

Spree and I walked along the lake again that morning, but we didn't stay out long. I wanted to begin my quest. First, I took my tire to Fleck's Tire Store for repair. Then I went back to the Archer house on Scruffsdale Road. I parked my Hyundai by the curb and walked to the gate.

By daylight, the house was breathtaking, reminding me of an art museum or some type of stately government building, standing three stories high. Imagine a private residence being three stories high. How could one possibly use all the rooms in such a house?

A long, spotless, concrete driveway circled up to the front of the house. Six elongated stairs led up to an open porch that had several expansive pillars extending the entire height of the house.

After a few minutes of staring at the house, I went over and pressed the buzzer plate that had the orange tree engraved on it. Within a few seconds, a gruff voice answered, "Who is it?"

"My name is Ken Driscoll. May I speak to Samuel Archer, please?" I was slightly embarrassed, for I think I had awakened this person. Most sane people are in bed at eight-thirty on a Saturday morning. That's where I should've been.

"Samuel Archer doesn't live here," she curtly responded.

"But this is the address that was given to me," I retorted in complete surprise.

"He hasn't lived here in years," she brusquely said.

What? My mind was confused. What was she telling me? Had I heard her correctly?

I asked her, "What did you say?"

Rudely she replied, "I said Samuel Archer has not lived here in years."

Quickly, I said, "That's impossible. A boy named Avery Archer is in trouble and trying to locate his father. He says Samuel Archer is his father."

"Is this some kind of sick joke?" There was buzzing in my ear from this rude person disconnecting me from the intercom.

I was stunned. I stood in that exact place for a few minutes, staring at the orange tree buzzer, the electrodes dancing like fireflies in my brain, not comprehending what was going on. I had to make sure she had said what I thought she had said. I must have misunderstood her. So I rang the intercom again.

The same rude voice answered bluntly. "If this is your idea of a joke, it is not funny. If you do not leave immediately, I will call the police."

Again the ringing in my ear from the disconnected intercom.

Bewildered, I shook my arms wildly as I turned in circles several times. I could not even guess what was going on, and this woman was not going to help me out. I went back into my car and sat for a full ten minutes, trying to imagine what was happening while insane scenarios crept into my thoughts.

"Okay," I reasoned. "Beth is right. This is too much for me to deal with on my own. I'm going to the police right now."

At the downtown Orlando police station, I parked the car, fed the parking meter, and ventured inside the police headquarters. A woman casually dressed in jeans and a Grateful Dead T-shirt was sitting behind a glass window. She was busy with some paperwork and paid no attention to me. I startled her when I knocked on the glass window. She turned around rather suddenly.

"Can I help you?"

"Uhh...I think I'd like to report a kidnapping." I stammered as I tried to think of how to explain.

"What do you mean?" She looked at me with a confused expression on her face.

"I'm not sure that there actually has been a kidnapping, but I think so." I even sounded ridiculous to myself.

"Can you be a little more specific?" Now she sounded condescending.

"Ma'am, may I talk to a policeman or a detective?" I gave up trying to find the right words to describe the situation.

"I'll see who's available." Yes, she thought I was a weirdo.

She was gone for several minutes. I glanced around the lobby. A poster of McGruff, the dog detective, hung on the wall, giving children advice about how to cross the street. Wanted posters were tacked to a bulletin board with photos of some of Florida's most notorious dirt bags. Several plaques and commendation awards were mounted on the wall across from the posters. A pay phone was over in the corner. It looked like one of the dirt bags from the posters was trying to make a phone call. He was digging in his filthy pockets, searching for some change.

He turned to me and asked, "Hey, bud, you got a quarter?"

My name isn't 'bud,' but I didn't bother to tell him. I dug in my pocket without saying a word and trying to avoid looking at his gross appearance. I handed him a quarter, avoiding his grimy, greasy hand. He silently took the change and turned his back to me.

The maintenance people apparently had not cleaned the night before, for the large cylindrical ashtray near the telephone overflowed with cigarette butts. The scummy poster man was helping it out a little by looking for a butt large enough to smoke.

I was taking in all these sights when the woman from the front desk returned, accompanied by a man slight in stature, dressed in a brightly colored shirt covered with replicas of fish. He wore suspenders, probably because he had no ass and his pants would have fallen off without them.

"Good morning. I'm Detective Pete Griffin. What can I do for you today?"

"Detective Griffin, I'm not exactly sure. I think there's been a kidnapping."

"Mister uhh, uhh?" Detective Griffin stammered as he waited for me to say my name.

"It's Driscoll. Ken Driscoll," I helped him out.

"Mister Driscoll, why don't you come back with me, and maybe we can clear this up."

I followed him down a corridor past several desks, some empty, some occupied with men and women engrossed in paperwork or talking on the telephone. He led me to a small room where a worn table, the top marred with cigarette burns and coffee cup rings, rested in the middle. He gestured for me to sit on one of the wooden chairs while he sat across from me.

"Now, Ken, what is this all about?" He poised his pen against a note pad he had removed from his shirt pocket and placed on the table.

I began with the first telephone call from Avery. I told him the boy's name and his parents' names. I told him about the calls, the frequency of them, and the content of them. I told him about the *69 incident. I told him how I was unable to locate Samuel Archer through the telephone number. I told him about going to the Scruffsdale residence, and lastly about the remark made by the woman at the house that Samuel Archer hadn't lived there for many years.

I told him everything. Every detail. And I waited for his reply.

The entire time I was reciting my experiences, he was rubbing his two thumbs up and down the inside of his wide suspenders. He probably did this often, for the suspenders were frayed along the edges. He had not written anything on the note pad he had placed on the table.

He did not respond to me immediately, so I continued talking.

"I'm very confused. I've tried to get information out of the kid. He seems forced to hang up before I can get much detail."

Detective Griffin was staring at me, fiddling with his suspenders.

Not knowing why he wasn't speaking, I continued. "He said he was an only child and that he had two cousins he played with named Gerald and Margaret Archer, the children of his dad's brother, Harold. He said his family had five servants, Fritz, the…"

"Ken. Mister Driscoll." The detective finally interrupted me. "No need to go on."

"Why? Have you found Avery? Is he okay?" My face lit up with relief. Everything was going to be okay.

He stood, staring at me in a very strange way. When he still did not speak, I asked, "What's going on?"

Detective Griffin gave me a very scathing look. "Mister Driscoll, we get a lot of crackpots like you in here. Why are you wasting our time?"

I was bewildered. A crackpot!

"What do you mean? I think this boy is in real danger. Can't you help me find him or his father? I don't think we have much time. He's afraid the kidnappers are going to kill him."

Griffin arose from his seat, pushed in his chair against the table, gathered up the pen and the blank note pad, and started toward the door. As he was turning the knob, he turned to face me. "I think it's too late for that."

He walked out the door leaving me in the room alone with my mouth wide open, wondering what he meant.

I quickly got out of my chair, almost knocking it over, and followed him out the door, asking as I caught up to him, "What do you mean, it's too late? Is the boy already dead? Oh my God, no!"

Still walking and not bothering to turn in my direction, Detective Griffin said, "Yeah, he's dead all right."

"Oh, no! Did you notify his parents? My God! This is awful!"

I was having a hard time coping with his response. I had just talked to Avery a few hours ago. Now this. And I was angry with myself. Surely, I could've done more to save him. What a stupid jerk I'd been! I was so concerned he was just prank calling me that I let the boy die. I felt just as guilty of his death as if I had actually killed him.

While all this was going on in my head, I was following Detective Griffin, hoping for some explanation from him.

At last, the detective stopped walking away and

turned to face me. Observing me, he said, "You really don't know what the hell you're talking about, do you?"

For several more seconds he looked at me, at last realizing that I was completely baffled by his reaction. Then he bluntly said, "Avery Archer was shot in the head, thrown in a lake, and eaten by alligators."

"What! No! It's not possible." In my mind, I was envisioning the gruesome scene of Avery's death. But I just talked to him! I was utterly confused.

Griffin went on, "He was murdered on July 4th. That is, July 4, *1931*. That was over sixty years ago. Someone is playing a very sick joke on you, Driscoll."

I could not have been more shocked if he had physically slapped me in the face.

Standing there like a man who had just lost his best friend, I yelled, "No way! No way!"

This man was talking utter nonsense. I was getting quite loud. Heads were turning in our direction.

"I'm getting phone calls from a kid named Avery Archer, and he's very much alive. Maybe the kidnapping is similar to that case from 1931, but this kid is only eleven. He told me so. A dead kid can't talk."

The detective sympathetically tried to explain. "I'm telling you. It's some kid playing a prank. The Archer case was the case of the century in the Orlando area. It was all over the newspapers and radio, worldwide. You must not be from around here, or you would've recognized it as a prank right away. I suggest you tell that kid if he calls again that you're calling the police on *him*. Scare him a little. Make him think twice about doing this to someone else."

"I can't believe this is just a prank. You didn't hear

his voice. You didn't hear him pleading and begging for help. He couldn't be that good of an actor."

Detective Griffin was not as anxious to walk away now. He sat at a desk and started going through some of the papers on the desk. "Listen, why don't you go to the library and look up some newspaper articles on the story? As I said, it was a big case back in the thirties. Put your mind at ease. You know, some kids these days are very sick. They'll do anything to get a rise out of an adult."

I didn't know what to say. I could not accept what he was telling me. I think I thanked the detective before I walked out the door completely in a daze.

After I left the police station, I needed to walk for a while to sort out this mess. I had no destination, just started walking. I played back the many phone calls repeatedly in my mind, trying to recall every detail the kid, whoever he was, had told me. Then I recalled the new knowledge that Detective Griffin had given me. Gradually, I began to believe Griffin. The more I walked, the angrier I became at the kid. I thought about all the time I had wasted trying to help him. Most of all, I thought about how he had made such an ass out of me. I resolved that I would get even with him, kid or not. Nobody makes an ass out of Ken Driscoll and gets away with it.

That was my state of mind when I ended up on Church Street. Calmer and more determined, I felt as if a load was lifted from my mind. I was no longer responsible for saving some kid's life. I was also ashamed of myself for believing the kid in the first place. How gullible can a person be?

Feeling much better, I went into one of the café

style restaurants and had a ham sandwich and a bottle of iced tea. Then I strolled resolutely back to my car near the police headquarters, my mind so much more at ease.

I spent the entire drive home deciding my strategy for dealing with this punk kid. Should I humor him until I was able to locate where the call was coming from, and then retaliate with some malicious trick, like showing up at his house with the police? Maybe I should get in touch with his real parents and inform them of the little bastard's malicious activity. After much deliberation, I decided I wouldn't put myself on his level. Therefore, I would simply call his bluff, inform him that I was wise to him, and disconnect the phone if he continued to bother me. Then if he did continued, the next step would be to report him to the police for harassment. That should put a scare into him, the little smartass.

When I got home about two, I let Spree out in the back yard. Then I sat on the couch to wait for the inevitable telephone call. I didn't have long to wait. Maybe the harasser was somebody in the neighborhood who knew when I got home. Could be they were looking out for my Hyundai to enter my driveway. Maybe it was even lawnmower man trying to get even with me for Spree's barking. Within five minutes, the phone rang. It was Avery, or whoever the hell he was.

Immediately in his pleading, whiny voice he said, "Did you find my house, mister, did you talk to my dad?"

I didn't answer right away. I wanted to create some suspense. The pint-size bastard! I guess I did want to lower myself to his level a little.

In my most reprimanding voice, I said, "Listen, kid, I found your house all right, but your dad wasn't there. In fact, he hasn't been there in over sixty years! You sure had me going for a while. You are a sick little bastard! Go bother somebody else, or I'll report you to the police. And if I get my hands on you, I'm going to wring your creepy, little neck."

I hung up the receiver so hard I'm sure it hurt his eardrum. Maybe that will keep the little creep from calling back. I can play this game too.

The phone immediately rang again.

This couldn't be the little brat. He'd be nuts to call back.

In a terrified, sobbing voice, which was fake, of course, I heard, "Are you sure you went to 1201 Scruffsdale Road? Did you get the right house? My dad *has* to be there! Please, mister, I'm not funnin' you. I wouldn't bother you, but I can't call anybody else. No matter what number I dial, I always get you. Was it a big white house with lots and lots of windows and pillars and a long driveway that curved up to the front door? There's a big white statue in the front yard. My dad's new Cadillac might be in front of the house. Was that what you saw? Mister? Please! Please! Mister? Help me!"

"Give it up, you little scum bag!" I hung up a second time.

I hoped that was going to be the end of it. I went to the back door and let Spree back in the house. After getting a glass of iced tea, I was just settling down to watch the Angels play the Padres on television when the phone rang again.

"This is probably Beth," I thought to myself. "I

should have called her at her parents' house."

It wasn't Beth. It was the little bastard *again*. He wasn't going to give up easily.

"Mister, I tried my Aunt Sophie's number. I tried my friend Trevor again, but every time I get you or nobody. Please, I'm not funnin' you. Please help me!"

"Listen, Avery, or whatever the hell your name is, I've had enough of this. Give it a rest. You call one more time, and I'm calling the police on *you*."

I hung up, but this time there was a slight hesitation in my actions.

Five minutes later the phone rang again. It was Eric.

"Hey, you doing anything this evening? Melanie is still mad at me. I heard Warrant is playing at Janie Lanes' tonight. How about it?"

I could use a break from this fiasco. "What time were you going?"

"We could stop to eat at Angel's maybe about eight-thirty, and get to Janie Lanes' about nine or ten."

"Sure, sounds good. Are you picking me up?"

"Yeah, I'll be there at eight or eight-fifteen."

I'm glad Eric called. This will keep my mind off what I would like to do to that little creep. I called Beth at her mother's house. They were busy discussing the menu and the bridal shower. I didn't want to keep her on the phone too long. I briefly told her about my trip to the Archer house and the police station. After telling her the abbreviated version, she also was convinced it was some smartass kid.

I then took Spree on a walk along Lake Ripple. They were making headway on the Kouprianov house. I was surprised to see the painters were working on a

Saturday. I wondered what the rush was to get it completed.

I played a few games with Spree. She loves to catch the Frisbee. We romped and played for about forty-five minutes before starting back to the house.

When Eric picked me up, he asked, "So what have you been up to this weekend?"

"You would not believe what I've been doing! Remember I told you about the kid who has been calling me?"

"Oh yeah, I forgot about that. What happened?"

"Well, I found out that it's all a sick joke. This Avery Archer character was kidnapped sixty-seven years ago, shot, and dumped in a lake where alligators ate him. This bastard kid was just messing with me all this time."

"That's sick. How did you find out?"

I told Eric about my visit to the house on Scruffsdale and the police station.

"You are so gullible. I bet you still believe in the tooth fairy."

"Yeah, but I think I've learned my lesson. I've convinced him not to call back again. I threatened to call the police."

With that, our discussion turned to work matters, then to Melanie and Beth.

Chapter Four

Sunday, June 28, 1998

After the concert, Eric dropped me off at home about one-thirty in the morning. Dragging my body through the motions, I let Spree out, took a quick shower, and went to bed.

The telephone rang at quarter after two. I could not believe it was the kid again. He was crying so hard that his speech was incoherent. Finally, I understood his pleading. "Mister, please, please! I wouldn't bother you, but there is *nobody else*. I can only dial your number. Every number I dial is your number."

It took all my willpower not to give in to his piteous wailing. I knew in my mind he was just some obnoxious kid, yet I felt sorry for him. Where were his parents? Didn't they know what he was doing? It was after two in the morning, and he was calling a perfect stranger. Some parents don't deserve to have kids if they can't take care of them and keep them out of trouble. This was nonsense, him being up this late, even if it was a weekend.

Finally, I got tired of hearing his bellyaching. What would it hurt to listen to his bullshit? I was awake anyhow. "Okay, kid, cut it out. I'll talk to you, but first tell me the truth. Who are you, and why did you pick on me? You could've called any number in the phone book. Why me? Why don't you bother somebody else for a change?"

"Mister, *I told you*. My name is Avery Archer. I live at 1201 Scruffsdale Road in Winter Park, Florida. All I want you to do is find my dad. Then I won't bother you anymore. Ever again. Please. I'm not funnin' you."

How can you feel sorry for somebody who you know is jerking you off? I decided to play his game again... If it was a game...

"Okay, Avery, if that *is* your name, what do you want me to do? I went to your house. Your dad doesn't live there anymore. There was no Cadillac in the drive. I went to the police. They think I'm nuts."

"I don't know...I just don't know... My dad would be there. I know he would. I know he lives there. You probably went to the wrong house. That's it. You went to the wrong house. No, maybe he's out looking for me. That's it. He must be out looking for me. I don't know. Oh, I don't know."

He seemed to be rambling and very confused, but he went on.

"I just know if my dad doesn't give them the money, they said they're going to kill me. They hit me tonight. I didn't do anything bad. They just hit me. The short man said I looked at him funny." Again, he was sobbing almost uncontrollably.

"Avery, who are they? Who's hitting you?"

"Those two men who threw me into the back of the truck."

"Okay, tell me in detail what these men look like?"

His voice sounded a little more controlled now that I was listening to him.

"They're dirty, really dirty. The big man wears this old, red shirt. His head is very big, but every time I see him, he has a lady's stocking on his head. And he has this pocket watch. He's always twirling the chain in my face. He keeps saying, 'Kid, if your pop don't pay up, you're dead meat.'"

"You said two men. What does the other man look like?"

"He has a lady's stocking on his face too, but I can see a dark mustache underneath. He's kind of short, and he smells like he peed his pants. He wears dirty overalls and an undershirt most of the time, and there are Chesterfield cigarettes in his overall pocket. They dropped out one time when he was bending over."

"Oh, here they come. I must hang up."

What was I to do? When I talked to Avery, I believed him, but when I talked to Detective Griffin I believed *him*. Then when I thought about all the other evidence, Avery simply could not be telling the truth. I wanted to call Beth to talk to her, but I knew better than to call at that hour. After fighting with myself for another hour, I finally decided I would go to the library tomorrow and find out all that I could about this Avery Archer thing back in 1931.

For whatever reason, I received no more calls that night. About nine in the morning, I called Beth. "Hi, sweetheart, are you awake?"

"Barely. I'm on my first of many cups of coffee. Is everything okay?"

"Actually, no. The kid called me again last night several times. No matter what I say to him, he keeps telling me he's not lying. You know, as weird as it seems, I halfway believe him. Am I going crazy? My brain tells me to hang up on him, but my heart tells me to do something to help him. How can that be?"

"But all the indications point to the fact he is definitely lying to you," she lectured.

"I know, I know, but you haven't heard the begging and pleading in his voice. After I told him I was going to call the police, he didn't call for a while, but when he did call back, he said the men who kidnapped him had hit him. It was so difficult to understand him he was crying so hard."

"You can't let him get to you. You know it's impossible for him to be telling you the truth. He's just a good little actor and an expert liar. That's all."

"I know...I know..."

"Just forget about him, and maybe go to a movie or something today."

"No, I'm going to the library and look up all I can on that 1931 case. Maybe I can catch him in a lie or something. Then I'll know he's just a bratty kid who needs his ass kicked."

"Well, if that's what it'll take, then do it. I hate that you are like this. Hey, I have an idea. Why don't I fly down for the Fourth? With it being on a Saturday this year, we'll get off Friday too. I miss you so. Maybe the two of us can work this out together."

I couldn't believe what I was hearing. I should have thought of it.

"That would be the best thing in the world. I can handle anything if you're around. Call today to get a flight, and let me know as soon as possible when you'll arrive so I can pick you up. Fantastic! I feel much better already."

"Good, it's settled. I'll try to get a flight out

Thursday night and come home Sunday. I gotta go now. I'm going over to Rachel's to make some more earth shaking wedding decisions, and then we're going to a movie. I love ya, guy."

I felt much better. I hadn't seen Beth since last March. Maybe we could get together with Eric and Melanie for a cookout on the Fourth. My mind was so busy thinking about Beth's visit that Avery and his problem became less important. Maybe I shouldn't go to the library after all. What good would it do? I knew it was all a lie anyhow. Oh, well, I had no other plans for the day. Besides, now I was too anxious for Beth to get here that I wouldn't be able to sit around all day.

At the downtown Orlando library, I got directions to the newspaper archive department. I asked the assistance of the woman at the desk, Mrs. Agnes Snuffley, according to her desk nameplate. She was about sixty years old with very short, white, curly hair.

"I'm looking for copies of the *Orlando Sun* from 1931. Can you help me?"

"Are there any particular dates in which you are interested in 1931, or do you want to see the entire year?

I thought for a moment. If the boy disappeared into the lake on July 4, 1931, there should be other articles before that date. Maybe a week in advance should get me all I needed. Then I had a revelation. Perhaps this woman knew about the case. No harm in asking.

"Ma'am, I'm trying to find articles dealing with the death of a young boy, Avery Archer, on July 4, 1931. Are you familiar with the case?"

"Oh, yes I am. Of course, I was not born yet, if you can believe that, but countless times my parents told me about the boy's death. You know, they never apprehended the kidnappers. I was born in 1937, and even at that time, parents kept a close watch on their children. I remember my sisters and I were never permitted to be alone in our yard without one of my parents being outside with us."

"So would you know when it first appeared in the *Sun*?"

"Let me think. Perhaps we should try a week and a half in advance. Let's see. That would put us at June 24, 1931. Let's try that."

She led me to a large cabinet, opening a drawer and pulling out a roll of microfilm. At the microfilm machine, she gave me brief instructions on how to insert and forward the film into the machine. I started with the microfilm for Wednesday, June 24, 1931. There was no mention of any kidnapping. I went on to Thursday, June 25. This, too, had no articles dealing with the case. Finally, in the Friday, June 26, 1931, edition, the article I was looking for was on the front page.

Son of Wealthy Orange Grower Missing

The eleven-year-old son of Samuel and Esther Archer was reported missing yesterday. Samuel Archer is a wealthy and influential orange grower in Orange County. Avery Archer, his son, was last seen playing ball in his back yard. The only clues thus far are large tire tracks found on the path leading to the wooded area behind the Archer mansion. Law enforcement agencies have checked the woods thoroughly. No signs of the boy were found, but small tree branches were broken, and the brush and weeds in the area were crushed, indicating signs of a struggle. Police have issued an all-points bulletin for the apprehension of the abductors.

That was all the information in the Friday, June 26, paper. I was perusing the other articles in the paper when my eye caught the name "Kouprianov." That large mansion on the other side of my lake, Lake Ripple, is called the Kouprianov Mansion. My interest was perked, something with which I was familiar. I read that article also.

Ivan Kouprianov to Purchase Large Land Area
South of Orlando

This paper has learned that Ivan Kouprianov plans to follow his father's example as a prominent land developer. He has recently signed a contract for the purchase of ten thousand acres of land south of Orlando. Our sources tell us that he plans to build a large hotel and an amusement park on the property.

Interesting. Maybe he had Walt Disney's idea before Walt Disney.

I forwarded the microfilm to the Saturday, June 27, 1931, edition,

Sheriff Looking for Leads in Archer Kidnapping

Sheriff Wallace Denton has asked the public for help in finding Avery Archer, the eleven-year-old son of Samuel Archer, the renowned orange grower of Orange County. If anyone has any information on the whereabouts of the Archer boy, please contact the Orange County Sheriff's Department immediately.

Samuel Archer has been in the orange growing business since moving to Orange County from Georgia as a lad in 1910. He went to work for the Calvin McNally Groves, and eventually, he became foreman of the McNally Groves. When Calvin McNally passed on, he left the Groves to Samuel Archer, who has since built up his orange groves to the successful enterprise it is today, the largest in the state of Florida.

Archer is responsible for many new developments in the citrus industry and holds several patents on innovative citrus processing machinery.

In 1918, Samuel Archer took a wife, Miss Esther Dussen, of the prominent Miami Dussen family. They begot Avery Archer, their only child, on March 19, 1920.

This paper has been informed that a reward of $5,000 is offered for information leading to the safe return of Avery Archer.

There could not be *two* Avery Archer's having the same parents, Samuel and Esther Archer, but it was inconceivable that the Avery I talked to could be this Avery I was reading about from 1931. There had to be another explanation. I continued with the microfilm for Sunday, June 28, 1931.

Ransom Note Delivered to Archer Estate

On Saturday morning, a messenger delivered a ransom note to the family of Avery Archer. The amount of the ransom was not disclosed. The sheriff's department has located the messenger and has detained him for questioning.

Avery Archer, the son of Samuel and Esther Archer, was abducted from the woods adjacent to his yard. It has been determined that Avery was playing baseball in his back yard. Orange County deputies speculate that Avery went into the woods to retrieve his baseball. The time of the incident is placed at approximately 3:30 P.M. on Thursday, June 25. The area was cordoned off while the search for clues continues.

Amazing! Everything the kid told me is in this paper. Either he read these microfilms the same way I did, or… I don't want to think of the other alternative. I forwarded to the next day's article and went over to talk to Mrs. Snuffley.

"Excuse me, may I ask you another question? Has anyone else recently asked to see those particular newspaper articles about the Archer kidnapping?"

"I only work in the library on weekends, so I can't speak for the other days of the week. I've worked in this department for twenty years, and to my knowledge, you are the only one who has requested those specific microfilms. There is no way of keeping track of who views them, however, since they do not leave the department. Therefore, it *is* possible that during the week someone may have used them."

I thanked her and went back to my viewing task for Monday, June 29, 1931.

Messenger Claims No Knowledge in Kidnapping

The Orange County Sheriff's Department has extensively questioned the messenger who delivered the ransom note to Samuel Archer, the father of Avery Archer, who was abducted last Thursday. The identity of the messenger was not released, but sources revealed he is a panhandler who lives on the streets. He informed the sheriff that he was approached by two men who gave him a quarter to deliver a letter to the Archer home. The messenger described the two men. One is a large man with pronounced facial features. The second is of small stature, having dark hair and a mustache. When asked why he had not come forward earlier with his information, the messenger said he feared retaliation from the criminals. The sheriff has released him but has told him not to leave the area.

Each article that I read made me more confident that Avery was telling the truth. I knew he could have easily read these microfilms as I was doing, but somehow, I was growing more certain that was not the case. Of course, I was also growing more confused. This was absolutely an impossible situation. No way in hell could I be talking to a dead kid. Not only dead, but also dead sixty-seven years!

I went to Tuesday, June 30, 1931, on the microfilm.

Still No Clues in Archer Kidnapping

The sheriff's department has not found any more clues in the disappearance of Avery Archer, son of Samuel and Esther Archer, the renowned orange grower of Orange County. He has been missing since Thursday, June 25. The sheriff is asking the public to be on the lookout for two men, one large man with large features and the other of slight built with dark hair and mustache. If these men are spotted, do not attempt to apprehend them, but contact the police or the sheriff's department immediately.

From the implications in the articles, I was certain the sheriff's department was getting nowhere with solving the case. I went on to Wednesday, July 1, 1931.

Archer Family Contacted by Kidnappers

The abductors of Avery Archer, the son of Samuel and Esther Archer, contacted the family by telephone Tuesday afternoon. Samuel Archer demanded to speak to his son to verify that he was still alive. The abductors permitted Samuel Archer to have a brief conversation with him. They also reiterated their demand for a large *ransom from the family, which this paper was informed to be $100,000. Archer has agreed to pay the ransom and has been in touch with his financial advisors.*

One hundred thousand dollars. That's a lot of money even in today's market. I bet it's about the same as a million dollars today. This Archer dude must have been loaded.

There seemed to be a conflict in this article. It stated that Samuel Archer was willing to pay the ransom. Then why did the kidnappers kill Avery? I had to read on with the microfilm from Thursday, July 2, 1931.

Archer Kidnappers Spotted in Area

Witnesses have reported that two men matching the descriptions of the abductors of Avery Archer were seen making a telephone call outside Squirt's Filling Station west of Orlando on Route 50. A boy was also seen entering the telephone booth. They reportedly were seen driving an old truck with multiple scratches and dents. The license number was not ascertained, nor was the year or model of the truck. Witnesses spotted one of the men paying for gas at the filling station. The other man was seen seated in the truck. The person who saw a boy entering the telephone booth did not see any truck. The person who saw two men in a truck did not see any boy. Sheriff Wallace Denton believes the men were hiding the boy in the truck somewhere. He believes the abductors are still in the area. He asks that the public use extreme caution if these men are spotted. They are assumed armed and dangerous. Do not try to apprehend them, but contact the police or the sheriff's department immediately.

After reading this article, I noticed that the name

"Kouprianov" again appeared on the front page of this paper.

Kouprianov to Return to Russia
for Russian Servants

Mr. and Mrs. Ivan Kouprianov will be returning to Russia today to hire a new set of Russian servants. In their philanthropic endeavors, each year they return to Russia to hire new servants. They bring them back to America to give them a start and eventually help them obtain other jobs in the community. Mrs. Olga A. Kouprianov, the widow of the late Vladimir Kouprianov, who came to America in 1890, will remain in her home in Nawinah. She is seventy-eight years old, and her son thought it best that she not make the trip this year. The trusty servants will be caring for her in the absence of her son.

Very interesting.

I needed a break, and my parking meter was about to expire. I asked Mrs. Snuffley if I could leave the microfilm in the machine while I fed the meter. She said she would watch it for me. Besides, no one else had been looking at microfilm the entire time I was there.

As I walked to where I parked my car, I tried to piece together all the things Avery had told me. Was it possible that a kid just playing a prank could remember all those details that were in the newspapers? Or was it more believable that those details were reality to him? But how could that be? I don't consider myself the most brilliant man in the world, but I'm no dummy either. No way could the real Avery be calling me repeatedly. First, this all happened sixty-seven years ago. Second, (the biggie), according to Detective Griffin, Avery was dead. Shot, thrown in the lake, and eaten by alligators. So how could a dead kid, who really wasn't a kid if this happened sixty-seven years ago, be calling me today? What bothered me the most was why was he calling me. Of all the people in this city, why me?

I fed my parking meter and went back to the library. My microfilm was still in the machine, and I continued on to Friday, July 3, 1931.

Archers Receive Another Call from The Kidnappers

The abductors of Avery Archer have again contacted his father, Samuel Archer. Archer spoke to his son briefly verifying that he was still alive. It is believed that the call was made from Okie's Diner along Route 50. Witnesses spotted two men and a boy in an old truck. This paper was informed that arrangements were made to transfer the ransom for the boy. Police are confident that Avery Archer will be returned to his family unharmed.

The next article was in Saturday, July 4, 1931.

Clues to Kidnapping Found;
Kidnappers Believed to Still Be in Area

This paper has learned that police found Chesterfield cigarette butts on a roadway along the wooded area behind the Archer resident. The sheriff's department believes these to be the first physical evidence belonging to the abductors of Avery Archer. The cigarette butts confirm that one or both of the abductors are chain smokers. It is believed the tire tracks also found are from a truck in very poor condition. Police are combing the area for other clues.

This was not news to me. Avery had informed me that one of the kidnappers was a heavy smoker. I was beginning to think I could anticipate what the articles would contain. I continued with the Saturday, July 4, 1931 article.

Police Narrow Search for Missing Archer Boy

A truck matching the description of the truck reportedly used to abduct Avery Archer was seen at the Nawinah General Store on Thursday. The clerk at the store claimed the man who was driving the truck questioned him regarding what type of medication to administer to a child of eleven who was suffering from a chest and head cold. The clerk described the man as being short, untidy and having a mustache and dark hair. Police are urging those living in Nawinah to lock their windows and doors and stay inside as much as possible. Police are concentrating their search in that area.

Nawinah. Shit! That's where I live.

I continued with the article for Sunday, July 5, 1931. That one should answer many questions.

Body of Avery Archer Believed to Be in Splash Lake

It is believed that Avery Archer, son of Samuel and Esther Archer, was shot and thrown into Splash Lake late last night. An extensive search of Splash Lake is still being conducted in hopes of recovering the body.

This paper has learned that Samuel Archer and his son's abductors arranged to meet and exchange Avery for $100,000 in ransom money at 10:00 p.m. on July 4. Samuel Archer was to meet the kidnappers alone at Splash Lake off Route 415 in Nawinah near an old oak tree. Deputies from Orange County and police from Nawinah and Orlando were hiding in the brush nearby. It was reported that the abductors wore silk stockings over their faces to avoid recognition. They ordered Samuel Archer to drop the money by the oak tree. While this took place, one kidnapper held onto Avery Archer with a gun to his head. The other kidnapper slashed all four tires of Samuel Archer's Cadillac.

The exchange went awry. The kidnappers spotted the police and deputies in the brush. Shots were fired. Samuel Archer was wounded in the left arm. Two policemen were also wounded. It is believed that one of the abductors was shot in the leg. It is also believed that Avery Archer was mortally wounded with a gunshot to his head. Witnesses say that one of the abductors shot the boy, and his body fell into Splash Lake. His shoe was found caught on a bush in the brush along the lake's edge where his body entered the water. The abductors were seen fleeing the scene with the money. Police and deputies followed in pursuit but were unable to apprehend them.

At approximately 12:00 a.m., two Orange County deputies found a 1915 Ford truck outside an abandoned farmhouse on Lake Ripple off Sunnyland Highway in Nawinah. Lake Ripple is approximately a half-mile from Splash Lake. The kidnappers were seen repeatedly in the Nawinah area. Upon entering the house, the deputies ascertained that the farmhouse was unoccupied at that time. In a small bedroom, evidence was found that led police to believe Avery Archer was held captive in that farmhouse. Sheriff Wallace Denton informed this newspaper that the house was infested with roaches and rats. It appeared that Avery Archer survived by eating soup. A pile of empty cans was discovered in one corner of the room. Chains were found linked to the bedpost. A telephone with cut wires was near the bedside. Sheriff Denton believes the kidnappers had a second vehicle and have escaped the *area. An all-points bulletin was issued for their capture.*

Almost in a trance, I stopped the microfilm.

So Avery was killed. Shot in the head and fell into the lake. And he was held captive in a farmhouse on Lake Ripple off Sunnyland Highway in Nawinah. What did that mean? What did it mean that I was receiving phone calls from a kid who was killed sixty-seven years ago? The fact that he was held captive so close to where I live gave me a very uncanny feeling. I also live on Lake Ripple off Sunnyland Highway in Nawinah. The farmhouse had been located on *my* lake somewhere! This was all undeveloped land back in 1931 except for the Kouprianov house across the lake.

I could not come to grips with my situation. I am a realist. I don't believe in fantasies, reincarnation, or even fortune telling, none of that mystic or voodoo stuff. Therefore, it was very difficult for me to comprehend what was going on. In order for me to believe, I would have to throw out all my preconceived ideas about life and death. I always thought that a person is born; he lives; he dies. Once his body is buried in the ground, or he is cremated and scattered where his relatives decide to dispose of him, then that is the end of him. Kaput. Nil. Zilch. That is my dilemma. I would have to throw these beliefs aside to make room for an altogether different mindset, one that placed Avery Archer and me somewhere near the same physical location but separated from each other by sixty-seven years, yet being able to communicate with one another. Not only were we separated by time, but also Avery was dead and I was alive. How is that for a mind-boggling exercise? Would anyone blame me for being doubtful? I was simply not quite ready to give up my reality. I had to learn more.

I continued looking at the microfilm to find if any new information was in the Monday, July 6, 1931, newspaper.

Police Spend Day Searching Splash Lake

Police and deputies spent yesterday searching Splash Lake for the body of Avery Archer assumed to have been shot in the head and fallen into the lake on the night of July 4. Police also combed the brush and dense growth along the edge of the lake, but no body was found. The search would continue until darkness, and, if unsuccessful, will begin again today.

Sources have informed us that Samuel Archer is recovering from a gunshot wound to his arm. He has refused to talk to reporters.

He and his wife must have been going through hell. And to have it all end like that.

I continued on to Tuesday, July 7, 1931.

Search of Splash Lake
for Archer Body Unsuccessful

Police had help from three neighboring counties in their unsuccessful search of Splash Lake for the slain body of Avery Archer. One more attempt will be made today. Splash Lake runs into the Peach River. Efforts are being directed along its riverbanks in the chance that the current may have carried Avery's body down the river.

Samuel and Esther Archer have remained in seclusion.

I continued with Wednesday, July 8, 1931, wondering if I could learn anything else about the case.

Part of Archer Boy's Shirt Found Caught on Branch

A gator hunter discovered a piece of material

believed to be part of Avery Archer's shirt. While hunting near an inlet emptying into Misty Lake, the hunter spotted the black and red material. Police have confiscated the piece of cloth for further investigation. The search for Avery Archer's body has now been extended along the Peach River banks to Misty Lake.

I then read Thursday, July 9, 1931.

Search for Body to Be Suspended

Police have called off the search for the body of Avery Archer. They speculate that the body was eaten by alligators in the infested Peach River. River wardens patrol the river daily. They will be on the lookout for the boy's body.

There was nothing in the next several days of papers. Then in the Saturday, July 11, 1931, paper, the following article appeared:

Samuel Archer Issues Statement on Death of Son

Samuel Archer issued the following statement to this newspaper on Friday, July 10.

"My wife and I would like to thank the Orange County Sheriff Department, the Orlando Police Department, the Nawinah Police Department, and all the surrounding counties for their joint efforts in searching for our son, Avery. Unfortunately, those efforts were unsuccessful, and two ruthless kidnappers killed our son. We are offering a $25,000 reward for information leading to the capture and conviction of these monsters.

"At this time, we are unable to continue with our lives as they had been before this tragedy. I have decided to take my wife to Europe to help ease her pain in dealing with Avery's death. We will be returning in October. I would like to thank each of you for your

prayers. You have been very thoughtful."

The Archers were to embark on their trip today. They asked that no reporters be present for their departure.

I guess the best way to help you forget *would* be to change your surroundings. Not that you would ever forget, but maybe a change of scenery would ease the pain somewhat.

I removed the microfilm and shut off the machine. I wondered what had eventually happened to the Archers. Perhaps I could continue to read the microfilm, but my eyes were starting to get tired from the strain. I wanted to read the ones I had already read again, but I wasn't up to it just then. I approached Mrs. Snuffley.

"Ma'am, is it possible to make copies of the microfilm articles?"

"Yes, just tell me the date and the articles you want copied, and I'll have them for you in about an hour."

"Do you know what became of Samuel and Esther Archer after they went to Europe?"

"Word was that the family moved away several months after the incident. I don't remember where. Sold their home and business. It might be in the newspaper back then…about when and where they moved."

I thanked her and told her I would be back to pick up the copies. While I waited, I went to the police station to talk to Detective Griffin again. I asked the officer at the front desk, "Is Detective Griffin available?"

"If you will have a seat, I'll check to see if he is in."

I sat near the outside door, glancing around the

room. It was still cluttered. Apparently, the maintenance people didn't work on the weekends. The ashtray was now so full that some of the butts had fallen on the floor.

Within a few minutes, the young woman returned. "I'm sorry Detective Griffin is unavailable. Can someone else help you?"

Fleetingly, I thought that I didn't want anyone else thinking I was an unbalanced crackhead. It was bad enough that one detective already thought I belonged in the psyche ward. "No, I don't think so. Do you know when Detective Griffin will be in?"

"Actually, he is off duty until tomorrow afternoon. Would you like to make an appointment to see him?"

She wrote my seven o'clock appointment on a large scheduling calendar hung on the wall. I hoped that when Detective Griffin saw my name he wouldn't conveniently find a case to go on or go out for donuts and coffee. He hadn't been too impressed with me the day before.

Since I couldn't talk to Griffin, I ventured back to the library to pick up the newspaper articles, and then drove home.

Before studying the articles, I took Spree for a walk around the lake. We went to the Kouprianov mansion to see the progress of the renovation up close. The painters were doing a fantastic job. Work was just beginning on the gazebo on the lake. The workers were replacing the rotted wood, keeping to its original design. I sat down on the grass near the lake while Spree romped back and forth, throwing a long stick up in the air, and running in and out of the water. My eyes perused the scene. I looked across the lake at my small bungalow, nestled cozily near the tall, full weeping willow tree in my back yard.

Then I thought of Avery, and I realized how complicated the circumstances were becoming. I outlined a plan of action. First, I would reread the articles from the library, memorizing every single detail. When Avery called back, I would verify his authenticity as much as possible through these articles. I wouldn't tell him that I had read them, just ask him questions about them. One of the reasons I believed him was his willingness to answer anything that I asked. If he were lying, would he not be hesitant to respond to the questions? Then after work tomorrow, I would meet with Detective Griffin and maybe get whatever information might be in the county records that was not in the newspapers. Then I could question Avery about incidents unknown to the public.

Now that I somewhat had a plan, my mind was a little more at ease. "Spree, let's go." She came dripping out of the water not with a fish, but with a plastic Coke bottle, all mangled and dirty. She dropped it on the shoreline and followed me.

Instead of walking back around Lake Ripple, we walked around to the front of the Kouprianov house. I had never seen it from that angle. It was an outstanding house. The gables; the height; the ornate craftsmanship. I looked around the area. Only a few other houses were on the street, and they were far apart, not like my subdivision on the other side of Lake Ripple. We walked across the street to a cement walkway lined with tall, black, decorative lights. Several benches were placed at intervals along the walkway. No signs were posted claiming it was private property, so we walked down it. We ended up at a small park with picnic tables and a playground. A few mothers were watching their children play on the playground equipment. A large sign read "*Splash Lake. No Alcoholic Beverages Allowed.*" I looked straight ahead. Sure enough. There was a giant, expansive lake, probably four times the size of Lake Ripple. Then it registered in my brain. *Splash Lake*! The lake where the kidnapper killed Avery!

We got home about five o'clock, I checked my answering machine, but there were no messages. I didn't expect to hear from Beth anymore that day. If Avery called, for whatever reason, he would not leave a message. I put a frozen pizza in the oven while I sat on the screened porch to read the copies of the microfilm articles again. I read them thoroughly before the pizza was done. I read them again while eating the pizza. By that time, I was sure I knew all the facts they offered about the case, and I felt a little more comfortable about just what to ask Avery.

I also came to the final realization that this was not a kid's prank. All this was happening for a reason having nothing whatsoever to do with mischief or harassment. I didn't know what that reason was yet, but as sure as hell, I was going to find out. It had taken the newspaper articles and that strange walk over to Splash Lake to wake me up to the fact that yes, a heinous crime was committed back in 1931. However, now in 1998, I was called to do something somehow about that crime. I didn't know how. I didn't know when, and I didn't know what. I only knew it was totally up to me. For some strange reason, Avery had contacted me from sixty-seven years ago. Me and only me. Why he was unable to reach anyone else, I didn't know. Hell, I didn't know anything. Only that I was deeply involved in this situation through no fault of my own.

Avery had said that no matter what number he dialed, he reached me each time. Was I supposed to save Avery? Could I save Avery? According to the newspapers he died. Shot in the head and eaten by alligators. If that conclusion were final, why was all this happening? If they weren't to initiate some form of action on my part, what could possibly be the reason for Avery's phone calls? Now, I was anxious for Avery's call.

I picked up the newspaper articles again to read them. All the facts and information I had learned were swimming in my head. Suddenly, it became clear to me. Somehow, all these facts and events would be my guide to saving Avery. Chronologically, I knew the chain of events. With Avery's help, I could fill in any missing details. We would use this information to free him somehow. Of course, how we would accomplish this, I simply had no clue.

About eight that evening while I was reading the articles again, my wait was over.

"Mister, did you find my dad? Did you tell him about the money? Is he coming to get me soon?" Avery bombarded me with questions as soon as I picked up the phone.

"No, Avery, I can't find your dad anywhere. I went to the police station, but I wasn't able to talk to anyone. I've made an appointment to speak to a detective tomorrow night."

"Oh, mister, what am I going to do?" He sounded so frightened and despondent. "They're getting meaner and meaner. I don't know how much longer it'll be before they kill me. I really need my dad."

"I'm trying, Avery. I'm trying very hard, but until tomorrow there isn't anything I can do. You'll have to hang in there a little while longer. What I would like, though, is for you to give me as much information as you can. Then maybe I'll have a better clue as to where you might be. First, my name is Ken Driscoll. You don't have to call me mister all the time. Now, I know you told me about your relatives and your servants, but maybe we can think of something else that will help the police to find you. Let's start with the kidnapping. Tell me exactly what happened."

He tentatively began, "I...I...was playing ball in my backyard. Nobody else was around. Once in a while, Isabel—she's the maid—would look out the door to make sure I was okay. Mother says there are bad men in the woods all the time, so I'm not allowed to go there. We have a fence around the yard, so it's hard to go there anyhow. I wouldn't have gone over the fence, but when I threw my new baseball against a tree, I thought it would come back to me, but it didn't. It bounced over the fence into the woods. I didn't know what to do. My dad just gave me the ball last week as a special present. Dizzy Dean autographed it. He's my favorite baseball player. He plays for the St. Louis Cardinals. They're my favorite team. I knew Dad would be mad if I lost it. Mister, are you still there?"

"Yes, I'm still here. I'm listening. Go on. Tell me what happened next." I wrote what he said on paper as quickly as possible. I wanted to get all the information I could before he had to hang up.

"I waited until Isabel looked out the door again. I

know it was a bad thing to do, but I just had to get that ball back. I figured I'd jump over the fence and get the ball before she looked out the door again. I didn't see anybody in the woods when I looked around before I climbed the fence. But when I reached down to pick up the ball, somebody grabbed me from behind. He put his hand over my mouth and nose. I could hardly breathe, and he smelled so bad I almost threw up in his hand. He was really mean and rough. He tied a handkerchief over my eyes so I couldn't see him and stuffed another one in my mouth so I couldn't talk. I was choking and gagging, but he didn't even care. Then one man grabbed my arms and another man grabbed my legs, and they dragged me through the woods. They threw me into the back of a truck and tied my hands together with a skinny rope, and one man held me down while the other one got in the front of the truck to drive. The man kept crushing my face down on the truck. It really hurt. I just kept wishing we would get to wherever they were taking me so he'd stop pushing my face down."

I interrupted him. "Do you have *any* idea where they took you?"

"No. It was really a bumpy ride, and I was too scared to think of anything."

"Do you remember anything when you got to where you are? I suppose they kept you blindfolded, but maybe you remember something you smelled or heard when you were walking to the place." I was grasping at straws, but I hoped to suggest anything that might awaken a memory.

"I didn't get to walk. They dragged me again. They were so rough, and I don't remember any smells or sounds."

"Okay. Let's change the subject and start talking about the room where they keep you. Can you describe it?"

"Uhh…It's not very clean. The man that smokes keeps putting out his cigarettes on the floor. After he leaves, I make sure that I step on them again so they don't start a fire."

"What kind of furniture is in the room?"

"There's just an old, rickety bed with a smelly mattress. They don't even have any sheets on it. Not even a pillow."

"What kind of bed is it? A wooden bed, a metal bed?"

"It's a metal bed. The posts are very loose and squeaky when I move."

"Is there any other furniture in the room?"

"Just a little table near the bed. The telephone is on it, but nothing else. When they give me food, I have to sit on the bed to eat it."

"So they are feeding you?"

"Yes, they give me some food, but not very much. I'm always hungry. They never give me any meat. Just stale bread and cold soup or beans in a can. At first, I didn't want to eat, but I got so hungry. Then they never take the empty cans away. I put them on the other side of the room 'cause all the bugs and mice crawl in them, and I don't want them crawling on me."

Avery stopped talking briefly. Then he asked, "Mister, can I ask you a question?"

"Sure, Avery."

"Do you think you'll be able to save me before they kill me?"

How could I answer that? I didn't know what I was

doing. Since I now knew of the crazy circumstances of our conversations, I was more confused than the kid was. However, I couldn't let Avery think he was destined to die.

"Somehow or other, I'm going to get you out of that place. I'm not sure how or when, but it will happen. You just have to do what those men tell you until I can get help or come up with some idea myself. I know it's very difficult for you. You miss your mom and dad. I wish I could do something about that, but I can't. You have to be strong. In the meantime, I want you to think of anything that will help. Anything that you can remember. Also, be very alert as far as those men are concerned. Try to remember everything they say and do. Hopefully, that will help determine who they are and where you are."

Then it occurred to me that we had been talking for quite some time.

"Avery, do you know where those men are now?"

"No, but they left right before I called you. I tried to open the door after they left, but they locked it. I even tried to kick it, but it wouldn't open."

"Another thing you can do, Avery, is look around your room to see if there's anything that might give me some clue to your location. Can you see outside?"

"There's one window with broken glass in it, but they have boards nailed to it from the outside."

"Can you see between the boards?"

"No they're too close together."

I had an idea. "Are the boards new or old?"

"They look like they're old and wet. Sometimes, I peel pieces of them off."

There had to be a way for him to see out that

window. I asked, "What do they give you to eat your soup with?"

"Just a bent spoon."

"How about when you are sure the men aren't around, use the spoon to shave off the edge of a board at your eye level so you can see through the crack? Be careful not to cut yourself on the glass left in the window. Then you can look out to see what's outside. Maybe that'll give me some clue to where the house is. Be sure to hide the wood shavings somewhere so those men don't know what you're doing. Let me think. Uhh…What about the hole you create? They'll surely notice that. How can we conceal it?"

I was silently thinking when Avery suddenly spoke, "I know. I left a little bit of soup and beans in the cans. I can mix the wood I shave off with the beans and soup and smash it in the crack."

"Great idea, Avery! You really are a smart kid."

"Thank you," he shyly said, but I could tell he was proud of himself.

"Now you know you'll have to go near those bugs and mice in the cans if you do that, don't you?"

"Yes. I can do it," he said with confidence.

"Then it's settled. Get some rest, and the next time they leave, start to work on the wood. I have no idea how long it'll take you, but I know you can do it. I have to go to work and to the police station tomorrow, so I won't be home until about nine at night. You don't have a clock or a watch, do you?"

"No. This place doesn't have electricity like at my house. Sometimes at night, they come into the room with an oil lamp, but they never leave it."

"Well, if I'm not home when you call, keep trying.

I'll hurry home after I talk to the police. I'm hanging up now. You're very brave. Just keep it up. Good-bye, Avery."

"Good-bye, Mister Driscoll."

So much for getting rid of the "mister"

I felt much better. At least, we had a partial plan. I wasn't quite sure where we were going with it, but it was something anyhow. Even Avery seemed a little less scared since he had something concrete to do to help with his release.

I let Spree out back while I showered. I was going to retire early. This stuff was draining me physically and emotionally

Chapter Five

Monday, June 29, 1998

The next morning, I didn't awaken until the alarm rang at six o'clock. No phone calls from Avery all night. I hoped he was getting a well-deserved rest also. Optimistically, I thought perhaps he was confident I was going to help him and he too had something productive to do to help himself.

I was out the door by a quarter till seven. I waited patiently at the corner of Routes 434 and 436. Nothing was going to get me down. I stopped for my favorite bagel and coffee at Dunkin' Donuts and arrived at the office at seven-thirty. Now, I had to concentrate on my work for eight hours without any sidetracks with thoughts of Avery. I was to meet with a new client, so I had to get in gear. I retrieved their files to study before their arrival at nine o'clock. I was doing just that when Eric arrived late and stopped in my office. Melanie must have made up with him.

"So how did you like the Warrant concert Saturday?" he asked.

"Hey, it was great. I'm glad they sang some of their old songs. The new stuff is okay, but I like the old stuff better."

I wasn't in the mood for small talk, but Eric is a good friend. I didn't want to blow him off.

"Yeah, you're right. I like the old stuff better too. Oh, by the way, what's new on that kid thing? Anymore phone calls?"

I had been so engrossed with working out a plan of action with Avery that I had forgotten to consider how I was going to handle this matter with Eric and others that I might have to deal with regarding Avery, so I had to think quickly and make a judgment call.

"Yeah, he did call back, but I think I have him convinced that I'm wise to his game. I threatened to call the police. I think he'll leave me alone now."

I hated to lie to Eric, but I wasn't sure he would understand if I told him the truth. Who would? I didn't even understand.

"Kids will be kids, but he was carrying his prank a little too far," Eric lectured.

"I don't expect him to call again. Maybe he'll bug somebody else now," I sternly responded as if the Avery thing was over and done.

"Yeah, guess I'd better get to work before Kincaid gets here. By the way, Melanie and I made up. I bought her two dozen yellow roses and a box of Lady Godiva chocolates. She *loves* me now, and it was so easy."

"Finally, you're learning. Oh, by the way, Beth is flying down for the Fourth. I thought you and Melanie might come over to meet her. We can have a cookout. I'm not a great cook. I'll push that job on Beth."

"I'll check with Melanie and let you know tomorrow. I know she hasn't made any plans yet. I really have to get to work now."

Mr. Kincaid and I had a successful meeting with the new client. In fact, Kincaid complimented me on my demeanor. The client would be dropping off several months of the work the next day.

I got through the rest of the day okay. Since there was nothing I could do about Avery until I talked to the police, I resigned myself to doing what was necessary at work.

I left the office promptly at five o'clock and grabbed a bite to eat before going to the police station. After careful thought, I decided it best *not* to tell Detective Griffin that I believed the phone calls from Avery were real. He would think I was crazier than when I talked to him originally, and he'd probably lock me up in a jail cell with all the druggies and convenience store burglars. Therefore, I decided to tell him the phone calls merely perked my interest, and I wanted to find out all that I could about the case.

The police officer at the front desk was about my age, but very muscular and rugged looking. I wondered why the department would put him behind a desk. He looked like he could beat the shit out of any criminal. I told him who I was and who I wanted to see.

"Have a seat. I'll get Detective Griffin."

This guy would get no argument from me about *anything*.

Ten minutes later Detective Griffin opened the heavy door to the operations area. He had on the same worn suspenders as the last time and was wearing a bright green shirt with golf clubs and golf balls all over it. I'd have to find out where he purchased his clothes—and avoid that store.

"Come in, Mister Driscoll."

I followed him back to the same office where we had spoken before.

"What can I do for you this evening?" he asked.

I could tell he was wary of what my reason for seeing him would be, giving me more fuel to lie to him.

"Since I was here the other day, this kid claiming to be Avery Archer has called me several times. With the threat of reporting him to the police, I think I've finally convinced him to leave me alone. However, all these calls have really perked my interest in the case. I went to the library and read the newspaper articles written on it. I'm more intrigued now than ever. I was wondering if it would be possible to look at the police files on it from 1931."

His face and stance relaxed. He seemed relieved that I was not going to insist on the authenticity of the calls again. Maybe that was why he seemed so accommodating.

"To tell the truth, I really don't know. No one has ever asked to see records that old. Those records are well beyond the statute of limitations, so as far as I know, if they are maintained somewhere, you'd be able to view them. We computerized our records about thirty-five years ago. I don't know what happened to anything before that time. Maybe they put them on microfilm. Since that case never went to trial, the court system would have no court documents on it. However, since the crime actually occurred in Orange County, maybe the county has a file on it somewhere. I believe they have an archive record department located somewhere near John Young Parkway and Thirty-third Street, but I don't know how far back they go either. Your best bet is to call down there. Maybe they can direct you to where the records can be located."

He took his pad and pencil out of his pocket. "Here's the Orange County Sheriff Department telephone number." He handed me the paper.

"Thanks a lot. I really appreciate this. You've been very helpful."

This record thing did not seem like an easy task. I thought all I had to do was walk into the police department, and there they would be.

By the time I left the police station, it was too late to do any calling to locate the records. I had to postpone it until the next day. I'd call from work the first thing in the morning.

Arriving home, I felt that I was wasting time, but I could do nothing until morning. And the hours were ticking away for Avery. He was relying on me so much, and he needed action, not worrying or fretting.

I tried to watch television but couldn't get interested in anything. Picking up the newspaper, I read each sentence three times before it stuck in my head. It was just after eight o'clock, much too early for bed. I ate a frozen dinner and took Spree down near Lake Ripple. Darkness seeped into the sky, and the setting sun streaked ripples of light across the gentle waves on the lake's surface. The air was hot and humid, but the slight breeze kept it from being unbearable.

We walked around the lake to the other side. All the while, my thoughts were on Avery. I stopped to admire the gazebo and the progress of its renovation and decided to view it close up. Spree followed along after me, running in and out of the water. I walked onto the dock. They had repaired missing and weathered wood with new lumber. The job was so intricate and so artistic. They still had not painted the structure, but it looked like they had very little repair work yet to do. I envied the workmanship. Me? My carpentry ability is such that if I were pounding nails into wood, I would end up hitting my fingernails instead of the metal nails. However, if I were asked to add in my head twenty numbers of two and three digits each as quickly as possible, I could do it in less than one minute. Or if I were asked what day of the week January 5, 1945, or March 18, 1969, fell on, I could give the answer in less than a minute also. However, when it comes to carpentry, plumbing, or any of the manual skills, I'm a complete moron. By the way, January 5, 1945, was a Friday, and March 18, 1969, was a Tuesday.

Resting on the new lumber, I looked across the lake at my house. I had left the kitchen light on above the sink that looks out onto the lake. The house looked so cozy and comfortable. Beth will love it. I was in deep thought, when suddenly, from behind me, someone spoke.

"Hey, you live in that big house back there?"

Startled, I jerked around. Two boys had walked onto the dock. They looked about twelve or thirteen. One was slightly shorter than the other one. They were dressed in cut-offs and T-shirts and carried fishing poles and a tackle box.

"You kids caught me by surprise. I didn't hear you coming up behind me. No, I don't live here. Wish I did. I live across the lake in that house with the light on. I was admiring the house and this gazebo and wanted to see it up close. Do you guys live around here?"

The boys came a little closer. The shorter one carrying the poles answered, "Yeah, we live over on Camilla. We come over here to fish. I caught a real big bass last week. We come about this time almost every night. I thought maybe you lived here and was gonna chase us away."

"Well, I guess whoever does own this place will be chasing all three of us away. I like to walk over here with my dog."

"Is that your dog? He's a beauty. I've seen him around here before. What kind is he?"

"He is a *she*. The vet told me she's part Lab and part Shepherd. That's about all I know."

The taller boy then asked timidly, "Can we play with her. My mom won't allow me to have a dog. She says they're too much work. I told her I'd take care of him, but she doesn't believe me. Guess I'll have to wait until I get old like you and buy my own."

Chuckling, I said, "You can play with her. She'd love it. Her name is Spree. What're your names? I'm Ken Driscoll."

The smaller one answered for both of them as they went to throw the stick to Spree. "I'm Robby Garrett. This here is my best friend Matt Spinoza."

"Well, glad to meet you, Robby and Matt."

They had a great time playing with Spree, throwing the stick back and forth, and chasing her in and out of the water. She enjoyed it as much, if not more than they did. I also enjoyed watching them. It was relaxing somehow to watch these two boys and a dog use up such energy, yet never seeming to run out of it. Every boy should have a dog. Maybe I should have a talk with this kid's mother to inform her of what he is missing. Maybe I should just mind my own business.

It grew dark as the boys romped with Spree. The moon and the reflection of the streetlights on the lake cast a small amount of light around us. As usual, I had brought my flashlight. I know how dark it can get around the lake. I turned it on, providing more light for Spree and the boys to play.

I grew melancholy thinking of how Avery's life was snuffed out before he had a chance to enjoy many of the things young boys do, such as what these boys were doing. I thought of how Avery loved baseball, how his dad would have taken him to many games as he grew up, but how he never got that chance.

Eventually, the boys and Spree grew tired, and they came over on the dock to sit with me.

"I sure like your dog. Can we play with her again, maybe?" asked Matt Spinoza.

Standing to get ready to leave, I responded, "Hey, that's a great idea. Remember, I live right across the lake in that house with just the one light on. You guys come over any evening, and Spree will be glad to play with you, won't you Spree?" I looked down at a tired, worn out dog.

"It's getting dark. Don't you guys have to go home?"

"Yeah, we'd better go or our moms will be mad at us," spoke Robby, regretfully.

They gathered their fishing poles and tackle box, which hadn't gotten any use that evening.

"Well, we'll see y'all, maybe in a couple of days," yelled Robbie as they walked away.

Our trip back around the lake was much slower than when we came. It wasn't my fault either, but it had done the poor dog some good. Both she and Beth had not received much of my attention lately. Also, those boys are more energetic than I am anymore. I guess I'm getting old like Matt mentioned. Maybe when Beth gets here, we'll both join the health club. Maybe not.

Chapter Six

Tuesday, June 30, 1998

"Hello, Mister Driscoll, this is Avery." He sounded very tired and despondent.

"What's wrong? Are you okay?"

"I'm pretty tired. I've been shaving that wood on the window all day until those men came back. I tried to sleep earlier, but they were having a loud party. They kept coming in my room and trying to spill beer down my throat. I was gagging, but they didn't stop. Now I smell terrible. They finally left me alone and went to sleep. I just can't go back to sleep now, and my stomach hurts from that awful beer."

"You've got to keep your strength up. Are you eating the soup they give you?"

"Most of it. Sometimes they give it to me after it sat out open all day long. Then bugs are crawling in it. I have a hard time eating it then, but sometimes I pick out the bugs. I don't like bugs very much, and I sure don't want to eat them."

"Avery, I know you have no clock or calendar there, but do you know what day it is?"

I had memorized the dates and events in the newspaper, and I wanted to see where we were in relationship to those events.

"I'm...not sure. The days and nights are all mixed

together. I know it was Thursday afternoon when they brought me here because I went out to play ball about two o'clock. I...don't know. Maybe a week has gone by. Maybe it's Thursday again."

"I guess you would be mixed up. You probably haven't seen daylight since you've been in that room. Have you shaved off enough wood to know if it is day or night?"

"I can't see out, but I know it's dark out now, 'cause when I was shaving the wood before a little bit of light started to show through the crack. There isn't any light now. So it must be night."

"Yes, in fact, it is very early in the morning, about two-thirty Tuesday morning. Do you know what month it is?"

"Let me think. It was Thursday, June 25, when they took me, so if it isn't Thursday again yet and it's only Tuesday, then it must be the last day of June. Yes. It's June 30th."

"Yes, that's correct. You're very smart to be able to work that out so quickly. You must do well in school."

"Yes. I get very good grades. Father wants me to be a doctor when I grow up, but I'd rather be a baseball player."

"A baseball player is good too, but you have a lot of time to think about that. Didn't you say you were eleven?"

"Yes. I'll be twelve on my next birthday on March 19."

"I'm going to ask you a silly question now. I have my reasons even if it sounds strange to you. Do you know what year it is?"

"It's 1931, of course."

My heart started racing. I had known he was going to say 1931, but actually hearing it made me get apprehensive. From the newspaper articles, I knew that on Tuesday, June 30, 1931, the kidnappers would be taking Avery to a telephone somewhere to make a phone call to Samuel Archer. This was our first chance at changing the course of history. A plan formed in my head.

Excitedly, I said, "Avery, I can't tell you how I know this, but I know positively that those men will take you to a gas station sometime during the daytime today. They will make a telephone call to your dad, and he will demand to speak to you."

He interrupted, "My dad? You talked to him? Oh, thank you. Thank you."

I could hear his voice tremble with emotion. I hated to disappoint him after he had thought I had contacted his dad, but I had no choice.

Quickly, I stopped him before he got too elated. "No, no, I haven't talked to your dad. I'm sorry if I misled you."

"But…But…how do you know they're gonna talk to my dad? Did you talk to those men? I…don't understand."

"No, I didn't talk to those men. You'll just have to trust me on this. It's very complicated."

What else could I say? He'd never understand the truth. I didn't understand it. How could he?

I replied, "Listen carefully. They will take you to this gas station. I think they will let you sit in the cab part of the truck this time. If they make you go in the back, try to put your arm under your face so you don't scratch it any more. The important thing is you have to try to get a message to someone at the gas station to let them know who you are and maybe some idea where you are."

I could hear the sobbing in his voice. "But I don't even know where I am."

"I know. I know."

Now the hard part. To tell him that I knew where he was, but that I couldn't get to him. There were sixty-seven years in our way. Since I couldn't tell him that, the best thing was to pretend I, too, didn't know where he was. I also thought it was important to keep his mind occupied while on the short trip with his kidnappers. In that way, he would stay more alert and perhaps take advantage of any situation where he might be able to contact someone, or, better still, to escape. So I "pretended" instead of actually lying. Sometimes there's a difference.

"I know you don't know where you are now, but when they take you in the truck, try to remember every time they turn a corner, whether it turns left or right, how many times it stops at a traffic light, how many times it stops at a stop sign, if they go over a railroad track. In other words, try to map out in your mind how they get to where you are now to the gas station."

"I...don't know if I can do that."

"Just try. Try your best. That's all I ask."

We had to do more. I had another idea.

"Avery, look around the room. Is there anything at all on which you can write? Paper? A book? A piece of light cloth? Anything? And something to write with? A pencil? A pen?"

"I don't see anything."

"I'll stay on the line. You give the room a thorough search. Everywhere. Under the bed. In the closet."

He was gone for several minutes. I could hear slight, muffled noises through the receiver. When he finally returned, he seemed in better spirits.

"I found a tiny pencil stub. It doesn't have much lead. Maybe I can sharpen it with my spoon. I found an old envelope too. It has some writing on it, but it's all blurry. It says…uh…Nawinah, Florida. Do you think that's where I am? I don't know where that is, do you? Maybe you could tell the police I found this envelope that says Nawinah, Florida, on it. Maybe they might know where to look for me."

The kid was clever. I had to get out of this one.

"You're right, Avery. I'll get in touch with the police as soon as I'm done talking to you, but Nawinah is a big town. We'd better not rely on them to find you. What we have to do is try to get somebody's attention at the gas station. The envelope should work perfectly. You need to write your name on it and something like 'help me' as big as you can on the envelope. Be careful not to write over the words 'Nawinah, Florida'. Then when they take you to the gas station, after you've talked to your dad, drop it on the ground. However, it's very important those men don't see you drop it. I don't mean to scare you, but they may even have a gun, maybe in their pocket out of sight where a passerby couldn't see it. So, if it's too risky, don't do it. We'll think of something else. Also, one of them will probably have his hands on you at all times, so you may not get a good opportunity. Try to keep the paper crumpled in your hand so they don't see you carry it. Then maybe toss it behind you after you've talked to your dad. I know you'll be all excited, getting a chance to talk to him, but you can't forget about the note. Be sure you drop it only if you think it's safe. Can you repeat what you're supposed to do?"

"Uhh…I'm supposed to write my name on the envelope as big as I can, and also HELP ME and not write over Nawinah, Florida. Then I'm supposed to remember how they drive me to the filling station, like traffic lights, and left and right turns, and stuff like that. After I talk to my dad, I'm supposed to drop the note, but I'm not supposed to let the bad men see me drop it. If I don't get a chance, I'm not supposed to do it. Is that right?"

"Perfect. Again, I can't promise that this will work. If it doesn't, we'll try something else. Just try not to worry anymore. We're going to get you out of this. We're a team now."

"A team?" He sounded puzzled.

"Yeah. That means we will work together. You know, like a baseball team does to win their game. They work together. That's how we will win too. How does that sound?"

"I guess that's okay," he answered, rather unsure of my analogy.

"It's getting very late, Avery. You have a big day ahead of you. Just remember everything I said, but tonight get some rest. Call me when it's all over. I do have to work, but I'll get home as soon as I can."

"Good-bye, Mister Driscoll. Thank you."

Sure, I told him to call me after it was over, but how would that work? If he did call me, did that mean he was unsuccessful in his escape attempt? Was it even possible for him to contact me from the police station or his dad's house? How the hell did all this work? This was brand new territory for me. Hell, for anybody.

I awakened to the blaring alarm, the sound I love so well. Maybe I had four hours sleep total. I staggered out of bed and put the coffee on, sleepwalking through the morning ritual. Then I remembered that I hadn't checked my message machine or my mailbox. First. I looked at the machine. Two messages. Both from Beth, wondering where I was. I couldn't believe she had entirely slipped my mind. How ironic that just a couple of days before, my thoughts were consumed by her and our coming wedding, which now seemed trivial in comparison to trying to save a life. I knew she would still be in bed, so I postponed calling her until the evening.

I opened the back door for Spree and let her roam around the back yard. I would have many piles of shit to clean up whenever I got around to it. I retrieved my mail from the mailbox. Just my credit card bill and an envelope from the telephone company, probably the printout I had requested from those incoming calls. I quickly ripped it open, hoping for some sort of revelation. No such luck. No calls whatsoever from Avery were listed. At least I knew why now. I remembered what a stupid ass I must have sounded like to the telephone company, although they didn't sound much better.

After rescuing Spree from a vicious stick, I gave her some food and finished my morning activities before letting her out to get rid of the food I had just given her. Then off to work.

Shortly after eight, I dialed the number Detective Griffin had given me for the sheriff's department.

Surprisingly, a cordial voice answered.

"Could you connect me to the Archive Records Department, please?"

Without hesitation, she connected me to a ringing telephone. A female voice answered. "Archives."

"Could you tell me if you have records there dating back to 1931?"

"No, sir. Our records only go back to 1950," she said.

"Where would you keep the records for 1931?"

"Did you check the courthouse? Do you know the case number? They may have the information you need."

"The case was never solved or even brought to trial."

"Oh. What type of records are we talking about?"

I told her the case was a kidnapping that occurred in June of 1931.

"Was there a juvenile involved in the kidnapping?" she asked, trying to get more information.

"Yes, an eleven-year-old boy."

"Then that would be under federal jurisdiction. You'll have to contact them. They keep all files on juvenile kidnapping cases," she advised.

"Do you know who I could contact?" I asked.

"No, I don't. You might try the FBI. Their number is listed in the telephone book."

"Thank you." I hung up. No luck there, so I got out my trusty telephone book and looked up the FBI in the blue pages.

"Federal Bureau of Investigations" Another live person. Surprise again.

"Yes. I have a rather strange question to ask. Do

you know where you might store old criminal case records that date back to 1931?"

"Oh my! I don't know the answer to that. Let me connect you with an agent. Perhaps he can assist you."

I love the telephone.

"Agent Landmier speaking."

"Yes, Agent Landmier, my name is Ken Driscoll, and I'm trying to find out where you might store criminal records that date back to 1931."

"What type of crime was it?" He wanted to know.

"It was a juvenile kidnapping."

"Where did the crime occur?" More questions.

"The boy lived in Winter Park, but the crime actually occurred in Orange County," I informed him.

"Have you contacted Orange County?"

"Yes. They told me the federal government keeps records of all juvenile kidnapping cases."

"That's not necessarily so. We are not always called in on cases," he contradicted. "Was this a prominent case?"

"Yes it was. It was the kidnapping of the son of Samuel and Esther Archer. It's my understanding that it made news nationally."

"I'm sorry. I'm not familiar with that case. Did you try the Orange County Court House?"

"The case never went to trial. The police never caught the abductors, so I doubt if the court house would have any records." I tried to explain the circumstances.

"Well, Mister Driscoll. I don't know what to tell you. As far as I know, we would not have records dating back that long ago. How about the newspaper?"

"I've obtained whatever I could from the

newspaper, but I wanted to get more detailed information."

"I'm sorry. I can't help you. I'd check back with the county. Maybe talk to the supervisor of their records department. I'm sure they would know."

"I guess I'll try that. Thank you." Another dead end.

I called back the Archive Record Department. "Hello. I just called regarding finding out where you might maintain records from 1931."

"Yes, this is Karen. You talked to me."

"Karen, I called the FBI, and they were unable to give me any information."

"You mean the information is classified?" she asked.

"No, he just told me he didn't know where those types of records are kept. He also said that they're not always called in on juvenile kidnapping cases."

"Let me see if I can get you an answer. Can you hold?" She pressed a button to administer more wordless music to my ears.

Of course, I can hold. You will then come back and tell me to run right down there because you have the file in your hand. Who am I kidding? I held anyway.

Several minutes passed, and Karen finally returned. "I've talked to my supervisor. He has informed me that we don't keep records dating back that far."

"You mean that in an unsolved case, the records would've been destroyed?"

"That's my understanding. I guess they feel that everybody concerned with the case is dead now."

"But this was a very prominent case, publicized throughout the country. Perhaps you heard of it. It was the kidnapping of Avery Archer, son of the wealthy orange grower, Samuel Archer and his wife, Esther. It was in all the papers throughout the country."

"I'm sorry. I'm not familiar with the case. Hold on. Let me ask my supervisor again." She was gone for several more minutes, and I heard more music.

Then the music stopped, and a man answered. "This is Don Wyckoff. To whom am I speaking?"

"I'm Ken Driscoll."

"Mister Driscoll, Karen told me you are interested in finding the files on the Avery Archer case?"

"Yes, I am."

"Well, as Karen told you, we don't maintain records dating back that far at this facility. I'm not sure if they are maintained anywhere. I'm vaguely familiar with the Archer case and know that it was quite well known. I'll give you the telephone number of the local storage facility of the Florida Records Storage Center. We currently use a state-operated, secured storage facility for inactive files and large items of evidence collected from a crime site. The state-of-the-art facility contains a climate-controlled vault for microfilm and magnetic media. I know files dating back that long ago were not put on microfilm. However, since it was such a publicized case, there's a possibility that something might be available."

"Thank you very much, Mister Wyckoff. I appreciate your effort."

I tried the number he gave me. It rang several times. I was about to hang up when the phone finally answered.

"Good morning. Florida Records Storage Center, Orlando Division."

Probably another dead end.

"Hello. I'm trying to locate the police files on a case dating back to 1931. Would you have them at that location?"

"Hold please. I will connect you with the Bureau of Archives and Records Management."

I waited.

"This is Osha Minnuppa. Can I help you?"

"I sure hope so, Osha Minnuppa. I'm trying to locate a police file dating back to 1931. Would you happen to have those at your location?"

"It depend what file you be looking for. We don't have many. That a long time ago. Most everything gone from way back then. What be the one you want?"

"It's the Avery Archer kidnapping. He was the son of Samuel Archer, the orange grower, and his wife Esther. The kidnapping occurred in June of 1931, and the boy was killed on July 4 of that year."

"Hmmm. You wait. I check."

She left the line for nearly ten minutes. There was no elevator music, so I thought she had hung up on me. I started adding a column of numbers from the client's worksheet I had on my desk and waited just in case she came back.

Finally, she returned. "I not sure we have that file. My computer say something available, but I have to search location. You want to see files?"

"Yes, I would very much like to actually see them if you have any."

"I tell you. Computer say we have something. I look and call you back."

"That would be great." I gave her my name and telephone number. It sounded promising. I just had to contain myself until I heard from this Osha Minnuppa babe with the weird accent. It was probably another dead end.

I went about my work as usual. I talked to Eric briefly at lunch. He mentioned that Melanie had agreed to join us for a cookout on the Fourth. With all else going on in my head, I had completely forgotten about it.

"Great. Beth will be pleased." I acted interested.

"What would you like us to bring? Melanie is a mean brownie maker."

"That's perfect. Chocolate is Beth's weakness. She'll kill me, but I like to watch her fight with herself over eating it. She'll probably devour them all. You'd better bring one batch for her and one batch for the rest of us, but hiding ours."

"What time should we come over?"

"I'll have to get back to you on that. I'll talk to Beth when she gets in. You know, we need some time to ourselves before we are invaded."

"Hey, are you uninviting us already?" he said in his mockingly hurt manner.

"I could handle keeping her in bed for the entire weekend. But, seriously, I'll have to let you know the time, probably early afternoon."

We went back to work. At least I expect that Eric did. I accomplished very little.

At three o'clock Nancy buzzed me. "Ken, you have a call on line three from an Osha Minkpuppy, or something like that."

"Thanks, Nancy. It's Minnuppa," I corrected her.

"Whatever."

"Mister Driscoll, this be Osha Minnuppa. I call you

about Archer kidnap files."

"Yes, Osha, I've been waiting for your call."

"I find old, old sealed box on case. It been here since building built in 1985. Don't know where it was before that, but it be cataloged in computer. I find it in vault of very old files."

"That's great. I assume that in most cases the public doesn't have access to criminal cases. But what about this one? It happened so long ago. Can I see it?"

"Yes. Statute of Limitation be up. You can see. Only need to submit form LLT5F303 to us. Can fax, telephone, or mail."

"I wanted to see them today. Would that be possible?"

"Yes, you come. We fill out form here. We not open all the time for people, but we open most time for the people who need to see files. What time you come?"

I probably could get out of work an hour or so early, claiming I had some personal business to attend.

"Where are you located?"

"We on John Young Parkway."

She gave me directions, and I told her I would be there at five o'clock.

At least, I had a physical location. Whether or not anything would be left to see in the files was another story, but I had to take the chance.

I left the office at four, telling Nancy I wouldn't be back for the rest of the day. Mister Kincaid had left with his family for a vacation in Canada, so he definitely wouldn't come looking for me.

I found the Florida Records Storage Center with very little difficulty. It was a huge building, taking up the space of a football field. It took me quite some time to find an entrance that was accessible to the public. I found a massive metal front door, but when I tried the knob, it was locked. I looked around the door and discovered a buzzer about two feet off to my left with a small sign saying "Ring Bell for Service." I did just that and waited for a response. Soon a security guard opened the big, metal door.

"What is your business, sir?"

"Osha Minnuppa is expecting me."

We entered the building into an expansive room. Half dozen computers and their uniformed operators occupied the large workstation in the center of the room. The security guard led me to the reception desk in front of the workstation.

"Your name, Sir?" asked the uniformed receptionist.

"Kenneth Driscoll. I'm here to see Osha Minnuppa."

"One moment please." She called Osha Minnuppa on her telephone.

"Captain Minnuppa will see you now. Please follow the guard."

He led me down a long hallway with numbered, metal doors on both sides at intervals of about fifteen or twenty feet. The floor was of a nondescript terrazzo, and the sound of our heels clicking echoed in the quiet hallway.

We stopped at number 243. The security guard knocked on the door. I heard from inside that distinctive accent I had heard earlier on the telephone. "Come in, please."

The guard unlocked the door with a large key from

his belt loop key ring and then held the door for me. The door locked behind me, leaving the guard to go about his business elsewhere.

Osha Minnuppa was at her desk. She was a huge, black woman, wearing an ornate African headdress and a bright orange, green, and yellow muumuu in an intricate, angular pattern. She looked exactly like her voice sounded. As I came up to the front counter, she waddled out of her chair toward me. She must have weighed four hundred pounds. The dress was probably made out of two sheets to cover her massive body. Maybe a tent.

"You be the young man who call this morning?"

"Yes, I am. Ken Driscoll, ma'am. I hope you can help me. I've been searching all over Orlando for the police files on the Avery Archer case."

"Like I tell you on telephone. Something here in sealed box. You fill out this form."

She handed me a two-sided form that required very specific information. First, there was the usual stuff: name, address, and telephone number. Then came the hard part. What was the reason that I wanted to see these files? I stared at the question for quite some time. Osha Minnuppa noticed I was not completing that part of the questionnaire.

"You have problem with form?"

"I...don't quite know how to answer this question." I pointed to the one giving me the problem.

"That a hard question for you?"

"Yes, I guess it is."

"They just want to know why a young man like you want to look at that old file. You have reason, I sure."

I don't know why, but I had a feeling about this woman. She looked like someone who would believe me. I could have lied and used the old excuse about writing a paper or research on some other case, but as reckless as it may seem, I decided to tell her the truth. I think I did so because it was just a tremendous burden on my mind, and I hoped that by saying it aloud, it might ease the burden somewhat. As I said, I had a feeling she was the right person.

"I don't know how to say this, so I'll just blurt it out. That murdered boy, Avery Archer, calls me on the telephone asking me to save him from his kidnappers."

Have you ever seen a black person turn white? Osha Minnuppa did. I could tell she believed me immediately. Even though I knew it was an enormous shock to her, it actually felt good finally to say it aloud to someone who didn't think I was a psycho.

She waddled back to her desk, and with a big thud, sat into her chair. She was sweating profusely. I had to apologize.

"I'm so sorry. I didn't mean to upset you. Please forgive me. You looked like someone who would believe me. Detective Griffin of the Orlando Police Department thinks I'm crazy. I had to tell him I was merely interested in the case. Here, take my handkerchief. I'm so sorry."

She did some deep, rhythmic breathing, then hoisted herself out of the chair, waddled back to the front counter, and took my handkerchief.

"Can I get you some water or something? I'm so sorry." Now, I was beginning to feel guilty. I hadn't expected her to be that upset.

Finally, she said, "No, I be okay now. You give me

big scare. I not think you say that. I let you in my office. You tell me more. Then we decide how to fill out form."

She unlocked and opened the counter entrance and went back to her desk. I followed and sat at the chair opposite her.

"Tell me now. Why you say that boy call you?"

I recounted my entire experience to her, trying not to leave out anything. She listened attentively. When I finished, she put her big brown hand over my hand. "You have big job. How you gonna do it?"

I knew then that she believed every word I told her.

"I really don't know. That's why I wanted to look at the files. Maybe they can give me some idea. I've been to the library and copied all the newspaper articles. Would you have any suggestions? I'm sort of having a hard time with this."

Her forehead crinkled up in a mass of wrinkles. The droplets of sweat went into the creases and flowed like tiny streams across her forehead, then down to her cheeks. She was staring at me, but I knew she really wasn't seeing me.

At last she spoke. "I tell you, man. You got to stop what the newspaper say. That what God want. That why that boy call you. God want you save that young boy. He want you change the past. That what you must do. You read each day of paper. You think how to change what happen."

"That's what I thought too, but how can I do that if it has already happened?"

"Don't know, but you *must*."

"I guess the first place to start is the files. What should I put down on this form?"

Her bulbous nose crinkled and wrinkled. Her tiny eyes closed to little slants as she thought. "We just say 'research'. That be enough. I go get box."

That was okay by me. I finished filling out the form while she retrieved the files. Rows and rows of shelving lined the area behind where I was sitting. She disappeared from my sight behind them. When she returned, she carried a tattered, old, cardboard box about the size of a ten-ream copier paper box. As soon as I saw her, I quickly got up to relieve her of it.

"Great! You found it!" I was elated.

"That be very big case. I think somebody decide we keep files. It back in room for many years, but we not destroy. Maybe think solved someday. Maybe somebody right."

"You don't know how thankful I am that you have this! Can I look through it?"

"That room over there. There be table you use."

I carried the box into the small room after she unlocked the door. It was only big enough for a small table and two straight back, wood chairs. She left the room as I sat on one of the chairs.

I stared at the box for several seconds, dreading, yet excited about what it might contain. Then after rubbing my hands together, I stood and slowly and gently removed the crumbling, dried tape away from the top of the box. It was so brittle that most of the glue had already disintegrated. I opened the box.

At the top were papers, wrinkled and yellow with age—small scraps of paper from the note pads of officers on the case and typed pages with faded letters. I sat down and read each typed sheet and each scrap of paper. Most of it was repetitious of itself or the newspaper articles. I had brought a three ring binder and a pen to write down any significant information that couldn't be copied.

Next, I looked at pages and pages dealing with the questioning of Samuel and Esther Archer and their staff, probably to determine if any of them had any connection to the crime. The consensus of the officers on the case was that neither the Archers nor their staff had been involved. The files also recounted conversations with neighbors, coming up with another dead end. No neighbor seemed connected in any way, and no one had witnessed the kidnapping. The essence of the files was that two men cased the Archer residence and knew who their victim was well in advance of the crime. It was no random act, but well planned and carried out.

The box contained pages on the testimony of the messenger who dropped off the ransom note. The police also determined he was just that, a messenger who needed money for coffee or booze. He too knew nothing about the crime.

I also read testimonies of all the eyewitnesses mentioned in the newspaper. Aside from reinforcing the descriptions of the two men that Avery had given me, I found no new revelations in these either. The eyewitnesses described the truck the men drove, but that too, was in the newspaper.

Then I came to the sheriff's plan for the exchange of the hostage for the ransom money. It contained details on how the police were stationed in and around the area of the exchange. According to the report, it sounded foolproof. I guess they didn't count on the kidnappers slashing Samuel Archer's car tires. I guess they also didn't expect to be found hiding in the brush around the area of the exchange. Myself, I think it was a very poor plan. Of course, not knowing much about covert police activity, I didn't have any better suggestion. However, it just seemed that with all the trained minds they had on the case, the outcome should've been better.

I put aside the paper work that I wanted to copy. I also wrote down the names of all those closely involved on the case. Wallace Denton was the Orange County Sheriff; Jeb Whiting was the captain of the Orlando Police Department; Calvin Mason was the deputy and main officer on the case; and Luther Billings was his junior partner. Wilbur Duncan and Eubbey Litomen were the police officers who found the farmhouse where the kidnappers held Avery captive.

The next group of papers dealt with the search for Avery's body by the combined law enforcement organizations, going into detail describing where they targeted and intensified their search. The newspaper had mentioned a piece of material believed to be part of Avery's shirt found on the banks of Peach River. These papers described the condition of the cloth as bloody and shredded.

The report then described the farmhouse, listing the address simply as a farmhouse off Sunnyland Highway near Lake Ripple. It stated that a long drive led to the farmhouse with an overgrowth of trees, bushes, and shrubs surrounding it, making it impossible to see the house from the highway. The drive itself was overgrown with weeds. The officers found it by accident when Eubbey Litomen got out to piss, great reading that in a police report. It described them finding the truck near the dilapidated farmhouse. It also described the condition of the house itself; how it was rat and roach infested; and how a pile of cans lay in the corner of the bedroom. It mentioned how the window was broken away and how the boards covering the window were chiseled with some type of tool, probably the spoon found on the table beside the bed. It described how part of the window frame was torn away and how it appeared the boards were re-nailed up to the window. The bed itself contained a vomit and urine-stained, bloody mattress with the batting worn loose. No pillows, sheets, or blankets were on the bed. Bloody chains hung from the bedpost.

The telephone base was on the small nightstand next to the bed. It had the number 358L printed on it, the exact numbers Avery had given me during our early conversations. The receiver was off its cradle, dangling from its base down the front of the small table. The telephone wires leading into the wall were cut.

I pulled out the black and white photographs next. Even though they were sixty-seven years old, they were as clear as if they were taken yesterday. They graphically showed the condition of the room where Avery spent so much of his last days. They showed the bloody, stained bed on which Avery existed during those days. They showed other rooms in the farmhouse. The filth was indescribable. How could anybody live there for five minutes let alone the week Avery spent there? Unconsciously, I still had the photographs in my hand when I walked over to the door. As I exited the room, I saw Osha Minnuppa at her desk with her head back and her eyes closed.

At first, I thought she was asleep, but she opened

her eyes as I drew near.

"You finish?" she asked me.

"No," I answered somewhat reluctantly. "I found these."

I didn't think. Stupidly, I dropped them on her desk in front of her.

"Oh God be merciful!" she cried out very loudly. "What monster make a boy live in this filth?"

Now I'm no wimp, but I had a difficult time coping with these photographs. I was beginning to identify with Avery, and looking at these photos, I realized what he endured before they shot him. He told me about the room, but seeing these photos made it a reality.

Osha Minnuppa realized I was having trouble. "You need coffee."

She had recovered more easily than I had. Maybe she was used to seeing this stuff. Probably worse.

I was still staring at the photographs when she returned with coffee.

"That enough. You saw. You look no more." She took the photographs away from me.

I drank the hot coffee. "Thank you. I don't know what came over me. I apologize for showing you those pictures. I wasn't thinking."

"That okay. I see worse before. Not new. In South Africa violence everywhere. I see too much. I see photos here too. People do bad things to each other all the time. Terrible things."

She looked at me in a motherly way. "You finish. It be late. Almost nine o'clock. You go home now."

I hadn't realized it was that late. Still somewhat in a daze, I looked at my watch. It was ten till nine. I had read and looked at the files and photographs for almost four hours! And Osha Minnuppa patiently waited for me to complete my task. I had to finish tonight.

"No. There isn't too much more. That is, if it's okay with you. Do you have to leave?"

"You finish if you must. I wait."

I took the remainder of the coffee into the room. I also picked up the photographs but carried them face down.

Back in the room, I looked into the box to see what remained. At the bottom was a large, bulky, sealed envelope, also very wrinkled and torn on the corners and creases. I don't know what I expected to find. What could be worse than those photographs except seeing Avery's dead body? I carefully pulled back the sealed portion. The glue, like the tape on the box itself, had mostly disintegrated. Gently, I reached my hand inside. The first thing I grasped was a baseball. It was yellow from age, and the threads on the seams were tattered, but what was most surprising, yet not a shock to me, was that Dizzy Dean had autographed it. No one except those who had seen these files and Avery's family knew about this autograph, but here it was. Just as Avery had said. I no longer had any doubts about the authenticity of those telephone calls.

After thoroughly examining the baseball, I retrieved the rest of the contents of the envelope. I pulled out a scrap of red and black plaid cloth, bloody, faded, and frayed, about five inches long and an inch and a half wide. A slip of paper pinned to the cloth noted the date of its discovery by the alligator trapper on the Peach River bank. I then removed a smaller envelope from the larger one. Upon opening it, I found pieces of cotton batting stained a brownish wine color and a dark mustard yellow, most likely from the mattress. Another envelope contained some cigarette butts, the brand of which could not be determined. Finally, the last item was an old bent, metal spoon so worn down it was almost unrecognizable as a spoon.

I carefully re-examined each item as I replaced them into the envelope. I put the photographs face down into the box. I took the papers I wanted to copy out to the main office where Osha Minnuppa was still at her desk.

"I'd like to have a hard copy of these papers. Is that permissible?"

"Sure, man."

Osha Minnuppa made the copies for me, and I put everything back into the box. I brought the box out to her to return to the archives. From a nearby cabinet, she retrieved a roll of wide, clear, blue tape. She mentioned it was a special tape that wouldn't crack or loosen with age. I watched as she orderly arranged the material in the box and put some additional filler in so no air remained in it. Then she sealed it with the tape and carried the box back to its place of origination.

As she was replacing the box, I thought how helpful she was. Partly because of her trust in me, a perfect stranger, I finally was able to resolve the tumultuous conflict going on in my mind over Avery. What I saw that evening thoroughly convinced me of the dangerous situation surrounding Avery then and as time would have it, now also. I had to express my gratitude to her.

When she returned I said, "You don't know how much your support has meant. I didn't think anyone would believe me. I want to sincerely thank you for your help and your kindness."

"I glad I be able to help. You need me, you call. Just ask for Osha when you call this building."

"I will definitely keep that in mind. I really don't know how or what I'm supposed to do, but I damn sure know I'll do something. And somehow save Avery."

"Good for you."

With that, I gave her a hug, or actually, she hugged me. With her massive body, I could not get my arms around her. I said good-bye and left the building.

I arrived home at ten-thirty. As I walked into the kitchen, I realized I hadn't even eaten dinner. I was so engrossed in those files that eating didn't enter my mind. I quickly made a peanut butter sandwich, let Spree out, and took a shower. I knew with all certainty that I wouldn't be able to sleep well tonight, but I went to bed anyhow.

As I lay in bed, I picked up the copies I had obtained at the archives and read them several times until I had them almost memorized. I compared them to the newspaper articles. Just as Osha Minnuppa had said, I had to change the course of history. Avery and me. Together. Day by day, we would work at it until we were successful. Let's see. Today was Tuesday, June 30. He was killed on July 4, so we had four days to accomplish the unthinkable. The impossible. How is that for optimism? My confidence started turning to despair. Four days. We could at least have used a week, maybe a month, maybe sixty-seven years. How could we do anything when neither of us knew what we actually *could* do?

While feeling sorry for myself, the telephone rang.

"Hey, guy, where have you been? You're never

home anymore. Do you have something going on that I don't know about?" It was Beth.

"Hey, sweetheart. Do I denote a bit of wishful thinking in that statement?" I mockingly responded.

"There's no way in hell you are going to get out of this wedding, after all the work I'm going through. Even if I have to carry you here from Florida on my back and hold you captive in my cellar until the wedding day," she threatened.

"Oh, that sounds exciting, but that won't be necessary. I'm ready, willing, and able. Oh, boy, am I able. Just talking to you makes me able," I responded, trying to sound more excited than I actually felt.

"You're making me blush again." Beth always blushes when I talk dirty.

"No. No. Save that so I can see," I begged.

"Seriously, where have you been?" she asked.

"You would not believe what I've been up to." I knew I'd eventually have to explain to her.

"Try me," she said.

"It's that Avery thing." There. I said it. Let me hear how she responds.

"What do you mean? I thought you were going to hang up on him or report him to the police?" she questioned.

"Well, I was. That is, I was until I went to the library Sunday and read about the case. Then tonight I saw the old police records and reports," I explained.

"Why did you want to see them?" She sounded curious yet perturbed.

I didn't know any other way to tell her, but straight out, believable or not. "Beth, this kid is telling the truth."

"What? You're crazy! Do you realize what you're saying? How could he be telling the truth? I thought the kidnapping occurred over sixty years ago." Now I know she was upset.

"Yes, it did. I can't explain it, but Avery is talking to me in 1998 from 1931. I'm the only person he can contact. I don't know how or why, but that's the way it is."

"Listen to yourself. Do you know how ridiculous you sound?"

"I know. You wouldn't believe how many times I've told myself that same thing, but it's the honest to God's truth. He is contacting me, and I know without a doubt that I am supposed to make every effort possible to save him."

"You told me he was killed. How is it conceivable that you can save him?" She was asking the same question that I've asked myself countless times.

"That's what we're working on."

"We? Who is we?" I was definitely confusing her.

"Avery and me. My plan is to get him to respond and react to the newspaper articles *before* the events occur. Today, I mean sixty-seven years ago today, he was supposed to drop a note with a plea for help on it. The kidnappers were taking him to call his dad and demand a ransom of one hundred thousand dollars. I told him to drop the note after they left the telephone booth."

"This is stupid. There must be some other explanation," she argued.

"Believe me. I've gone over every possible scenario. I've tried to call his bluff several times, but it comes down to simply he is not bluffing."

"I'm sorry, but I guess you have to experience it to believe it. It just sounds absurd." Looks like I can't expect any help from her.

"I can see how you would feel that way. You're right. I guess you have to be part of it to know it's for real. By the way, since you'll be here in a couple of days, you may just have that opportunity. However, I sincerely hope that it's all over by then. Avery will probably call me back tonight to let me know how our plan worked. Maybe, just maybe, someone will find the note."

"I really think you'd better back off this thing. You sound crazy," she scolded.

"I think I am a little crazy. This has made me that way, but I can't back off if there's even a hint of a chance to save him. I know I was meant to help him some way."

"Stop! Ken! I don't want to hear it," she shouted.

"I'm sorry, but it's true. No matter how crazy or absurd it sounds. It's true. It's the only thing I can think of anymore."

"I guess that explains why I haven't heard from you." She sounded angry and offended.

"I'm sorry." All I did these days was apologize. "I'll make it up to you when you get here. By the way, did you book your flight yet?" It was time to change the subject.

Still sounding upset, she said, "It arrives at the Orlando Airport at eight-fifty Thursday night, Delta Flight 2515. Do you think you'll have time to pick me up?"

"Of course I will. Don't be angry. You know how I'm looking forward to seeing you, sweetheart."

I tried to smooth things over. Actually, as callous as it may sound, I wanted to hang up, for I was anxious to hear from Avery. I thought it best, though, for Beth to make the overture, since she was already pissed at me.

Changing the subject again and trying to appease her, I said, "Oh, I forgot. Eric and Melanie are coming over for the Fourth. What time do you think I should tell them to come? How about one o'clock?"

"I guess that sounds okay. Are we going to have a cookout?"

"I bought a small Weber grill last month just for such an occasion. I'll pick up some steaks, potatoes, and corn. Should I get anything else?"

"You do have all the condiments, don't you?" she asked.

"Condiments?"

"Silly! Ketchup, mustard, pickles, that kind of stuff." She was sounding a little less upset.

"Uhh...No...I guess I'll be buying them too."

"Get a couple of nice ripe tomatoes too. And maybe some other veggies for a good, healthy salad."

"Jeez. How much do you plan to eat? Don't you cook up there anymore?"

"Actually, not too often. I go over to Mom's a lot. Then I just have a salad sometimes. I guess that'll have to change in a couple of months. We'll have to take turns with the cooking."

Ohh ohh. That wasn't what I had in mind. It was best not to inform her of my thoughts on that subject right then. I'll postpone discussing our duties and chores of married life until we are married.

"Well, guy, some of us have to work in the

morning. Guess I'll say good-bye."

"Love ya, sweets. I'll call you Wednesday after work to make sure your plane is leaving on time. Bye."

That wasn't the best phone call we ever had, but she'd get over it. I took a beer from the fridge and paced in the kitchen, hoping Avery would call soon. I unconsciously stopped in front of my kitchen window. My backyard light was on. It was a large, mercury light, illuminating my entire yard and the lake near my property. Lawnmower man was probably not happy with it, for it seemed to shine directly into his back bedroom window. I looked out my window, staring at the lake. Staring at the house and gazebo across the lake. Staring at the huge weeping willow tree at the bottom of my yard that was planted years ago. Weeping willow trees are not indigenous to Florida. In fact, when I moved into the house I was amazed there was one in the yard. That's my favorite tree, if you could have a favorite tree. You could have favorite colors, favorite foods, and favorite songs, so I guess you could have favorite trees. Anyhow, the weeping willow is my favorite tree, and I felt lucky to have one in my yard.

As I gazed across the lake, I wondered why Avery could only reach me and no one else. My telephone number was not the same as the number he called. We were unrelated. My name was unfamiliar to him, and his name and his father's name were unfamiliar to me. Hell, I'd never heard of the Archers before. I didn't know anybody with that last name either here or in Illinois. Then what was the connection? I didn't live near his father's house, nor would I ever, considering the size and the wealth of that neighborhood. Surely, it wasn't just some random freak of nature, fate, or whatever it's called. Then, again, why not? What would make that any stranger than all the other aspects of this crazy relationship? Yet there had to be some link between Avery and me. It just didn't make any sense.

Gradually, while staring out the window an idea came to me. I recalled that according to the newspaper and the police records. Avery was held captive in a farmhouse in Nawinah off Sunnyland Highway. Could it be? I was extremely anxious for Avery's call to ask him about my new revelation.

Chapter Seven

Wednesday, July 1, 1998

When Avery called after midnight, he was agitated and very upset. "Mister Driscoll, they found the note! They saw me drop it! They hurt me, real bad. I…don't know what to do…"

"Take it easy, Avery. Calm down. I know you're upset, but slow down. Start from the beginning."

"They blindfolded me with a smelly handkerchief and shoved me into the back of the truck again. This time they put a big box over me. The one man stayed in the back with me and told me not to make any noise or move around. I was so scared. I tried to do what you told me, about remembering the stops and starts, and the directions they turned, and all that stuff, but I got so mixed up. They just seemed to be turning and stopping all the time. The only thing I remember was we turned left when we got off the bumpy place around the house, and the first time they stopped, they turned left again. Then they went real fast. I couldn't see, and I was bumping up and down. I hit my back against something in the truck. It hurts so much."

Wanting to keep him calm, I interrupted. "You did fine, Avery. I didn't expect you to remember everything. I knew it would be hard. What happened when you came to where they made the phone call?"

"He parked the truck in some trees. They got me out of the box and took the handkerchief off my eyes. Then I saw their faces for the first time. The big man who was the driver said I'd better button my lip or he'd knock my block off. I think maybe he had a gun 'cause he kept his hand in his pocket all the time, so I didn't say one word. The short man put his arm around me and held me real tight so I couldn't even move either of my arms. They told me to look straight ahead and walk to the telephone booth near the road. I tried to look around me. I saw that we were at a filling station, and there was a gray car getting gas. I couldn't see the whole name on the sign on the building, but it started with S...Q...U... I didn't get a chance to see the rest. I didn't see any people either."

He was calming down and sobbing less as he continued.

"The big man went into the telephone booth by himself while the little man held me so tight I could smell his cigarette breath. After a couple of minutes, the big man opened the booth and took me inside. He whispered that I was supposed to say 'Hello, Daddy' and nothing else if I knew what was good for me. So that's all I said."

He started to cry again. "I wanted to talk to my dad so bad, but I knew they would hurt me if I did, so I just did what he told me. Then he shoved me out of the booth and closed the door and talked to my dad some more. I couldn't hear the words he was saying, but he was talking real loud. Finally, he came out of the booth and grabbed my other arm. I had the paper crumpled in my hand. I didn't know when to let it go. I...I'm sorry. I guess when I dropped it the big man felt my hand open up 'cause he looked down at the ground and saw the paper fall. I was so scared. He looked at me so mean. He didn't say anything then but just looked at me. I thought he was gonna shoot me then, but he started squeezing my arm so tight that I thought he would break it. It's all black and blue now, and it hurts when I touch it. They made me get back in the truck. They didn't put the blindfold back on me yet. I saw their dirty, old truck. I was really scared now 'cause I saw their faces and I saw their truck, and they saw me drop the note."

This wasn't good. Now the kidnappers knew Avery could identify them and their vehicle. Nevertheless, I didn't want him to think I too was worried.

"That's okay, Avery. They knew you would see their faces and their truck since they had to take you with them. They had to prove to your dad that you were safe. So don't worry. That was just part of their plan. What happened when you got back to the truck?"

"They were real rough with me. The big man told me to get on the floor near the other man's feet. There wasn't any room, so I...I...said I couldn't do it. He hit me in the head, so I did it. I squeezed and squeezed until I got all tangled up in the little man's feet. Then they drove over to the filling station and got some gas. The big man got out to pay for the gas while the little man kept one of his feet pushing on my head. When the big man came back, they kept me all pushed down in that little space. It was worse than being in the box in the back. When we got down the road a piece, the man pulled over and stopped the truck. The little man yanked me out of the front and put the blindfold on me again. I could hardly stand up 'cause my legs hurt so much. Then he put me back under the box in the back, but I was glad. It was better back there. When we got back to the house, the big man was very angry. He threw me on the bed and tore off the blindfold. He had my note in his hand. He was saying all kinds of bad words."

I could hear Avery's voice trembling again, trying to get the courage to go on.

"Avery, it's okay. You're the bravest kid I know. I don't know anybody, even any adult who would be as brave as you are. Maybe we should talk about something different for a while."

Reiterating the events so soon after they occurred was taking its toll on his composure. Perhaps if I got him interested in some unemotional conversation, he would be less troubled.

"Why don't you tell me more about what you like to do? Like what games or sports you like to play. You told me you like Dizzy Dean and the St. Louis Cardinals. Did you ever go to a baseball game?"

"Yes, my dad took me to see my team play the Pittsburgh Pirates last September. It was the last game of the season, and Dizzy Dean pitched the whole game. The Pirates only had three hits and scored one run. We went on the train all the way to St. Louis. We slept on the train and ate on the train. My dad said we'll go again this year. He says the St. Louis Cardinals are gonna win the World Series, and we can go see one of the games. Last year the Philadelphia Athletics beat my team in the World Series, but my team is gonna win this year. That's what my dad says, but I don't know now if I'll ever see my team play again. Will I, Mister Driscoll?"

He was starting to cry again. This was not working. I had to think of something else. The poor kid had gone through enough agony for one day.

"Avery, I think you should get some rest. You've had quite an ordeal today. I want to hear the rest of what happened, but I think it's best if both of us try to sleep. What do you say?"

"Maybe you're right. I don't feel so good. Maybe I'll call you in the morning. Will you be home?"

I knew I had to go to work after taking off early today. I was taking an unpaid vacation for the wedding, so I couldn't afford to stay home any more. I hadn't worked long enough at Kincaid & Company to accumulate any paid vacations yet, so I didn't have a choice. However, I wanted him to know that he still could reach me before and after work.

"I have to go to work tomorrow. I know you said you don't have a watch or a clock, but if you keep trying me whenever you have an opportunity, I'll be home as soon as I can, definitely in the evening."

"Thank you, Mister Driscoll. I don't know what I would do without you. I get so lonely and afraid all the time. If I couldn't talk to you, I just don't know what I'd do."

"I'm glad that I'm here for you, and sooner or later, we'll get you out of this mess, hopefully sooner. You get some sleep, and I'll make some plans for our next move."

"Yes, I'm really tired, and my head hurts. I don't think I'm gonna be able to work on the boards at the window tonight."

"That can wait until you feel better. You have to get enough rest to keep up your strength. Good night,

Avery."

"Good night, Mister Driscoll."

Things were not going well. Besides the abuse from those two assholes, I think Avery was getting physically sick. He didn't get the proper sleep, and he definitely didn't get the proper nutrition. Then with those jerks beating up on him all the time. Poor kid. A plan to get him out of this mess was becoming more crucial, and time was running out. July 4 was just four days away. I had wanted to talk to him more, but because he was so tired, so upset, and apparently ill, it was best if he rested.

I woke up again by the ringing of the telephone about three in the morning. Avery was hysterical. It was very difficult to understand him.

"They beat me…and they…burned me with cigarettes… I hurt so bad, Mister Driscoll. I think they're gonna kill me. Please, please, can't you do something? Please, please find my father!"

"Avery, take it easy. I know it's really rough on you, and you know I can't find your dad."

"But why? Why? He must be looking for me. When I talked to him for just that little bit yesterday, I know he was worried. I just know it. I don't know what I'm gonna do. I can't take this much longer. They hurt me so bad, my head hurts, and my stomach hurts. What am I gonna do?"

"Okay, where are the men now? Did they just beat and burn you?"

"Yes…a little while ago. They were drinking again. The big one came in first. They don't even wear the ladies' stockings over their heads anymore. He had the scrap of envelope that I wrote the note on. He shoved it in my face, and then he made me eat it. I was gagging, but I finally swallowed it. I think I'm gonna vomit. Oh, I'm so sick."

"Can you lie down while you talk to me? Maybe that'll help you feel better."

"I'm sitting on the bed, but I'm so sore. He punched me in the arm and in the stomach 'cause I wouldn't eat the envelope fast enough. Then the shorter man came in with a cigarette in his mouth. He told the big man that they had to teach me a lesson. Then he took his cigarette and burned me all over. I screamed and screamed, but they wouldn't stop. Then I think I fainted 'cause when I woke up they were gone. Now it's quiet out there. They probably fell asleep finally. I'm so glad when they go to sleep or leave. Then they don't bother me anymore."

"Avery, I'm so sorry you have to endure all this. If there were *any* way that I could come and get you this very minute, I would be there, but I just don't know where you are or how to get to you. I do have an idea, though. If you get a chance tomorrow, do as much scraping on the window board as you can, but don't let them catch you, or they'll hurt you again. Work at it when you're sure they're not around. Do they leave often?"

"Yes, they usually leave like at meal times. Sometimes I think they even leave me here all night long by myself 'cause it's so quiet."

"It's important to get that wood shaved off, but it's more important that you don't get caught. If you don't get it done, we'll think of something else."

He had calmed down. "What did you want me to do, Mister Driscoll?"

I wanted to give him some type of encouragement. Everything that had been happening to him had been so horrific and traumatic. He needed something to lift his spirits.

"I thought when you get enough wood scraped off, you could look out the window and describe to me what you see, maybe I'll recognize something. Maybe there'll be a landmark of some kind, a house, a barn, a road, anything that might help me locate you."

"Do we have to hang up now?"

"No, not if you don't want to. I did want to ask you some other questions anyhow. We could just talk about what we're interested in and what we like to do. You said you like baseball. Now, me, I like basketball. My favorite team is the Chicago Bulls, especially Michael Jordan. They've won the championship six times in the last eight years. They beat the Jazz last year and this year again."

"I don't know much about basketball. I never saw any games. What's the Jazz? Is this Michael person a good basketball player, like Dizzy Dean is a good baseball player?"

"The Jazz is the Utah Jazz. They're a good team, but not as good as the Chicago Bulls. As far as Michael Jordan, oh yes, he's probably the best basketball player ever. I used to see him play when I lived in Chicago, but that's too far away now. When Chicago plays the Magic, I plan to buy tickets for my girlfriend and me. But Michael Jordan may retire this year, so I don't know if I'll get a chance to see him play again."

"You have a girlfriend? What's her name? And what did you mean the Magic? Do magicians play basketball too?"

I couldn't help but chuckle. My strategy was working. He was forgetting about his pain and his predicament. I didn't know if he would be interested in my life, but I thought it might help to pull him out of his misery.

"My girlfriend's name is Beth. We're going to be married in October. She's the prettiest girl in the entire world."

"Wow! I wish I could see her!"

"Maybe someday you will. When we get you out of this." Oops! I quickly changed the subject.

"As for the Magic, they're another basketball team. That's just their nickname. They are the Orlando Magic, and they really aren't magicians, although I think they'd like to be so they could win more games. They aren't nearly as good as the Bulls."

I still needed more information from him, perhaps anything that might give me some clue as to who was behind this whole operation. Maybe then, I could think of some way to try to stop it.

Hoping not to upset him, I asked, "Avery, do you know anybody that might want to hurt you or your mom or dad?"

"No. I don't think so."

"Can you name any of the people who come around your dad often?"

"Mister Pratt…He's my dad's foreman. He lives at the house in the orange groves, but he's over our house all the time. He'd never hurt my dad or me. Sometimes he even plays catch with me."

I'd file that name back in my mind. Maybe Mister Pratt wanted more of Archer's money than he was getting from a paycheck. Plus, he knew Avery played ball. He probably saw him play in his back yard often enough.

I asked him more questions regarding his dad's acquaintances. "Can you think of anybody else who your dad knows well?"

"I…I don't know. Mama and Dad have parties sometimes. I'm allowed to come downstairs to get some food, but they don't like me to stay around with all grownups. I usually eat in the kitchen with Isabel. Lots of people come to the parties. Winfield Appleton —he's gonna run for governor—he's at almost all the parties. Buster Keaton came to one of the parties. Dad let me stay up to meet him. He's a very funny man. And one time Charles Curtis, the vice president of United States of America was there. Dad called him 'Charlie.' I was scared to meet him 'cause he's so important. I just peeked at him from the staircase. Dad said he'll probably be president after Herbert Hoover."

He was quiet for a while, calming down. Maybe I could get more information. "How about neighbors, Avery?" Do you see much of them?"

"No. The wall is so high around the house that I can only see the top of the houses next door."

"Do your neighbors visit much?"

"Sometimes Mama plays bridge with Mrs. Weller, who lives next door. Some other ladies come too, but I don't know them. They're all old."

"How about you, Avery? Do you have any best friends?"

"Well, I guess Trevor Clinton is my best friend. If he's at the country club, I play with him. Then there's my cousin, Gerald, who I told you about. I guess he's my best friend too. But not his sister Margaret. She's a pest. She always wants to play with us, but she's a girl. Girls can't play baseball or climb trees or anything fun."

"I know what you mean. Beth, my girlfriend, doesn't like basketball much either, but she feels like she has to go to the games with me. It's no fun to take her, though. I'd rather go with my brother or a buddy of mine instead. She doesn't understand the game and always asks dumb questions."

"Yeah, girls are too silly."

He paused for a little bit. I waited.

"Maybe someday I could go to a basketball game with you."

He was conversing normally with not much fear or pain in his voice. This was good.

"I'd really like that Avery. You'd be more fun than Beth."

I changed the conversation back to cousin Gerald. I didn't want him to start thinking too much about the future. "How often do you get to see Gerald?"

"Maybe once a week. Sometimes Clayton, our chauffeur, takes me over to Gerald's house. Sometimes Uncle Harold brings Gerald over to my house, but Margaret always has to come too. I wish I had a sister. Then Margaret would play with her and wouldn't bother us all the time."

"Yes, that'd be better. Then you boys could do what you wanted to do. I just met two boys in my neighborhood last night. Their names are Robby and Matt. They were going fishing, but when they saw my dog, they wanted to play with her."

That was all I needed to say. Avery was so excited. "You have a dog? Oh, boy, I wish I had a dog. Dad said maybe for my next birthday if I'm good and don't get into trouble. He'll probably change his mind now since I'm probably in big trouble."

He was getting upset again. I had to get back to a more pleasant topic. Spree. "Spree is a Lab mix. I found her one night. We're good pals now."

"Was she lost?"

"Well, sort of. Her owners moved away and didn't take her with them."

"That's an awful thing to do."

"Yeah, but she's doing okay now."

"What color is she?"

"She's a dark brown, almost black. She was very bad when she first came to live with me, but I sent her to school. Now she's a good dog."

He sounded surprised. "You sent her to school? I didn't know they had schools for dogs."

"Yes, they do. To try to get them to behave better. It's like a people school, only it doesn't last as long. What grade of school are you in?"

"I'm going into the sixth grade in September. I go to Brookfield Academy, but Dad said he might send me to the public school. I'd rather stay at the academy. My friends are there. I don't see them much in the summer, but when school starts, we have lots of fun. My roommate last year was this boy from Gainesville named Herman Welcher. I liked him for a roommate. We would sneak down to the kitchen at night and get some food. One time the housemaster caught us and called my dad, but Dad wasn't angry. He just laughed. I guess he knew we were hungry. Herman wrote me a couple of letters this summer. He told me he wasn't going back to Brookfield this year. He didn't know why his parents weren't sending him back, but I don't think they had very much money. Dad said something about them losing all their money in the stock market crash a couple of years ago. I'll miss him. He was my best friend at school."

Avery stopped talking for a moment. I assumed he was remembering his friend, Herman. I waited for him to resume. As long as he wasn't agitated or crying, I thought it would do him some good to think about something other than his predicament.

Finally, in a subdued voice he spoke, "I'm tired now, Mister Driscoll. I'd like to go to sleep."

"Okay, Avery. I'll talk to you tomorrow."

After my conversations with Avery, I always had a difficult time going back to sleep, but the calls were very important. For Avery, I was his only link to civilization, his only hope of freedom. For me, it was the only means of finding a way to save him. The more I learned about him, the better chance I had of thinking up possibilities.

Eventually, I fell asleep, but the blast of the alarm rudely awakened me. Another almost sleepless night. I had to go to work again, which was the last thing I felt like doing.

I'm thankful the summer months are somewhat slow for accounting firms. Don't get me wrong. I had work to do, but nothing compared to the period between January 1 and April 15. With being less busy and with Mister Kincaid off to Canada, the atmosphere in the office was more relaxed. Normally, his presence didn't bother me. In fact, I preferred him being around. Then if a problem arose, I could get an answer from him the same day. However, since I was not giving my best effort to the job these days, I was glad he wasn't there to catch me staring into space, trying to come up with a solution to Avery's quandary.

Whatever, I was not getting much accomplished. In fact, I was doing just that, staring into space, when Eric put his head around the corner of my office doorway. "How does Applebee's sound for lunch today?"

"I don't know. I have so much to do."

"And I see how well you're doing it. Do you think the answers are written on that wall you're staring at?"

Guiltily, I admitted, "You're right. I'm not getting much accomplished today. I might as well join you. Anybody else going?"

"Yeah, Meg Harper, Dave McDaniels, and Alan Siegel. We leave in five minutes. I'll sign you out."

I quickly finished my current task and got out to the screen saver on my computer. Eric drove his Explorer, and we arrived at Applebee's before the lunch crowd. While waiting for our orders, we talked about various subjects, most of it work related.

Shortly after our food arrived, Eric unexpectedly asked, "By the way, Ken, have you gotten any more prank telephone calls lately?"

I wasn't prepared to discuss Avery in front of these fellow workers. I didn't even talk much about it to Eric anymore, but I had to respond. Eric had asked me if I had gotten any "prank calls." Avery's calls were *not* prank calls. Therefore, while still eating my soup, I simply said, "No."

Much to my chagrin, Eric didn't let it go at that. "You mean that kid who claims to be Avery Archer hasn't called you anymore?"

Before I had a chance to respond, Meg Harper

interrupted. "Hey, I know that name. Wasn't that the kid who was kidnapped and murdered years ago?"

Originally from New York, Alan Siegel, asked, "What happened? I never heard about it."

I continued quietly eating my soup, ignoring the conversation, and allowing Eric to field the question and answer period. He explained, "From what I was told, this kid, Avery Archer, was the son of probably the wealthiest man in Orlando back in the thirties. He was kidnapped and eventually killed."

"That's enough. Can't we talk about something else while we're eating?" Meg Harper shivered as she thought of the murder.

"So, Ken, you haven't received any more calls from Avery Archer?" Eric asked, jokingly.

I stopped eating my soup. I figured it would come to this. I wasn't trying to keep it a secret, but then, why should I tell every acquaintance of mine?

I replied, "Yeah, Eric, can't we talk about something else while we're eating?"

Eric squinted his eyes. "Ken, I thought you told that kid where to go."

I started eating my soup again without responding.

"Ken? Well?" Eric was not going to let it slide.

I guess I can't blame him. As far as he knew, it was some practical joke, and I had already put a stop to it. I could easily have said that Avery had stopped calling me or that my threat of the police had scared him off, but I didn't. How the hell do I know why I didn't? I guess my excuse is that I wasn't getting enough sleep or maybe that my mind was literally on overload. Normally, I'm more of a private person, and I don't blurt out my personal problems to strangers, as these co-workers almost were. However, I was in no mood to play games. Maybe I figured these guys would give me some suggestion how to free Avery. Most likely, these co-workers would simply think I had completely lost it. What did I have to lose if they did think that? Since the three of them did not know me well, they would just think I was weird and not want to get to know me any better. It would supply an unending topic for office gossip.

I put my spoon down and turned my head to face Eric, and I made an ass of myself. "I've been getting calls regularly from Avery."

For several seconds Eric and the others said nothing. They too had stopped eating and were staring at me.

Sounding bewildered, Dave McDaniels then asked, "Did you mean you were getting calls from the same Avery that was murdered in the thirties?"

I picked up my soupspoon and went back to eating. Looking down at the bowl, I said, "Yes, that's what I mean."

Smirking suspiciously, Meg said, "You're joking, of course, aren't you?"

Between bites of soup, I answered, "No, I'm not joking. The very same Avery Archer who was murdered sixty-seven years ago calls me daily on the telephone."

I knew that remark would only increase their curiosity and my lunacy, but so be it. I had started my humiliating descent. There was no turning back now.

A pause in the conversation occurred while my lunch partners tried to comprehend what I had said. I also heard a few chuckles. I finished my soup and put the spoon inside the bowl, waiting for the next bantering barrage.

"Are you saying that you actually believe the kid calling you is the real Avery Archer?" Eric questioned. The look on Eric's face proved he was stunned.

"Not only do I believe it, but I know it for a fact."

"Come on, Ken!" chided Alan Siegel. "You're a smarter guy than that."

Defensively, I asserted, "It's not a matter of being smart or stupid. It is simply a fact. Avery Archer is calling me on the phone, and I'm going to save his life." I know they thought I'd gone completely mad with that statement.

Meg carried on the attack against me. "Did you just hear what you said? You said you're going to save a kid's life who has been dead for sixty years. I don't really know you very well, but that's the most bizarre statement I've ever heard."

"You're right. That's exactly what I said. That's the sole reason Avery contacts me. He needs me to save his life. As far as it being a bizarre remark, yeah, I guess it is. But sometimes the truth can be hard to believe."

No one was eating his or her food. All four of them were staring at me as if I had suddenly turned into Dracula, or maybe blood was coming out of all the orifices on my face.

At last Dave McDaniels spoke, "Did I understand this correctly? I don't mean to sound like I'm patronizing you, but how the hell are you going to save a dead boy's life?"

"That part I'm not so sure of right now."

As I listened to my own remarks, I could definitely

understand how these people could think I was a lunatic. Even to me, saying it aloud sounded like the most ridiculous thing I'd ever said. No, it *was definitely* the most ridiculous thing I'd ever said, but that didn't make it any less true.

"Can you be a little more specific?" asked Alan Siegel.

"This isn't something that I'm taking lightly, or for that matter, think of as a game. This is deadly serious. This boy's life is in my hands. I'm not going to bore you with all the details. Let me just say that I have done extensive research. I even saw all the police reports and evidence available to the detectives who worked on the case in 1931. Believe me. I'm not joking. I'm going to save Avery Archer's life."

"Okay, suppose this is all true," said Meg. "Do you then expect to change history? That's ridiculous. What will happen to all the newspaper articles that say the boy died? What about the memories of all those people who know he died? What about my memory? I know he's dead. Are you going to brainwash me? Zap! I have a void in my brain as far as Avery Archer is concerned."

"Meg, I can't answer any of those questions." I admitted. "I don't know what will happen to any of the records, physical or mental. I don't even know how I got messed up in this, although I have my suspicions."

"What suspicions?" interrupted Eric.

"I'd rather not say right now."

"Why not? Do you think we'll think you're crazy? Of course not!" Alan Siegel said very sarcastically.

It was starting to get rough. I had enough of their persecution. Since I was on an end seat, I shimmied out of the booth, saying, "I think it's time to go. I've been enough of a scapegoat for one day."

The others quickly finished what food they planned to finish. I guess I spoiled their appetites. We divided the bill and made our way out to Eric's Explorer. They sensed that I didn't want to talk about the matter anymore.

As I walked into my office, Eric followed me, apologizing, "Ken, I'm sorry if I embarrassed you. I really didn't expect those responses to my questions about the Avery thing. I thought it was all over with."

"No problem. I didn't want to discuss it around all those guys, but I guess it really doesn't matter. So what if they think I'm unbalanced. I could be worse things."

"No hard feelings, then?" he timidly asked.

"No, it's okay."

He started to leave my office. "Oh, by the way, are we still on for the Fourth?"

"We sure are. I'm picking Beth up at the airport tomorrow night. You guys come over about one in the afternoon. I'll give you a call on the Fourth to verify."

"Gotcha." He went back to his office, but I saw him look back at me with a puzzled look on his face.

I spent the rest of the afternoon working on a couple of pension plans, looking at the clock constantly for five-thirty to arrive. When it did, I left immediately, saying good-bye only to Nancy, the receptionist, on my way out. Because of the heavy traffic, my Hyundai had trouble getting out of the parking lot. With a break in the flow, I swiftly gunned the motor and pulled into the combat zone. Who should be on my tail again but the stupid, redneck, monster truck driver from last Friday. He was just as obnoxious as the before, but this time I wasn't going to acquiesce without a fight. I was in no mood to be pushed around again. If he wanted to be childish, I could match his immaturity. He also must have recognized me. First, he was almost kissing my back bumper. I moved to get into the left lane. He followed directly behind me, cutting off a big Buick Riviera in the process. The guy in the Riviera was really pissed. He laid on his horn for a full ten seconds. However, that didn't faze our tough, stupid redneck. He had better games to play. He was after *me*.

I was going the speed limit of forty-five miles an hour, but I dropped to thirty-five for a block, then down to thirty. My redneck buddy stayed glued to my bumper, not even attempting to pass me in the right hand lane. I knew I was aggravating about twenty other drivers with my slow speed, but I had enough crap for the day. Finally, I dropped down to twenty-five miles an hour and crept into the left hand turning lane to make my U-turn to go in the opposite direction. At first, I thought the redneck was going to follow me. In fact, he came into the turning lane for a second, then changed his mind and swerved back into the driving lane narrowly missing a maroon van. Horns were blowing all over the place, but I had a break in the traffic on the other side of the street and smoothly pulled into the flow, leaving many angry drivers behind.

After my little game, I drove home rather quickly. I was anxious to talk to Avery again. I stopped first at Taco Bell to pick up a couple of fajitas for dinner. As I pulled in my drive, my new, young friends, Matt Spinoza and Robby Garrett, were walking up the driveway. Robby asked, "Hey, Ken, can we take Spree over to the other side of the lake and play?"

I hadn't thought they would request her company this soon after they met her. I wasn't sure whether to trust them to bring her back, but then I realized she knew her way home anyhow, even if they grew tired of playing with her and decided to go home. I told them that it was okay, but to bring her back before dark.

First, I opened the gate in the back yard in case Spree came home alone. Then I called Beth to appease her and calm any misgivings she might have about my possibly forgetting to pick her up at the airport on Thursday.

"Hi, sweetheart. Are you getting anxious to see your handsome fiancé?"

"I was wondering if you were going to call tonight."

"What do you mean? Of course, I was going to call. I'm so anxious to see you that I can't even eat. My appetite is only for you," I said as I was picking at my fajita, chewing lightly so she couldn't recognize the sound. "Is your plane still expected to arrive on time tomorrow night?"

"So far, yes, but you might want to call the airport to be sure before you start out."

"I'll leave directly from work, so I'll call from there. If I'm too early, I'll have dinner and a drink."

"Don't get drunk. You'll have to drive. I know nothing about the roads in Florida."

"Don't worry. I want to be completely sober when I see you because I'm going to get drunk on you."

"Ken! Stop that!" she pleaded.

"Seriously, honey, I'm so anxious to see you. I really miss you. This long distance courtship is wearing me thin."

"How thin *are* you? I don't want my future husband to be some scrawny wimp."

"Ha!" I chuckled. "Do you think I would ever be a scrawny wimp? I love food too much—except for now, that is." I remembered I was not supposed to be hungry, still munching the fajita.

"Well, guy, I have to get some packing done. Besides, you probably want to finish whatever you are eating."

Whoops! Caught red handed.

"Uh…it's just a little snack to keep me fit for you. I'm only thinking of you."

"Sure. Sure. Just don't forget to pick me up tomorrow night. Even if you have to hang up on your Avery." She said that quite scathingly, but I ignored it. I didn't want to get her in another bad mood like last night.

"I won't forget. I promise. See you, sweetheart."

Maybe when she got here, she'd realize how important Avery had become in my life. I couldn't expect her to believe me. Look how long it took me to make up my mind. I even hoped that perhaps Avery could talk to her. Who would know? Who would ever have thought I'd be in this predicament? Certainly not me.

The boys brought Spree back as I was finishing my cold fajita. I thanked them for taking her and assured them she would love to go with them again sometime. She was tired and drank a big dish of water before lying down at the foot of the couch.

About eight o'clock Avery called. "Hello, Mister Driscoll." He sounded very depressed.

"Hi, Avery. You don't sound so good. Are you feeling worse?"

"I guess so. My throat hurts, and I have a cough. The men don't like me to cough, so I try to put my face in the mattress so they won't hear me."

"Maybe they'll go to the store and get you some medicine soon." I remembered the newspaper article mentioning the kidnappers were seen at the Nawinah General Store.

"I...I...don't think so. They don't like me very much. I think they just want me dead."

It was apparent his physical and mental conditions were deteriorating. I had to help him keep his spirits up. He had to want to live. He had to *fight* to live. I needed to change the subject again.

"Avery, did you get a chance to work on the wood at the window anymore?"

"Yes."

He was obviously not going to volunteer any information. I guess I had to draw it out of him.

"Were you able to scrape enough so you can see outside?"

"I don't know." Short and to the point.

"It's still light out. Can you go to the window to check if you can see anything through the space you made?"

"Yes."

"Okay, then, I'll stay on the phone while you go check."

It took several minutes for him to maneuver into position. At one point, I thought he had hung up, but soon he came on the line again.

"Mister Driscoll?"

"Yes, I'm here."

"I'm at the window. I can barely see out of the crack, but if I squint I can look through the hole."

"Good. Now look all around and describe to me anything you see no matter how small or unimportant it may seem.

"First, there are weeds and grass. That's what's nearest the house. Then there's a lake. I can see across it, so it must not be too big." He was silent for a while looking around.

"What else can you see?" I asked.

"On the other side of the lake is a big house. Something like my house, only different. This one is funny looking."

"What do you mean funny looking?" I wanted him to go into more detail.

"It has these ice cream cone towers on the sides of it," he described.

Getting a little excited, I asked, "Ice cream cone towers? Can you be more specific?"

"Uhh…it's a big white house, and on each side are these high towers. At the top of the towers, it looks like upside-down ice cream cones for the roofs."

YESSS! I was so excited. I knew exactly what he meant. "Go on. What else do you see?" I was really anticipating his response.

"Uhh. There is a little tiny building on the lake right in front of the house. It's funny looking too. It's all open."

Eagerly, I said, "That's called a gazebo. Some people build them at the end of their docks on a lake. Is there anything else you see, maybe closer to the house? Can you see anything in the weeds outside the window?"

"No. Nothing. Just maybe a lot of junk. Five old tires are in a pile about half way to the lake. And…uhh…near the tires is a big can filled with garbage with some rats crawling in it. A real old davenport with all the stuffing coming out of it is also in the weeds, and a rusted set of bedsprings is leaning on the davenport. That's all, I guess."

"That's good, Avery. You're able to see quite a bit. Now, besides the weeds, is there anything growing between the house and the lake, any trees, flowers, anything like that?"

"Uhh…there are some bushes right below the window. I can see leaves sticking up. Bushes are down near the lake too, not too many, though, 'cause I can see the lake pretty good. Oh, there's a droopy tree, near the lake too."

I was tense. "Describe the droopy tree."

"It's not a very big tree, but taller than my dad's orange trees. The branches all bend down and almost touch the ground."

I knew it! I knew it! Avery was describing the exact location of *my* house! Avery was held captive in a farmhouse located on this very spot! The ice cream house was the Kouprianov house being restored across the lake right now, and he described my weeping willow tree when it was young.

How do I tell him I know where he is located without telling him I am unable to get him or to send the police or his father to his rescue? For several seconds, I was trying to think of how to respond to his descriptions. He noticed my silence.

"Mister Driscoll? Are you still there?"

"Yes, I'm still here. I was thinking about what you described to me. Uhh...now I have something to look for. There can't be too many houses like the one across the lake from you. I'll find it."

I hated to lie. Well, it wasn't exactly lying, but it was not admitting to him what I knew. However, I didn't want to compound the complexity of the predicament. He had enough to deal with. My quick judgment, then, was to let him believe I would be looking for his location.

"I'm tired now, Mister Driscoll. Can I go lie down?"

"Sure, Avery. Try to get some rest. It won't be much longer until we get you out of there. Just be strong."

"I'll try… Good-bye."

Things were getting much worse. I didn't know how to keep his spirits up.

I had to relax too. So much to do in the next couple of days—working; Beth flying down from Chicago; our Fourth of July gathering. And saving Avery. How could I handle it all? I tried to read the *Orlando Sun* but couldn't keep my mind on it. I made a pot of coffee, hoping that would relax me. The television provided no solace. I kept flipping channels, not really seeing whatever was on, but thankful for the background noise.

Finally, I gave up trying to relax and went for a walk. My body was tired from lack of sleep and from tension, but my mind did not want to obey what the body was telling it. Spree's little jaunt with her newfound friends wore her out, thus I left her at home.

The Kouprianov house drew me to it once again.

Since it seemed to be the only tangible, physical link between Avery and me, I guess I felt closer to Avery when I was near it. I walked around the house, peering in the windows with my flashlight. I couldn't see much. The house still needed a great deal of work inside. Paint cans, tarp clothes, and ladders were strewn around several of the rooms. The house was barren of furnishings except for an occasional folding chair or table in a couple of the rooms. Empty cans of Pepsi and Lays Potato Chip and McDonald's bags were scattered on the tables and the floor.

I walked around to the front of the house and climbed the stairs leading up to the wide porch that stretched the entire length of the house front. The odor of the new wood and the new paint was very pungent. I shone the light into the large bay window to the left of the grand entranceway. This room looked almost completed. The hardwood floors glimmered when my flashlight beamed off them. I spanned the room with the light. The walls were painted a velvety cream color. On the left wall was an enormous built-in bookcase. The woodwork was ornate and intricate. There must have been space for thousands of books.

Suddenly from behind, I heard a deep voice say, "Slowly drop whatever is in your hand, then turn around."

I did just that. I let the flashlight fall gently to the porch floor, then I straightened up my body and turned around. As I did so, a light shone into my face, blinding me to its source.

"What's going on?" I attempted to block out the light with my arm.

"I ask the questions. What are you doing here? Do

you know you are trespassing on private property?"

"Uhh…I guess I am," I stammered, being caught off guard and not knowing what to say.

He testily asked, "Is that all you have to say? What were you planning to do? Break in the place?"

"Could you please lower that light? You're blinding me. And no, I wasn't going to break in. There's nothing inside anyway. I was just looking at the place. I live across the lake. Back there." I pointed in the direction of my house.

Instantly, the man came closer. "Keep your hands down, and stand still."

"Sorry! But I was just showing you where I live."

"I don't care where you live. What I do care about is why you are on this porch peeking in this window."

"I told you I was just looking at the place. I've been watching the workers renovate it on the outside, and I just wanted to see what they've done on the inside. I wasn't going to break in. Can you *please* lower that light?"

Finally, he shone the light more on my midriff, and I could see that it was a police officer confronting me. What a surprise.

"Do you have any identification on you?"

I had changed into shorts upon coming home from work, so I knew I didn't have my wallet. It was across the lake on my bedroom dresser. Hoping to appease the officer, I patted the small back pocket of my shorts.

"No, sir, I don't. My wallet is in my house across the lake."

"What is your name?" he demanded.

"Kenneth Driscoll. My address is 1334 Razzle Road. Like I told you, it's just across the lake."

"Suppose we get in my patrol car and take a ride around the lake so you can get your identification."

"Sure, Officer, no problem."

He motioned for me to walk down the stairs.

I asked, "Are you going to handcuff me?"

"Do I need to?"

"No, sir, I was just asking."

I walked down the stairs and the long walkway to the patrol car, which was at the curb with its blue and red lights spinning. Dummy! Why didn't I see these reflecting in the window on the porch? At least, then I would've had some warning of my impending confrontation, but no, I had been too busy trying to think of a way to break in the house.

"Stop there," he ordered when I reached the car. "Put your hands on the roof of the vehicle."

I did as he demanded. He frisked me up and down. With shorts and a T-shirt, there wasn't much to frisk.

"Get in the back."

I obeyed. I wasn't in any position to argue with this man.

The patrol car had a heavy, wire screen between the back and the front seat. The radio was cutting in and out, as I entered.

The police officer picked up the receiver of the radio. "Sergeant Nichols, here. I have a peeping tom in custody at 1330 Sand Star Road. We are proceeding to his residence at 1334 Razzle Road to procure some identification. Over."

Whoa! This guy was serious. A peeping tom? At what was I supposed to be peeping? Naked paint cans?

I heard an inaudible response from the radio. Then he started the patrol car and drove around to my side of the lake, pulling into my driveway.

"Wait in the vehicle," he ordered. Then he got out of his door and opened mine. "Proceed to your door. Keep your hands to your side."

He followed me to the door.

"Can I get my keys out of my pocket?"

"Yes."

I opened the front door. He followed me into the house.

"My wallet is in the bedroom. Can I go get it?"

"I'll be right behind you. Don't try anything."

In the bedroom on the dresser was my wallet. I took out my driver's license and handed it to him. He studied it for several seconds.

"You know, Mister Driscoll, I could arrest you for trespassing."

"You're kidding. I...I...mean. I was just looking in the place. I wasn't going to break in. God! Do you think I'd do that, living right across the lake from it?"

"I don't know what you would do, but let this be a warning. You stay away from that house. If I catch you there again, I *will* arrest you. Do you understand?"

"Yes, Officer."

He returned my driver's license, walked out of the bedroom, and out my front door. I stood staring at the door after he had closed it. Some relaxing walk! Almost arrested for breaking and entering. Looks like I'd better change my walking destinations for the time being.

It was then ten minutes until eleven. I was definitely too keyed up now to sleep. I tried the television again. Maybe the news would help me relax. I didn't want to drink anymore coffee, or I'd never be able to sleep, so I made myself a cup of herbal tea Eric had given me about a month before. He said it would lower my sex drive. I guess he figured I could use it, not being with Beth for months. It didn't work. For the relaxing or the sex drive. It also tasted like grass.

After the news, I showered and went to bed, knowing I would toss and turn all night.

Chapter Eight

Thursday, July 2, 1998

I got up about two o'clock to get the copies of the newspaper articles and the police records on the kidnapping from the coffee table in the living room. I had to determine our next plan of action. According to the Saturday, July 4, 1931, newspaper, the abductors were spotted in the Nawinah General Store on Friday, July 3, 1931, buying medicine for a child with a cold. Okay. Looks like Avery will have to wait until tomorrow for any pain medication.

I read the copy for Friday, July 3, 1931, which would tell me what would happen on Thursday, July 2. The abductors were making another phone call to Avery's father, this time from Okie's Diner along Route 50. A diner is a very public place. There must be some way Avery could draw the attention of somebody in the place without alerting the kidnappers. I was sure they'd have some type of weapon on Avery or very nearby so the threat of using it would keep Avery from doing anything foolish. I also assumed they would not let him out of their sight. If he had to go to the restroom, they would accompany him. It also seemed reasonable that since they selected a diner to make the call, perhaps they planned to eat something there. If that was the case, the best person whose attention Avery should try to get would be the waitress. Perhaps when she was taking their order or when she brought their food to them. Maybe when they were paying their bill. At those times the focus of the kidnappers would be somewhat diverted from Avery to the waitress.

Aside from a possible way to escape, the diner presented an opportunity for Avery to eat some real food. I doubt if the kidnappers would want to draw attention to themselves by not ordering Avery something to eat.

Maybe Avery could make a mess of his food. Maybe pour ketchup all over it. Maybe he could spill his food, causing the waitress to come back to clean it up. No. Those were bad ideas. I wanted him to eat the food. He wouldn't want to eat it if it had gobs of ketchup on it or if it were splattered all over the table.

There must be some other way. What else was on the table at a diner back in 1931? There was usually a jukebox selector box hanging on the wall. That wouldn't do him any good. He didn't have any money. Besides, what could he select that would make somebody come over to their table or booth? Too bad, I couldn't slip a Metallica or Black Sabbath CD into the jukebox. That would draw some attention in 1931. I think they were listening to bands like Guy Lombardo or Duke Ellington back then. Big, big difference.

So the jukebox idea was out.

Also on the table probably were napkins, a sugar container, and perhaps salt and pepper shakers. Maybe he could do something with these.

I was still contemplating a plan when the telephone rang about three o'clock.

"Mister Driscoll?"

"Hello, Avery, are you feeling any better?"

"No. I tried eating the soup. I could only swallow a couple of bites. My throat is really sore."

"I know you don't feel very well, but you have to eat. You have to keep your strength up. Is the soup still there?"

"Yes, they never take any of the cans away. I just put them over in the corner for the bugs to eat what is left."

"When we are done talking, try to eat the rest of it. Even if it takes you a long time."

"Okay," he agreed.

"Listen, Avery, tomorrow those men will take you again to talk to your father."

I could tell his spirits had lifted by the tone of his voice. "How do you know that, Mister Driscoll?"

He was entitled to some type of explanation. Maybe just a simple statement would work.

"Avery, there is no way that I can explain to you today how I know some of the things that will happen. Just believe me when I say there are a few things that I know and many, many things that I don't know. If you can understand this, what we have to do is to take the things I do know, and try to make the things I don't know come out the way we want them. Does that make any sense?"

"No." He was being honest anyhow.

Chuckling a little, I said, "Well, if you don't understand me, do you at least trust me?"

"Yes." That was important.

"Okay. That's all that counts. Believe me. I'm trying my damnedest to get you out of there."

"I believe you, Mister Driscoll. I really do."

165

"Thanks, Avery. Someday you will understand all of this." I paused, hoping I was telling the truth.

"Like I said, tomorrow the kidnappers will take you to a diner so they can again ask your dad for money. I'm not sure what the diner will look like, but I expect that they will also plan to eat something. It's very important that if they buy you something to eat, you eat every bit of the food they order for you. You need something other than soup. So whatever else happens, make sure you eat."

I continued my instructions. "You have to get the attention of somebody in the diner. Since the waitress will come to your table, she is the most likely person. Don't do anything crazy to your food. Don't spill it or mess it up so you don't want to eat it. The only other thing I can think of is if you use something besides food on the table to draw her attention. Maybe the salt and pepper. Maybe your knife, fork, or spoon. Since I don't exactly know what will be available, you'll have to be creative and act quickly. I'm sorry I can't tell you exactly what to do, but I just don't know what will be there. Do you understand?"

"I think so."

"Good. Now I'd like to get back to finding out more about you. Remember I said I know some things, but not enough? Whatever you can tell me about yourself will be extremely helpful. You told me you love baseball, but you don't know much about basketball. Is there any other sport in which you are interested?"

"I don't think so. I like football, just a little. I never saw a real game, though."

"Besides baseball and playing with Trevor or your

cousin, what do you like to do in your free time?"

"I like to read. Sometimes Mama takes me to the bookstore and lets me buy as many books as I want. I like to read about people's lives. I read about Benjamin Franklin and Abraham Lincoln. I read about Ivan, the Terrible too. He didn't seem like a very nice man."

"I don't think he was either," I agreed.

"Is there anything else you like to do or maybe that you are good at doing? Do you like to go on trips? Do you like to listen to the radio? Do you like to swim?"

Almost before I got the last question out of my mouth, he interrupted. "Yes, I like to swim very much. I'm a very good swimmer. Especially underwater. I'm on the swim team at school, and I can hold my breath underwater longer than anybody else can in the whole school. We practice every day during the school year. We also have a pool at home. I swim and practice whenever Mama lets me. She calls me a fish. In the summer, she takes me to the country club pool at least twice a week."

My mind started thinking. This might come in very handy.

"That's very good Avery. I bet your parents are very proud..."

"Oh no!" Avery cried before he abruptly disconnected.

The men must have awakened or come home. At least we were able to talk about the diner. I simply had to wait until Avery called again to find out what happened.

I looked at the clock. It was nearly four. No way would I be able to go to work today. I hadn't slept at all, and my alarm was set to go off in an hour and a half. That was it. I would call in sick. I hadn't missed any days since starting last March. Maybe I wasn't sick, but if I didn't get some sleep, I would be sick while trying to work. I'd probably fall asleep on the computer. I'd call at eight and tell them I wouldn't be in. Besides, with Beth coming in tonight, I had to be "functional." Just in case it might have the reaction Eric said it would, Eric's herbal tea was off my drink list. I then changed my alarm to awaken me at eight and tried once again to fall asleep.

This time I was successful, for the deafening clock blasted at eight o'clock. When I called Nancy, she was very sympathetic. She hoped I'd feel better tomorrow. She'd tell Mister Kincaid when he called in from Canada.

With that out of the way, I went back to bed for a few hours.

The phone woke me around noon. There was anguish and pain in Avery's voice.

"Mister Driscoll, they caught me using the telephone last night. The big man grabbed the telephone out of my hand and hit me in the face with it."

I didn't quite understand why he was still calling me. "But, Avery, how come they're letting you call again now?"

"First, they were real mad. That's why he hit me with the telephone. Then the short man picked up the big part of the phone, and he started laughing so hard he was grabbing his stomach. When he stopped laughing for a little bit, he said to the big man something like, 'Jack, the brat should be in the looney bin. Look at this phone.' The big man took the phone from the short man, and he ran his hand down the wire. Then he started laughing real hard too."

"I didn't know why they were laughing so much. Then the big man shoved the whole phone in my chest and said, 'Hey, kid, call as much as you want. You really pulled one over on us. I knew I cut those damn wires.' Then they both went out of the room laughing and slapping each other on the back. The short one said, 'We'll have to put the brat out of his misery. He's nuttier than a fruitcake. Go ahead kid. Call your old man. Call everybody. Call the coppers, if you want.' So that's why I'm calling you. So what if they cut the wires. I can still talk to you. I don't care if they think I'm a fruitcake. They can think whatever they want, 'cause now I can talk to you and not even worry if they'll get mad. At first my face was too sore, but when it stopped hurting a little bit, I called you."

The cut wire explained it. We were destined to link up with each other. He could only reach me and me alone. For whatever reason, whoever controlled our fates decided that no matter a cut wire or a connected wire, Avery was going to talk to someone. As fate would have it, I happened to be in the very same location as Avery was sixty-seven years ago. I had to go on the assumption that whatever Avery and I were doing to free him was not all for nothing.

"Mister Driscoll, are you still there?" Avery shook me out of my reverie.

"Yes, Avery. I was just thinking how strange our situation is, but we're going to make the best of it, and get you out of that place."

"I sure hope so, Mister Driscoll. I hurt all over."

"It shouldn't be much longer before it will end. Do you still remember what I told you in our last conversation about the diner?"

"Yes."

"Well, I'll leave it up to you. You are a very smart boy. I want you to try to think of something there that will draw the waitress' attention. Again, most important is that you eat any food they buy for you."

"Yes, sir, I'll do my very best. Oh, they are coming in my room now. I don't want them to hear me talk to you, even if they call me a fruitcake. Good-bye, Mister Driscoll."

So maybe that was it. Maybe this would be the break we needed.

Since I now had the day off, I had to determine how best to spend it before picking up Beth at the airport. I retrieved all the paperwork on the Archer case. Perusing through the pages, I realized there was a slim chance that some of the police officers on the case might still be alive. I ruffled through the papers until I came to the sheet listing the officers by name: Wallace Denton—the Orange County Sheriff; Jeb Whiting—captain of the Orlando Police Department; Calvin Douglas—lieutenant and officer handling the case; Luther Billings—Douglas's junior partner; and Wilbur Duncan and Eubbey Litomen—officers who found the body.

If any of them were rookies back then, they were probably eighteen or twenty. That would make them eighty-five or eighty-seven now. It's possible to live that long. I had a Great Aunt Beatrice who lived to be ninety-seven. She was as sharp as could be too. I know because I experienced her wit first hand. Aunt Bea lived with us the last few years of her life. Mom fixed up the back bedroom for her. She could get around in her room quite well but needed a walker to maneuver about the house. Maybe I was twelve and Eddie was sixteen. We would move her walker around in her room so she would never know where to find it. She never complained or told Mom on us, but she must've schemed for weeks how to get even with us.

One day while she was napping on her chair, we moved the walker to the side of her desk. It really wasn't hidden, not exactly, but she had so much junk in the room that it was often difficult to find anything. She had stacks and stacks of trashy romance books on every available piece of furniture. It amazed Mom how the old woman's eyesight hadn't given out many years before with all that she read. It amazed my brother and me how this wrinkled, shriveled, old lady would still have any interest whatsoever in romance.

Anyhow, we put the walker on the side of the desk while she was napping. Whether it could be construed as hiding it or not, there are differences of opinion. Then we went into the kitchen to eat our lunch. Half way through lunch, we heard this blood-curdling scream coming from Aunt Bea's room. Mom was in the basement washing clothes. She ran up the stairs two at a time. Eddie and I had our sandwiches in our hands, with our mouths wide open, staring at each other when Mom came bursting through the cellar door.

"Boys! That's Aunt Bea! What are you doing? Come with me!"

We dropped our sandwiches and followed Mom into Aunt Bea's room. When we reached the doorway, Aunt Bea was lying on the floor in front of her desk with blood everywhere. Well, I lost it—screaming and jumping up and down like a lunatic. Eddie was almost as bad. He kept repeatedly muttering, "Oh, no. Oh, no." Mom quickly went over to Aunt Bea and knelt down beside her. Mom's shoulders started shaking with emotion as she covered her eyes with her hands, sobbing. All I could think of was that Eddie and I had killed Aunt Bea. She fell trying to get to her walker that we had hidden. I screamed, "I didn't mean it! I didn't mean to hurt her!" All the while, my mother's shoulders shook while she kept her hands over her eyes.

In the midst of all my screaming, Mom finally took her hands away from her eyes and turned Aunt Bea's face toward her.

Suddenly, Aunt Bea's eyes and mouth popped open. In a squeaky, shaky voice, Aunt Bea said, "Gotcha, sonny boys!"

I actually did faint and hit my head on the doorway. When I came out of it, Mom was helping me into a chair. She wasn't crying with grief while looking at Aunt Bea's supposedly dead body, but she was laughing hysterically. Aunt Bea had asked her at lunchtime if she could take the ketchup bottle into her bedroom. She wouldn't tell Mom why, but Mom knew the reason the minute she bent over Aunt Bea's "lifeless, bloody body," for she reeked of ketchup. She knew immediately what Aunt Bea was doing. She didn't know about our habitual, sick game with the walker, but she knew our capabilities concerning mischievous deeds. Of course, she also knew we'd done *something* to provoke Aunt Bea. With her feeble, ninety-seven-year-old body, how Aunt Bea was able to get down on that floor and assume the position of a dead person is beyond me. And I was definitely not going to ask her.

I'm not saying we never played any more pranks on Aunt Bea. She was a good sport about everything, and she teased us as much as we teased her, but we never hid her walker again.

Thus, since Great Aunt Beatrice at ninety-seven could still win a battle of wits against two young "whipper snappers," I figured somebody from the 1931 Avery case might still be alive. I wasn't sure exactly how to find out. I could call Detective Pete Griffin, but I had a feeling he wouldn't want me to bug him anymore. Then I remembered Osha Minnuppa. She had told me that if there was anything she could do to give her a call.

When I called the Florida Records Storage Center, the operator informed me that Osha would not be in her office until tomorrow. Looks like I couldn't depend on any help from her this afternoon.

I didn't have any other choice but to call Detective Griffin. Retrieving the files on the case, I found the paper listing the police officers involved, and I called him at the Orlando police station.

"Detective Griffin, here."

"Yes, sir, this is Ken Driscoll. Remember me? I talked to you a couple of days ago regarding the 1931 Archer case."

"Oh, I remember you."

"I wonder if you can help me out one more time."

"Mister Driscoll, I don't mean to be rude, but don't you have anything better to do with yourself? I'm a busy man. I don't have time for this shit."

"I know you are, and I'm really sorry to bug you, but I have one more question. I have a list of all the police officers who worked on the case, and I was wondering if any of them might still be alive."

"Christ! That was sixty-seven years ago. What do you expect?"

"I know. I know, but it's possible. Could you check your records? This will be the last time I'll bother you."

There were a few more moments of silence. Finally, he responded. "Shit. All right. Call me back in an hour. I'll see what I can do." He abruptly hung up before I could thank him.

An hour. I had enough time to get to Publix to pick up food for our cookout tomorrow. I also needed to clean the house a little too. The sheets on the bed hadn't been changed in at least two months. That would never do. I couldn't impress Beth that way.

I'm as good at grocery shopping as I am at cooking. I went to Publix's meat section to pick out the steaks. Believe it or not, I have never cooked steaks on the grill. That was Dad's specialty and far be it from me to take that pleasure away from him. Therefore, I now didn't even know what kind of steaks to buy. Had I thought in advance, I could've asked Eric's advice. Since I wasn't at work that day, and it wouldn't be wise to call and ask Eric about steaks, I had to wing it. I picked up several cuts of meat: T-bone, London broil, round, sirloin. How confusing. The butcher was nowhere in sight. As I was perusing my choices, a young woman also started examining the various cuts. She looked like she knew what she was doing.

"Excuse me. Do you know anything about steaks?"

She looked at me rather warily. Maybe she thought I was trying to hit on her. "Uhh, I'm sorry?" she questioned.

"I was wondering what kind of steak is good to

cook on the grill."

Suspiciously, she responded, "I like the London broil. It's my *husband's* favorite too." Her inflection on the word, "husband" was very pronounced.

Yep, I was right. She thought I was hitting on her. So who cared what her *husband* liked?

"Okay. I guess that's what I'll get. Thanks."

I picked up four London broil steaks, threw them in my cart, and hurriedly moved away before she accused me of sexual harassment.

I really didn't know what else to buy. This was not my usual method of shopping. My experience lies primarily in the frozen food section or the snack aisle. I picked up a bag of potatoes, some big tomatoes, and some other salad type vegetables. I got the condiments too, as Beth had requested. That would have to do. As an afterthought, I got a couple boxes of cereal, a loaf of bread, some milk, and some juice for our breakfasts in bed.

When I arrived home, I let Spree out in the back yard, put the groceries away, and then called the detective back.

"Did you have any success?" I asked.

"Yes and no," he answered. "Wallace Denton, Jeb Whiting, Calvin Douglas, Luther Billings, and Wilbur Duncan have all died. Eubbey Litomen is still alive, but he's in the Serendipity Oaks Nursing Home in Winter Park. I hope this is enough information so you won't bother me again."

"I know I've been a pain. I'm sorry. I won't bother you anymore. Thanks so much for all your help."

"Yeah. Sure." He quickly hung up before I asked him for something else.

According to my map, the Serendipity Oaks Nursing Home was off Aloma in Winter Park. It was about three o'clock, and I had to be sure I'd get to the airport when Beth's flight came in at eight.

The nursing home was a converted building made from two houses next door to each other. Several modifications were made to connect them together. The air outside was hazy from the smoke resulting from the fires in the area, giving the house a somewhat gloomy, depressing appearance. I parked my car and walked around to the main entrance, which had a small cardboard sign with magic marker letters, stating, "Walk In." I obeyed the sign and entered a small hallway containing a desk covered with a myriad of papers and files. The top of a filing cabinet to the right of the desk also housed a huge pile of the same. No one was at the desk, but I could hear conversation coming from an open doorway on the left. A gruff female voice was speaking.

"I don't care what excuse you have. You didn't need to call the ambulance. We could have taken care of the problem."

Another voice spoke. "But…"

"I *said*, no excuses," coming from the gruff voice. "We are a contained facility, and we don't need outside assistance."

I thought it best to let my presence be known before I heard something I shouldn't. I was already in enough hot water because of my involvement in someone else's problem. I quietly walked over to the door, opened it softly, but closed it forcefully so the occupants in the next room would think that I was just entering the premises.

It worked. A short, rather disheveled woman entered the room. She walked with a pronounced limp. Her left leg was considerably shorter than the right and about twice the size in circumference. In a deep voice, she questioned, "Good afternoon. How can I help you?"

"I was wondering if I could see Mister Eubbey Litomen."

She appeared somewhat surprised at my request. "Are you a relative of Mister Litomen?"

"No. I'd like to ask him a couple of questions."

"Mister Litomen rarely gets visitors these days. As far as answering your questions, I'm afraid that might not be very productive."

"Why is that, ma'am?"

"Mister Litomen is a very old man and suffers from Alzheimer's. He is oftentimes confused and incoherent. There are times, however, when he is aware of his surroundings, but there is no guarantee."

"If it's all the same with you, I'd like to try," I said.

"What is your name, sir?" She walked behind the cluttered desk. After moving some files aside, she retrieved a ledger type book from underneath the rubble.

"Kenneth Driscoll."

She wrote my name in the book next to a time slot, and put Eubbey Litomen's name in parenthesis next to my name. "If you'll have a seat in the room across the hall, I'll see if Mister Litomen is awake."

The woman walked toward a door on the right. I wondered why she didn't just pick up the phone and call someone in Eubbey Litomen's area. Since my visit was unexpected, she probably wanted to make sure Mister Litomen and his room were presentable before permitting a visitor.

The room I entered was a quasi-waiting room/file room/office. No one else occupied the room. Filing cabinets were located in a small, open alcove directly across from the entrance. Several unmatched chairs rested along the wall on both sides of the entrance. I sat on the cleanest looking of these, a black, vinyl office chair.

About fifteen minutes later, the same woman returned. "Mister Litomen is awake. If you'll follow me, I'll take you to his room."

I followed her to the area that housed the patients. The common room off which several other rooms were connected had numerous wheel chairs and walkers strewn about. The vinyl tile flooring was chipped and faded but clean. One of the rooms off this common area served as a nurses' station. A woman dressed in a uniform was putting medications on a cart.

We walked to the far end of this main room to the last room on the right. I followed her into the room. Eubbey Litomen was rocking back and forth on a worn, wooden rocking chair. He was a gaunt, old man with extremely wild, stark white hair. Some of it stood straight up from the top of his head. He had a thick mustache that stretched across his sunken cheeks. His mouth was open wide, and mucous-like saliva drooled from the opening in long strands. The woman spoke to Eubbey Litomen in a loud and pronounced manner. Even if the patient in the next room were hard of hearing, he could've heard her. "Mister Litomen, you have a guest. His name is Kenneth Driscoll. He would like to ask you a couple of questions."

Litomen stopped rocking and looked directly at me

with piercing blue eyes.

Quickly, he turned his gaze to the woman, then back to me, jerking his head back and forth between the two of us.

The woman spoke again, this time putting her hand on his shoulder. "Mister Litomen, calm down. Mister Driscoll simply wants to talk to you. No need to be upset."

To me she said, "As I told you, he doesn't get many visitors. He's also a little deaf, so you have to speak up."

So I noticed.

Mister Litomen visibly calmed down and resumed his rocking. He then kept his penetrating eyes exclusively on me. He also finally closed his mouth, for which I was quite grateful. That slimy spittle dripping in gobs was an unpleasant sight to see.

Judging from his current behavior, I was somewhat hesitant to speak. I didn't quite know what his reaction would be, but I figured I had nothing to lose. I started out rather simple, just to let him feel more at ease. I also wanted to see how rational he was.

"How are you Mister Litomen? I'm glad to meet you." I waited several seconds. He did not respond.

The woman spoke, "Sometimes Mister Litomen does not always *feel* like talking."

I'll give her credit. She seemed to know what she was doing. Even if the place wasn't as orderly as a hospital, perhaps she was concerned about her patients' welfare and circumstances.

She spoke again as she went toward the door. "I'll leave you alone to have your conversation. If there's a problem, Mister Driscoll, you can ring the buzzer next to Mister Litomen's bed, and the aide will come to assist you. Mister Litomen is not confined to the chair. He can walk using his walker, so if you'd like to go out on the patio, that could be arranged."

"That's probably a good idea," I agreed.

"Then if you'll wait here one moment, I'll send the aide to take him outside."

She left the room, closing the door behind her. Mister Litomen was still staring at me. I was at a loss on how to proceed with my conversation. There were several uncomfortable moments of silence.

Suddenly, Mister Litomen spoke, "You have no hair."

His statement took me by surprise. I'm ashamed to admit it, but my unintentional response was "Well, you're not too pretty yourself."

He cracked up. He started to belly laugh, and he didn't have much of a belly. Tears of laughter started to descend from the corners of his eyes, and the trusty, old drool started descending from his mouth. I didn't think my remark was that funny, but apparently, he did. His laughter was contagious, for I also started to smile and chuckle. However, I didn't drool.

The aide entered the room while we were both laughing. He was a black man about ten feet tall and just as wide. "Sounds like you be havin' a party in here."

Then I lost it. This big black man had a voice that sounded like Julia Child. So there we were—this feeble old man with drool running down his face, clutching his belly, and me, throwing my head back and shaking with laughter. The aide was staring at both of us. I think he wanted to admit me to that facility also—to the psychiatric wing.

Finally, I gained my composure enough to apologize to the aide and ask him to assist me in taking Mister Litomen to the patio.

He helped Mister Litomen, who was still snickering, out of the rocker and maneuvered him into his walker. They proceeded out the door with me following behind. The aide constantly turned his head to look in my direction as he walked. I'm not sure what he expected me to do. I guess he wasn't sure either, but he wanted to keep an eye on me to catch me at doing whatever I was going to do.

As we walked down the hall, between his chuckling, Litomen would yell back at me, "Come along, sonny." He moved slowly, but he kept striding forward. They walked toward a pair of French doors. When I saw the direction they were going, I quickly moved forward to open the door. I held the door while both of the men went through. The aide seated Litomen on one of the many white, resin, outdoor chairs scattered about the large patio. The one he had selected was under a faded gray and burgundy sun umbrella stuck in a metal cage to anchor and support it. I selected a chair to Mister Litomen's right but at an angle so I could look at him when I spoke.

The aide finished getting Litomen seated then turned to me. "I be inside if you need me. Just ring da buzzer next to da do'."

The aide then left us alone on the patio. Litomen had now stopped laughing and was somberly staring at me again. However, he was not agitated.

I had to gather my thoughts. Several seconds passed. "This is a nice place," I said.

"No, it ain't."

"Well, it seems like the people who work here treat you okay." I tried to make small talk while I thought of how to approach the reason I wanted to talk to him.

"Sometimes," he curtly replied.

"Do they feed you well?" I asked.

He didn't respond immediately. Then he said, "Whatchu want, sonny? Who are you?"

"I'm Ken Driscoll," I answered.

"I know that, damn it, but who is Ken Driscoll? Whatchu doin' here?"

"I'd like to ask you a couple of questions." Time to get down to business.

"What kind o' questions?" he asked.

"Oh, about when you were a policeman," I said.

"Whatchu wanna know? That was a long time ago. Ain't been a policeman in twenty-five years. Can't remember much. I'm old and sick, case you didn't notice."

"I noticed you were old, but I'm not so sure about the sick part."

"You caught me on a good day, that's all," he replied.

"I guess I should be glad about that," I agreed. I hoped that our conversation would continue that way.

"Yeah, I can be kinda mean, so Ole Morgan tells me." He was talking sensibly.

"Who's 'Ol' Morgan'?" I asked.

"She's my babysitter, the one with the gimpy leg." I guess that's how he thought of his caretaker.

"That's not very complimentary to her or to you." We were having a decent conversation, even though it wasn't exactly what I wanted to discuss.

"I ain't a nice man. And I'm old. When you're old you can get away with lots o' stuff that a youngin' like you can't. Besides, she is my babysitter. They treat me like a baby most of the time. And she sure does have a gimpy leg."

"These days they would call it physically challenged." I corrected him.

"Ha! That's a goodun'. Physically what? Challenged? Is that some kind of flowery way to say she's a cripple?" He was quite amused with my analogy.

"You might say that. Only I don't think Ole Morgan would appreciate being called a cripple either," I explained.

"Like I say, sonny, I call a spade a spade. She's a cripple, and that's what I say." He remarked in a strongly opinionated manner.

He stopped talking and stared at me again. Suddenly he said, "So whatchu wanna know 'bout my policeman days, anyhow? I was a good cop. Was on the force for forty-five years. Had to retire when I was sixty-two. Couldn't handle the rough stuff anymore."

He opened up the conversation I wanted to pursue. I proceeded with specifics. "Actually, I was curious about a particular case you worked on."

"What case? I worked on hundreds of them." I sensed that he was curious.

"This case was back in 1931 and was a much publicized case throughout the country. It was the kidnapping of Avery Archer, the son of the famous orange grower, Samuel Archer. Do you remember that case?"

I was looking directly at him when I started asking

him about Avery's kidnapping. It was utterly amazing how his face changed. When I mentioned the year, his head swiftly jutted forward, and his mouth gapped open. When I mentioned Avery's name, his eyes just about bulged out of his head. As I continued to describe the case, this blank stare immobilized his face, and he started to drool again.

He said nothing as I looked at him directly. I asked again. "Do you remember the Archer case, Mister Litomen?"

He continued to stare and to drool. It was as if he turned into a different personality right before my eyes.

"Mister Litomen?" I questioned.

He kept on staring at me.

Suddenly, he swiftly popped out of his chair, shaking unsteadily. I too got out of my chair and promptly went over to support him, but he batted me away with one arm while holding onto the chair with the other.

"Noooo! Piss Ant! Noooo! Leave it! Ain't no good! It'll cost you two bits. I don't know. Can't find him. Nooo. I don't know where he is. Piss Ant! He's gone. He's gone. They ran away. It'll cost you four bits. I can't do it. I won't do it. Shouldn't a done it. He's dead. They shoulda known better. Sons a bitches! They're all dead! Sons a bitches!"

He was lifting his feet up and down, one at a time very swiftly, sort of rocking from side to side as he did so.

"Mister Litomen! Calm down. Sit down. It's okay." I broke in and tried to steady him and maneuver him into his chair. He fought me for a while, and then he succumbed to my greater strength. The way he was carrying on, he was going to fall and seriously hurt himself. I didn't want to be responsible for that. He calmed down but was visibly shaken. I had truly disturbed him with my inquiry. I was very thankful when he gradually returned to his staring mode.

"I'm calling the aide to take you back inside."

He said nothing, just continued to stare. I quickly went over to the buzzer next to the door and rang it twice. Within seconds, the aide came out to the patio.

"Mister Litomen is ready to go back inside. I think you'd better hold onto him. He's a bit shaken up."

"Yeah," responded the aide. "He be dat way sometime. Someday he gonna hurt himself."

"That's what I was afraid of. He was almost jumping up and down. I thought for sure he was going to fall."

The aide placed the walker in front of him and almost lifted Litomen out of his chair. He placed Litomen's hands on the walker.

"Let's go back to da room now Misser Litomen."

The two of them went toward the French doors, Litomen, staring down at the ground as he shuffled his feet along. I opened the doors to allow their easy entry. They went off in the direction of Litomen's room, and I went in search of 'Ol' Morgan.'

She wasn't at the front desk, so I walked into the room where I had waited when I first arrived. She was standing at one of the filing cabinets, looking at a file.

"Ms. Morgan?"

"Oh! You startled me." I could see that I had, for she dropped several papers out of the file.

"I'm sorry. I didn't mean to surprise you. I wanted to inform you of how my conversation went with

Mister Litomen." I thought that she should be aware of how upset he was.

"He was talking to me very rationally until I started to talk about an old case he had worked on many years ago."

She picked up the papers that had dropped to the floor and put them into the file. Laying the file on the top of the filing cabinet, she turned. "Was it the kidnapping of the young boy back in the thirties?"

"Yes, it was." I was surprised that she knew about it. "How did you know?"

"At times, Mister Litomen can be very rational while at other times, he is delirious. Sometimes certain events or conversations bring on his erratic behavior. Sometimes it just happens for no reason. That's a trait of Alzheimer's. He's also very passive at times, but he can be very violent in his behavior. Inevitably, if that particular boy is discussed, he becomes irrational. Sometimes for no reason he'll cry, or sometimes he'll scream the name, Avery, in a blood-curdling manner. Whatever happened has caused him great anguish over the years. He has no living relatives, so we can't question anyone about it to get some insight into his torment. We try to deal with it as best we can. I don't expect he has too many years left. He has had a couple of strokes, and his heart is not strong. We try to make him as comfortable as possible."

Then she asked, "By the way, were you able to get the information from him that you wanted?"

"Actually, no. We were getting along great until I asked him about that kidnapping. Then he went berserk. Do you think I could come back another time to talk to him?"

"I suppose you can try. Perhaps next time the aide should stay nearby. He's a little more equipped to handle Mister Litomen's violent behavior."

"That'd be fine with me. In fact, after today, I would definitely prefer it that way. I was so afraid he would fall and hurt himself. However, it's vitally important that I talk to him about that case."

"If it's that important, we can try it some other time. When do you think you would be returning?"

"Could I come back tomorrow?" I asked.

She was visibly surprised. "That soon?"

"As I said, this is extremely crucial."

"I can't guarantee that you'll have any more success tomorrow than today, but I suppose you can try. We'll be sure Mister Litomen gets a good night's sleep tonight, and we'll give him his favorite breakfast of cheese and grits. Perhaps that'll help put him in a mellower mood. Also, tomorrow afternoon is Mister Litomen's time to go to the mall. We'll have to arrange your visit in the morning. Would eleven o'clock work for you?"

I had forgotten about Beth flying into Orlando tonight. Would she appreciate sharing part of her first day with me in months in the company of a slobbering, old man who perhaps would be ranting and raving like a maniac? I had no choice. She'd have to come with me or stay at the house. I'd figure out how to handle that situation tomorrow.

"Sure. That'll be fine. If for some reason I can't make it, I'll call you at least by ten o'clock." I started toward the door. "Thanks again for your help."

"Hopefully, tomorrow will be more successful for you."

"I hope so too," I said as I went out the front door.

When I got home, I was putting the mustard on my baloney sandwich when the telephone rang. It was Avery, and he was hysterical again, sobbing and gulping for his breath.

"Avery! Avery! Get a grip!"

"Mister Driscoll, they caught me! I tried to do it without them seeing me, but they caught me! They're gonna kill me! I know it! I'm gonna die."

He started sobbing uncontrollably.

"Avery!" I practically screamed into the telephone. "Calm down!"

I kept trying to talk to him. "You're still alive, Avery. They need you. They won't kill you because they want the ransom money. They have to keep you alive, or your dad won't pay them. Please calm down. Please."

Eventually, the sobbing subsided enough so that I knew he could hear me.

"Start from the beginning. Tell me what happened. If it's too upsetting, then just stop. Remember, you're still alive. They didn't kill you, and we'll have you out of there before they'll get a chance. Trust me, Avery. Do you trust me?"

He was still sobbing, but I knew he was listening. "Yes, but I'm so scared."

"You have every right to be scared. How many boys your age have ever gone through what you're going through? We'll get through this. Believe me. You have to hang in there a little longer."

"Yes, sir," he quietly responded between sobs.

"Can you tell me what happened at the diner now?"

"Okay. They blindfolded me again, and then they

dragged me out to the truck. I had to go on the floor in the cab of the truck again. The short man told me to stay down there until he told me to get up. Both my legs were falling asleep because I was so cramped, but I just kept thinking to myself about you and what you might look like and how you're helping me. Then I thought about my mom and dad and how worried they must be. Pretty soon, I forgot about the pain in my legs. When we stopped, the short man pulled me up onto the seat, but he held my head down. Then he took the blindfold off my eyes, and then he yanked my head up too. I had a little trouble seeing at first, 'cause the sun was so bright. I looked out the window and saw he parked way at the end of the parking lot. Maybe four or five other cars were there too. The big man told me not to be so nosy and to keep my trap shut, so I tried to look out of the corner of my eyes at everything. Then the little man pulled me out of the truck. He told me to smile and act like he was my father. I couldn't do that, Mister Driscoll! My father would never treat anybody the way they treat me." He started crying again.

"Avery, I know your father wouldn't mistreat anybody, and he's so worried about you. That's why we have to go through this. We have to figure some way to get you free. You're doing a good job. Take a deep breath, and start again."

I could hear his breathing in the background. He took several deep breaths.

"I tried to smile, but it was real hard. Out of the corner of my eye, I saw that the name of the diner had a big red "O" on the sign over the door. A man and a woman were coming out the door. The big man said to them 'Good afternoon.' They looked at us kind of strange, but they said 'Good afternoon' too. When we got in the diner, we sat in a booth in a corner. The booth was near the telephone way far away from the door. A lady in a red and white dress with a blue apron came to our table. You know what's funny? When I saw her in the red, white, and blue, all's I could think of was that the Fourth of July was in a couple of days, and I wondered if I'd ever get a chance to go with my dad to see the fireworks ever again."

I waited to see if he was going to break down again. He soon resumed, still in control.

"The lady was going to give me a menu, but the big man said he would order for me 'cause I didn't read too well. He lied, Mister Driscoll. I'm a good reader. I bet I can read better than he can."

"I know you are, Avery. They just didn't want you to say anything to the lady. They thought you might say the wrong thing."

"I was just gonna look at the menu to see what I wanted to eat," he explained.

"I know, but he thought you might tell her that he wasn't your father," I reminded him.

"I wouldn't do that. For sure they'd hurt me if I did. I was scared they had that gun in their pocket. Maybe they'd shoot the lady too."

"Well, you did the right thing. What next?"

"I looked around the diner to see if I could get somebody's attention, like you said, but nobody was near us. They were all sitting on stools at the counter, or at tables on the other side of the diner. When the big man saw me looking around, he told me not to get any big ideas. If I tried anything, I'd be real sorry. He said he had a gun in his pocket. So I stopped looking around 'cause I was scared."

He paused, took a breath, and then continued. "Then the lady came back, and they ordered their food. I was getting hungry just listening to them talk about food. Then the lady looked at me and at the big man and asked him what I wanted to eat. He said I wanted the meatloaf special with milk, but no pie. I didn't know what meatloaf was 'cause I never ate it before, but I was really hungry, so I didn't care what it tasted like. I didn't even care about the pie. I just wanted some food to eat. All I could think about after the lady left was that food. I didn't even think about what you told me. You know, trying to figure out a plan. I was too hungry. I'm sorry."

"Don't be sorry. I told you the most important thing of all was for you to eat. You needed food to keep up your strength. What happened next?"

"While we waited for the food, the big man went over to the telephone. He stood with his back to me, so I couldn't see his mouth. I heard him talking, but I couldn't understand what he said. He mumbled so nobody could hear. I forgot about how hungry I was 'cause I figured he was talking to my dad, and I wanted to talk to him so much. I kept hoping he would let me talk to him. The big man then told me to come over to the telephone. He grabbed my arm so tight it was going numb, and he told me to tell my dad how good he was treating me. He told me if I messed up I'd never see my dad again. I knew he meant he was gonna kill me if I said anything wrong, but I sure wanted to talk to my dad."

Again, Avery paused, presumably thinking about

his dad. Then he said, "My dad sounded so worried. That's why I can't understand why he wasn't home when you tried to see him. I think he was even crying. I tried to be calm, 'cause I knew I'd get in trouble if I wasn't. I told my dad I was fine and they were treating me okay and they didn't hurt me. I had to lie. I never lied to my dad before, but they would hurt me more if I didn't. Then my dad said he was gonna get me home soon. Then he asked me if they were feeding me enough. I started to say we were at a diner getting ready to eat right then, but the big man grabbed the telephone out of my hand before I could say anything else and told me to sit down.

"So I went back to the booth. I was real sad then. I was trying hard to hold back the tears. They'd be mad if I started bawling. Then the lady brought our food, and I remembered I was so hungry. I guess I must've been gulping my food, 'cause the lady looked at me kind of funny. The big man told her that meatloaf was my favorite food, and he told me to mind my manners. He called me 'son'. I didn't like him calling me his son. I'm not his son. I hate him. But I didn't say anything.

"Mister Driscoll, it was the best food I ever, ever ate in my whole life. Our cook never made anything that good. They were talking while I was eating, but I wasn't paying any mind to them. When my food was gone, I remembered what you said about trying to get somebody's attention, so I started looking around the booth. When the men weren't looking, I took my napkin and picked up the saltshaker and put them on my lap and unscrewed the lid of the shaker. It was kind of stuck, but I finally got it loose. Then I put my napkin on my plate, but I sort of bunched it up so they couldn't see on the other side of the plate. I made sure they still weren't looking, and then I dumped the salt on the table next to my plate, and started pushing it to say 'HELP.' I almost had it all done when the short man wanted the salt for his grits, and he saw that I spilled it on the table and was writing words. In a real mean voice, he told me to use the napkin to clean it up. I knew he was real mad at me again. Then we left. I was scared. I didn't know what they were gonna do to me.

"I got into the truck and sat on the seat. When the big man came into the truck, he told me I made a big mistake. When we got away from the diner, the short man shoved me down on the floor again. At the house, the short man pulled me out the door. I thought he was gonna rip my arm off. He kept shoving me up the path when I tried to walk. At the porch, he gave me a hard shove, and I fell on the steps, scraping my knee real bad. Then he dragged me into the room and shoved me onto the bed. He told me to sit there until he came back. Then he left and slammed the door. I didn't know what they were gonna do to me. I heard them shouting in the other room. Then the big man came in the room and slapped me so hard on the face that I fell down on the floor. Everything was spinning round and round."

He started to cry. I let him cry while I tried to figure something to say to comfort him. He was in such a predicament. I was at least thankful he had a decent meal, but one meal did not attempt to solve the long-range problem.

Before I could think of anything, Avery spoke between sobs. "The big man said if I pulled one more stunt, he was gonna kill me."

"Avery, that's what he had to say. He wants to

scare you, but as I told you, he won't kill you because he wants that money. He has to prove to your dad that you're okay, or your dad won't pay them. I know things don't look so good. I feel so bad that you have to be hurt repeatedly, but please, *please* believe me. We're going to get you out of this. We can't give up. We have to keep trying. Do you agree?"

"I…I…guess so."

I tried to give him a pep talk. "You know you want to see your mom and dad soon, and you want to go to another baseball game. I promise you that you will be free by the Fourth of July. Do you believe me?"

"How? What can we do? You don't even know where I am."

Ironically, I knew exactly where he was, but he would never believe that we were in the exact same place sixty-seven years apart.

"I know you're hurting. Don't give up on me now. Okay?"

There was silence for a while. Then he spoke. "I…suppose we can try something else."

"Good for you!" I was so proud of this kid. He had such spirit; he had more guts than anybody I ever knew. It was contagious too. With him trusting me, I knew we would get out of this somehow.

"You get some rest now. You've had enough trauma for one day. I'll try to come up with something else before tonight. I'm picking up my girlfriend tonight, but I'll be home later in the evening. Call back after you sleep. You need to maintain your health as much as possible. Now that you had some good meatloaf, maybe you won't feel so hungry or sick."

"I sure wish I could meet your girlfriend. I sure

wish I could meet you, too."

"Oh, you'd rather meet my girlfriend before you meet me, huh? Don't get any ideas, young man. I don't want you stealing her away from me."

"Oh no! I didn't mean that. I just meant I wanted to meet both of you. I'm sorry."

"I was just teasing you, Avery. I know if Beth ever met you, I'm not so sure she wouldn't dump me for you. She likes young, brave men. And that's exactly what you are. I'm going to hang up now. You get some rest."

What a dilemma! Why couldn't Avery have reached somebody more equipped to handle this type of situation? There I was—a meagre accountant, enjoying my life, my new job, and my plans of marriage, when now none of that seemed important anymore. And Beth? I love her so much, but I hardly had time to think about that love. As much as I wanted to see her, I almost wished she were not coming. I only had the next day to find a solution. How could I do that while entertaining Beth? In addition, she was refusing to understand. Maybe when Avery calls, she could talk to him. Maybe then, she'd believe me. But maybe I'm the only one that can talk to him. It would be great if I had some help because I sure as hell didn't know what I was doing.

I looked at the clock. Great. Six-thirty. I had wanted to be at the airport by then. I looked around the house. Damn! What a mess! I hadn't picked up any of the massive mounds of clothing, newspapers, or other junk that had accumulated over the past months. I had planned to do the laundry the night before. I hadn't done it. I scrambled through each of the rooms, picking up the clothes and tossing them in the laundry room. I grabbed a load of underwear, shirts, and socks and threw them in the washing machine. I hurriedly put a week's worth of dishes that had been idling in the sink into the dishwasher. Spree was whining at the door. I had forgotten all about letting her out this afternoon. Poor dog. She was being even more neglected than the house.

"Sorry, girl," I said as I opened the back door. I surveyed the house after my frantic attempt at straightening it. Everything looked presentable except the bathtub and the kitchen floor. The bathtub was a mottled shade of gray, and the kitchen floor was the same shade of gray with streaks of nondescript stains. I couldn't leave it looking like that. This was to be Beth's home in a couple of months. What an image to introduce her to the place where she was going to spend at least the next five years of her life.

First, I attempted to scrub the bathtub with a sponge from under the bathroom sink that looked and smelled like a small, dead animal. The attempt was only half-successful. I closed the shower curtain. Maybe she wouldn't notice.

Next, I grabbed the bucket and foul smelling mop from the laundry room. I looked under the kitchen sink for some type of soap to scrub the floor. Nothing there but dishwasher detergent and cleanser. I chose the dishwasher detergent. If it makes the glasses sparkle, maybe it would do the same for tile floors. I was not too successful there either, but at least the streaks disappeared even if soap film covered the entire floor. This only goes to show that men are not meant to clean house either.

As Spree was scratching at the back door to come in, the front door bell buzzed. I hurriedly opened the back door for Spree. Then she beat me to the front door to acknowledge our caller. I opened the door to see my friends, Robby and Matt, standing there each with a Frisbee in their hands.

"Hi, Mister Driscoll. Can Spree come out and play?" asked Robby.

I had neglected Spree considerably these last few days, but I had to leave at that very moment or I'd never make it to the airport on time.

"Guys… Guys… I need to leave right now."

Robby said, "But we'll watch her real good. We'll bring her back when we see your car in the drive."

"Problem is I'll be gone for several hours. It'll be dark, and you'll be tired of playing with her by then."

"Can we just put her in your back yard when we're done?" he begged.

"There's not enough shelter for her in the backyard. She'd get too hot. We'd better postpone it until tomorrow."

"Aww, we really wanted to play with her. We could take her to our house when we're done," sighed Matt.

"Sorry, guys. I don't think that'll work. Come back tomorrow. I really need to go now. I'm already late."

They walked away with their heads staring at the sidewalk and their Frisbees dangling at their sides. I was sorry that I was being so abrupt, but I had to leave. I had no time to worry about hurt feelings. Speaking of hurt feelings, Beth would never forgive me if I weren't there to pick her up. With luck, maybe the flight would be late.

Sixty-five is the speed limit in many places on the turnpike. I went seventy all the way. I didn't want to go too fast. All I needed was to get a ticket. I arrived at the parking garage at seven-thirty. I had a half-hour to park and get to the gate. Ample enough, assuming that I would have no difficulty finding a parking place. That was not the case. I ended up on the sixth level of the parking garage. Luckily, my car is a compact model because only those spots were still available. By the time I got out of my car, it was twenty until eight. Twenty minutes. I rushed to the nearest elevator. I waited several minutes before one arrived. Quickly, I entered the opened doors. As the doors were closing, someone shouted, "Could you hold that for us?"

I darted my arm out to keep it from closing. The source of the voice was soon entering the elevator. He was a short, rotund man about sixty years old. "Thank you," he said. "Hurry along, Mother, we're late."

"Mother" finally arrived at the elevator in what seemed to take a lifetime. My twenty minutes was dwindling fast. "Mother" was as short and round as "Father". She hobbled into the elevator, all out of breath. "Marvin, I told you we should've left sooner, but no, you had to watch the rest of that stupid television show. We're going to miss our flight now."

"Oh, Mother, we have plenty of time. The flight doesn't leave until eight-thirty. We have over forty-five minutes." He put his luggage down on the floor of the elevator, and I pressed the "To Terminal" button.

The elevator stopped at every floor on the way down. Five... Four... Three... Two... One... There must have been a dozen people on the elevator before it reached the terminal level. And five more minutes had passed.

Since I had been the first one on the elevator, I then had to be the last one off. All those from the other levels exited quite quickly, but Mother and Marvin, supposedly late for their flight, took forever to disembark. Finally, I was able to squeeze by them. "Excuse me, please." I hurried passed. I could hear Mother as I walked away. "Well, how rude these young people are today!"

I quickly walked across the causeway into the terminal building and found the escalator leading up to the gate level. Delta flights come in at gates in Terminal A, so I wove my way through the crowd to my destination. Travelers packed the lobby of Terminal A. All seats were occupied. Many people sat on the floor leaning against their luggage. I had never seen the airport that crowded. I looked at the huge Arrival/Departure display, searching for Beth's flight from Chicago. It was now eight o'clock. Yes! The flight's arrival would be a half-hour late at Gate 24. Maybe my luck was finally changing.

I still didn't have time to fool around. I stopped and took a leak, then went to Gate 24. Many people were awaiting the arrival of Flight 2515. Its next destination was St. Louis. I hadn't anticipated flights leaving that late in the evening. I walked around for a while until a young guy with a ponytail down to the middle of his back got out of his seat, taking with him a backpack the size of my bed. I sat in his seat to wait out the twenty minutes until the flight arrived.

Lucky me. Sitting next to me was this chubby girl about seven years old licking a sucker larger than her face, wearing a hot pink Mickey Mouse ears hat on her head. Actually, I think there was more of the sucker on her face and her hands than on the stick. Before long that sucker was also on my shirt and my arms. I leaned forward and rested my forearms on my knees, hoping to get a little further away from the sticky circle, but the kid fidgeted back and forth, in and out of her seat. She must have hit me twenty times with that damn sucker.

"Sissy, be careful. You're hitting the nice man with your lollipop." Her mother modestly scolded her.

However, Sissy did not listen. In and out. Up and down. With each turn, I got more goo on me than the brat got in her mouth.

I'd had enough. The seat wasn't worth it. I got up and went over to lean on a partition near the walkway. It was twenty after eight.

Leaning up against that wall, I realized how tired I was. It had really been a long day, and nothing was accomplished. I didn't get any information from Eubbey Litomen, and Avery had been unsuccessful in his escape attempt. I closed my eyes, thinking of the day's events.

Suddenly, I heard a squeaky voice close by. "Hey, mister, are you sleeping?"

I stumbled upright, almost losing my balance. It was Sissy, the fat sucker kid back to torment me. I guess I had dozed off, for I looked at the large clock overhead. It read eight-thirty-five.

Then a stewardess announced over the P.A. system, "Flight 2515 from Chicago O'Hare has just landed. Passengers will be disembarking shortly from Gate 24. Flight 3224 to St. Louis will be leaving at nine-fifteen as soon as the flight crew has a chance to freshen up the airplane. Thank you for flying Delta

Airlines. Enjoy your flight."

I leaned back against my wall. Sissy's mother called for her to go to the bathroom before boarding their flight. Lucky St. Louis. Luckier still her seatmate.

I think I dozed off again. Another announcement involving the St. Louis flight awakened me. I slowly opened my eyes and focused on the large, metal door that opened to the walkway leading to the airplane. The stewardess had opened it and passengers from Flight 2515 were scurrying out the door.

Suddenly, as if in slow motion, there she was, more beautiful than ever. Her dark hair had grown longer. Its soft curls surrounded her face like a waterfall clinging to a cliff, cascading in magnificent waves down her cheeks. I saw the brilliant blue of her eyes from where I was standing ten yards away. Frozen in my spot, all the emotions I had felt for her before the Avery incident were enveloping me again. The girl of my dreams. The girl with whom I was so madly in love. The girl with whom I was going to spend the rest of my life.

She came right up to me. "Ken?"

I stared at her for a few more seconds. Then I grabbed her so tightly, hugging her, and whispering in her ear how much I loved her; how much I missed her; how glad I was that she was finally in my arms. I could feel the tears gently flowing down her face.

Finally, I tenderly pulled back from her so I could admire her beautiful face. "Beth, I missed you so much. I don't ever want to be without you again."

She quietly responded between her sobs of joy. "Oh, Ken, I love you so. I missed you so much."

We went on and on, hugging, kissing, and sobbing, for a few more minutes. Then I felt someone tap me on the back. Not that annoying, little Sissy again. I turned around, looking down at about the sucker brat's height, only to be staring into a man's crotch. My eyes went upward to the face belonging to the crotch.

Sometimes there's just no end to the surprises in a man's life. There was my brother, Eddie, standing before me. I grabbed him and hugged him tightly. Then I punched him in the shoulder as we always used to do. He punched me back even harder.

"How the hell are you, Eddie? What are you doing here?"

"What kind of a greeting is that? Should we turn around and fly back to Chicago?"

We? What did he mean by "we"? I looked behind him. There was Theresa, Eddie's wife, and Zachary, my four-year-old nephew.

You could've blown me away! Never in my life! I don't think I was surprised this much since I won five thousand dollars in the Illinois Lottery.

"You guys are trying to give me a heart attack. Beth, why didn't you tell me Eddie and Theresa were coming with you?"

"How would you have been surprised if I told you? That would've spoiled all our fun."

"I have a bit of a surprise for you, also. You know I have a Hyundai. We need to load five people and your entire luggage into it."

They had only carry-on luggage, so we gathered it up and proceeded to the parking garage. We squeezed, shoved, pushed, crammed the luggage into the hatchback, then we all loaded into the car to head back to Nawinah.

Traffic was heavy on the Beeline, but light on the

turnpike. After exiting the turnpike, Beth was all eyes, looking around the area. When I pulled in our driveway, I knew she was sizing up our house.

"Well, how do you like it, sweetheart?" I asked.

"Can I see it in daylight before I'm cross examined? At least let me see the inside first," she scolded.

"This seems like a quiet neighborhood," offered Eddie.

"Yeah, it is," I said. I didn't mention lawnmower man next door.

We retrieved the luggage from the hatchback. It was almost as difficult getting it out as it was putting it in. Zachary had fallen asleep, and Theresa carried him with his head resting on her shoulder. When we got to the front door, Spree was barking. She was not used to company. I wasn't sure how she would react.

Beth looked a little frightened. "Does she always sound that mean?"

"She's not used to company. I'd better go in first to make sure she knows I'm with you. I think she'll be okay then."

I unlocked the door and entered first. She was so happy to see me that I had to pet and hug her to calm her down.

"She's a beauty, Ken. I hope she's okay with kids," Eddie said.

"Yeah, she is. A couple of neighborhood kids play with her. She loves it."

Spree sniffed our company from top to bottom while Beth stood in the living room looking around.

"Let me give you a little tour, honey. You'll love the place," I suggested.

Theresa laid the sleeping Zachary on the couch. I don't think Spree had noticed this little person in all the excitement, for she then gave Zachary her undivided attention. It's a wonder the kid didn't wake up with that cold, wet nose, rubbing against his face, but he stayed asleep, and Spree sniffed him thoroughly while I took the adults around the house.

"Well, are you impressed, Beth?" We were in the kitchen, and she was gazing around the room. Oh oh. She's going to say something about the dirty floor.

"I guess I can put up with it."

Spree had left Zachary's side and had eventually followed us from room to room, right at my heels. Beth then went over to her and bent down to her level, holding out her hand. "Come here, girl."

Spree was not sure at first what to do. She looked up at me. "Go ahead, Spree." She still looked at me.

Beth called her again. "Here Spree, pretty girl."

I guess Beth is irresistible to a dog too. Spree slowly walked over to her. Beth lightly rubbed her hands over the top of Spree's head and gently massaged her ears. Spree loved it and began wagging her tail. From that moment on, my two brunettes were fine with each other.

"How about some coffee? I hope you know I don't have much food in the house. We'll go out in the morning for some groceries. I do have bread and peanut butter. I ate the last of the baloney for dinner."

"Hey, peanut butter sandwiches sound great to me," agreed Theresa.

I filled up the coffee maker. Beth and Theresa familiarized themselves with the cabinets in search of the mugs. Then they found the bread and peanut butter and made several sandwiches. We gathered around the kitchen table, eating our sandwiches, drinking coffee, talking about old times, old friends, and the future. Spree fell asleep under the table.

For a time I forgot about the urgency of Avery's dilemma. I needed the reprieve to rejuvenate my determination. I had been concentrating too hard on the problem that my objectivity was suffering.

Soberly, Eddie asked, "Ken, what's this about a kidnapped kid? Beth tells me you're going nuts about some prank caller."

I guess the light camaraderie was over. Serious business now. I took a deep breath before answering his inquiry. Beth, Eddie, and Theresa were all staring at me.

"Eddie, have I ever lied to you?"

"Are you serious? You used to lie to me all the time, and I'd get blamed for things you'd do."

"I mean since we've been adults."

"Well, no, but then I don't know if any incident has ever come up that might force you to lie."

"Well, I've never lied to you as an adult, and I won't lie to you now. I'm going to tell you a very preposterous chain of events. Please don't interrupt me until I'm finished. Then, hell, I hope you do interrupt me and help me out. Agreed?"

"Agreed," he said.

Eddie is really a good guy, probably a much better individual than I am or ever will be. He always puts money in the Salvation Army buckets at Christmas. I don't know how many Walk-A-Thon's, Bike-A-Thon's, Skate-A-Thon's I've sponsored for him. He's just an all-around good person. If anyone could help me, it would be he. I started from the beginning and told them everything about Avery and everything I had learned. I ended with the last phone call from Avery. It took me a good forty-five minutes to complete the dialogue.

Chapter Nine

Friday, July 3, 1998

When I finished my entire discourse, there was complete silence.

Beth spoke first. "I didn't realize how much this meant to you, or how much you were involved. I'm sorry I didn't take you seriously when you first told me. I sincerely thought some young kid was getting the best of you."

I could tell Eddie was mulling it over in his mind. When Eddie is deep in thought, he unconsciously scratches his head and wrinkles up the left side of his face.

Finally, he said, "I can see why you've been going out of your mind. You know what you've got to do, but you can't do it." Then he leaned back on his chair and continued to scratch his head and wrinkle up his face.

Theresa, too, had been speechless. She then said, "Ken, I'm so sorry. We didn't know. You should've called us. Maybe we could've come sooner."

Most people would just say I was full of shit, but these three people I loved dearly didn't even hint at that. They truly believed me from the moment I finished my narrative, but they were just as baffled as I was.

Theresa meant well. It wasn't their fault that I was

in this situation. "Thanks, Theresa, no disrespect, but what would you do that I haven't already done?"

"You're right. But maybe now with the four of us, we can think of something," she added.

"I sure hope so." I stood up to freshen everybody's coffee.

I could tell something was on Eddie's mind. He was scratching his head and wrinkling up his face again. "When do you think this kid will call you back? Do you think I could talk to him?"

"I'm surprised he hasn't called back already. He was very distraught when I talked to him before I left for the airport. And as far as you talking to him, this is such I weird situation that I have no idea if that's possible."

"Let's think about this. You've done all you can up to this point. Now we've got to figure the next move." Eddie stretched his arms, folded them at the back of his head, and looked up at the ceiling.

Eddie was always good about taking over a situation. When we were kids, I used to resent it. I'd tell him to mind his own business and let me make my own mistakes. However, I truly didn't feel that way about Avery. I needed all the help I could get. And quickly.

Everyone was quiet, thinking what the next move should be.

Eddie suggested a different approach to an escape. "It seems you've tried to get him to escape when they have taken him out of the house where they are keeping him. Do you think there might be some way he could escape from the house itself?"

Theresa, following up on Eddie's idea, revealed, "I never told you this, Eddie, but when I was a teenager, my dad used to lock me in my bedroom so I wouldn't sneak out at night. I used to try all kinds of ways to escape. One night before I went to bed, I stuffed a matchbook firmly into the hole in the doorframe where the latch would go. Then after everybody was asleep, I tried the door to see if it had latched, and it hadn't. I was able to sneak out unnoticed. Of course, when Dad got up at two in the morning and noticed my door slightly open, it didn't matter how successful I was. I was congratulating myself so much that I had forgotten to close the door completely. Do you think Avery could try something like that with his door?"

"Ken, do you think he might have something he could shove into the hole in the door frame?" asked Eddie.

"I'm not so sure. The way he talks, the room only has a metal bed and a small table beside it. No bedding on the bed."

Then I remembered the cans of soup. "Hey, what about the labels on the soup cans?"

"That might work," answered Eddie. "He might need a couple of them to make sure they're packed in firmly, but it's worth a try. Do they ever leave him out of the room? It would take several seconds to jam it in the hole. Would he have the time to do it?"

"I don't know. The only time they leave him out is to take him to the bathroom or to talk to his father. I'm sure he doesn't have too much time. Whether or not it's enough time, is anybody's guess."

"Is there something he could do to distract them while he's in the bathroom or on his way back to the room that might allow some extra seconds? What if he pretends to clog the toilet, or maybe, really clogs it, and starts yelling for their help?" Beth added her suggestion.

Eddie thought about Beth's suggestion. "I guess we really can't predict what they'll do. We just have to try to anticipate different scenarios."

Theresa was concerned about the plan. "What if he takes the labels off several of the soup cans and stuffs them into the toilet? Toilets probably weren't made the way they are today. Then he tries to flush them down. Would that clog it up?"

"Actually," I said. "I'm not sure what kind of a toilet it is. What the hell did they look like back in 1931? Jeez! This is getting complicated."

I was getting agitated, frustrated, and worried. We didn't have time for trial and error. Whatever we decided had to work. The situation was getting extremely dangerous for Avery. I was sure the patience of his kidnappers was wearing thin also. They were not going to put up with much out of him in their edgy state of mind. Thus, I was afraid of the consequences of a botched attempt. I relayed my misgivings to the rest of them.

"I don't know. We can't say maybe this or maybe that. It has to be something definite. We can't screw around with this kid's life. We don't have the time."

I got up and paced in the kitchen, getting extremely upset. Maybe it was their presence. Maybe it was so close to when he was actually killed. Maybe it was my lack of rest. Maybe it was... Oh, how the hell do I know? But I was losing it.

Beth quickly came over to me. She grabbed my arm and turned me toward her. Then she put both arms tightly around my torso and hugged me. For a little bit of a girl, I was amazed at her strength. When she finally let go, she took my face between her hands and forced my eyes to look into her beguiling, baby blues. I began to drown in the depth of them. Then she reached around my neck and pulled my face to hers until our lips barely touched. She gave me the softest, gentlest kiss she had ever given me. When she finally pulled away, she then tenderly grabbed my head again and brought my ear down to her mouth.

"I love you, Ken Driscoll," she whispered in my ear.

It was enough. I came back to reality. I turned to Eddie and Theresa while putting my arm around Beth. "I'm sorry, guys. I guess I flipped out there for a minute."

Then Eddie joined Beth and me. He gave us a big hug also. With tears in her eyes, Theresa came over to the three of us for a group hug.

We were interrupted by little Zachary's cries from the living room. "Mommy! Mommy! Where are you?"

Theresa broke loose and went into the living room to appease her son. Spree followed her. Eddie and I sat back down at the table. Beth got us all another cup of coffee.

Then the telephone rang.

The three of us stopped everything. Beth had poured my coffee and was about to pour Eddie's. She held the coffee pot suspended in mid-air. Eddie had been reaching for his cup to move it toward the coffee pot in Beth's hand. His hand also froze in mid-air. I had just picked up my cup and was about to take a swallow of coffee. The cup stopped abruptly at my lips. Theresa came quickly into the kitchen carrying Zachary in her arms.

The phone rang again. I quickly put down the coffee cup and went to the phone.

"Avery, is that you?"

"Mister Driscoll?" He was softly sobbing.

"Are you okay, Avery?"

"Yes, sir. I'm just tired and sore. I'm having a hard time sleeping. Those men are just getting meaner and meaner."

In the background Eddie said, "What's he saying? Is he okay?"

"Mister Driscoll, is somebody there?" He sounded very excited. "Is it my dad?"

"No, no, Avery, it's my brother. Remember I told you I was picking up my girlfriend? Well, my brother and his family came to visit me too."

"Does that mean you aren't going to have time to help me anymore?" He sounded so forlorn and devastated.

I was his only link to any possible help in escaping, and he thought that I would abandon him. "Oh, no, Avery. I would never do that. In fact, they're going to help me get you free. We've been talking about it for hours."

He sounded surprised. "You have?"

Again, I heard Eddie in the background. "Let me talk to the kid."

I didn't know whether it was a good idea to have Avery talk to Eddie. Maybe that would frighten him even more. Also, with this time element thing spanning sixty-seven years, who really knew if Eddie *could* talk to him? I figured there was only one way to find out. First, I had to be sure it was okay with Avery.

"Avery, my brother, Eddie, wants to talk to you. He's my big brother, and he has helped me out of many bad situations in my life. Maybe he could help us out here too."

"Uhh. Do you think it's okay?"

"Yeah. I think it'll do you some good. You're probably sick of hearing my voice all the time."

"Oh, no, Mister Driscoll. If it weren't for you, I don't know what I would do."

"Okay, Avery. I'm going to let you talk to Eddie. I've told him all about you, so you don't have to explain anything."

Eddie grabbed the phone. Theresa and Beth both sat at the table waiting to see what would transpire. I stood nervously inches away from Eddie. I was worried something would go wrong, but I knew the more help we could get, the better.

With his normal self-confidence, Eddie said, "Hey, Avery, how ya doin'?"

Silence.

"Yeah, Ken told me all about it."

I guess Avery was able to talk to Eddie after all. One hurdle out of the way.

Eddie has the type of personality that makes anyone trust him completely. Countless times, he has helped me out of tough situations. One time when I was in the ninth grade, Scoot, a buddy of mine, and I were walking home from a basketball game our school had won. We were talking and laughing, not realizing that following behind us were six kids from the school we had just beaten. As Scoot and I were crossing this bridge over a small stream, the six boys surrounded us. We were startled and terrified, but we tried to act tough.

"What do you assholes want?" I bravely jeered.

They got closer and closer to us, pushing us up against the railing of the bridge.

"Hey, man!" yelled Scoot. Whatcha tryin' to do?" I could tell Scoot was scared too.

The biggest guy in the group spoke, "You dudes think you're hot shit 'cause you won a basketball game. We're gonna show you just what hot shit is."

He pulled out a lighter from his jean pocket and flicked it on an inch from my face.

I jerked back, but the bridge railing kept me from going anywhere. Two of the guys grabbed my arms. Two other guys grabbed Scoot. The sixth guy took out his lighter and did the same to Scoot as the big guy was doing to me.

"Come on," I pleaded. "We ain't botherin' you. Leave us alone."

"I'll leave you alone when I'm ready, you little shit."

Scoot and I tried to pull loose from the grip of the guys holding us, but we were overpowered. They started lifting us up. They were going to throw us over the bridge!

At that moment, I saw a beat-up, old, 1970 yellow Firebird barreling down the street. There was only one car like that in all of the Chicago area. It was Eddie's car. Eddie pulled up alongside the commotion. The six guys holding us hostage turned to see what had approached.

Eddie is four years older than I am. I was probably fourteen, and he was eighteen. His four buddies in the Firebird were also seventeen and eighteen. His four big buddies. One was Big John, who played tackle on the football team in high school. When those five guys got out of the car, our six predators immediately changed to six pussies. They let go of Scoot and me at once.

In his tough guy voice, Eddie spoke, "You havin' some trouble here little bro'?"

Normally I'd be bent out of shape, him calling me little bro', but not that time. I shoved the big guy with the lighter out of my face and walked over to Eddie and his buddies. I turned to the former predators. "Not anymore!"

Big John strolled over to them with his massive arms swinging at his side. "I think you *girls* better get out of my sight before I turn each of you into lumps of bloody flesh."

"Hey, man, we were only kiddin'. We weren't gonna do anything to them. Really," said the big guy with the lighter in a quivering voice.

Then Big John yelled, "Well now prissy *girl*. We won't be able to find out, will we? Because you are out of here. *Right now*!"

He shouted with such force that all six of them ran in all directions. Eddie, his friends, Scoot, and I buckled over with laughter.

So that was just one of many times Eddie has gotten me out of a bad situation. I was now counting on him to help me out of the toughest circumstances that either he or I had ever been in before.

Eddie continued to talk to Avery in a very calming manner. It was as if he were carrying on a conversation with an old buddy.

"Yeah, Ken, he's okay. We had some good times when we were kids."

Pause.

"Yeah, we fought some, but not much, because he was always smaller than I was. I didn't want to hurt him."

Then Eddie started to discuss our toilet clogging/latch clogging solution with Avery. Silence again.

"Oh, I see. That won't work then. Forget about the bathroom part. Can you still put the crumpled soup labels inside the lock seat?" Eddie was intently listening to Avery's answer.

"I guess that won't work either. I'll tell you what. I'm gonna let you talk to Ken while I think. I do my best brainwork on the toilet. I'll be back in about five minutes."

Eddie handed me the phone. "Here, talk to him while I go concentrate. Maybe I can come up with something while I take a shit."

I sat my coffee down and took the telephone. "Hey, Avery, so what do you think of my brother?"

He wasn't too quick to answer me. "I guess he's okay, but I'd rather talk to you. I know you better, and I'm used to you. Like I told Mister Eddie, I can't clog the toilet. There's no bathroom here like I have at home. I have to go outside to the outhouse, and the toilet is just a big hole in a wooden seat. One of them follows me into the outhouse every time. Sometimes I can't even pee 'cause they're staring at me. They even stand right next to me when I'm trying to, you know, that other, number two. So I haven't been able to do that for a couple of days. I'm sorry. Maybe I shouldn't talk about this?"

"No, no, that's okay. I understand what you mean. I have trouble if someone else is in the bathroom too." I knew he was embarrassed talking about such personal stuff.

"And I can't even wash my hands right either. They have this pail of dirty water on the floor of the outhouse. I swish my hands in it and dry them on my pants."

He then reiterated what he told Eddie about the door plan. "I don't think I'd have enough time to stuff those soup labels in the door latch either. For sure, they would see me doing it."

"Yeah, I guess that was a bad idea too," I agreed.

My mixed-up mind was trying to think of something else when Eddie came back from the bathroom.

"Let me talk to the kid," Eddie said.

I put my index finger up to Eddie to inform him to wait. "Avery, hold on a second, okay?"

Eddie said, "Tell him I have a plan."

I removed my hand from the mouthpiece to talk again to Avery. "Avery, Eddie wants to tell you about a plan he has."

Eddie took the phone. "Kid, let's scrap the bathroom idea. Ken told me there are old boards covering your window. He said you were able to scrape at them with a spoon. Do you think you'd be able to pry them from the window? They might not come off very easy, but if they're old boards, if you keep working at them, they might break free. It's worth a try. You'll have to find something in the room to break whatever glass is still there. How about those soup cans? They aren't the best solution, but at least they'll keep you from cutting your hand on the glass. To be safe, take your shirt off and wrap it around your hand before breaking the window with the can. Then any flying glass won't be as likely to cut you. You'll have to break out enough glass and the boards to crawl through the opening. What do you think of that plan, kid?"

Eddie was listening to Avery's response. The rest of us were waiting for Eddie's next words.

Eddie turned to me handing me the phone. "He'd like to talk to you."

I took the phone. "What's going on, Avery?"

"Mister Driscoll, do you think I can get those boards off the window? Remember, I really had a hard time scraping them. Sometimes my hand would slip, and I'd cut myself on the glass too."

I wasn't sure if he could do it or not. Hell, what was I sure about anymore? But do you think I would disappoint him and tell him that?

"I know you can do it. Remember what I told you? You are the bravest person I've ever met. I am so proud to be your friend. What I'd like you to do is to lie down and rest for a couple of hours. Try to sleep, and when you wake up, be sure those men are not in the house. Then pretend you're Hercules and just push at those boards as hard as you can. If you can reach the window with your feet, kick at the boards. You can do it. I know you can."

He was silent for a few seconds. "Mister Driscoll, say I get those boards off and say I'm able to get out the window, what do I do then?"

I answered with extreme confidence in my voice that I absolutely didn't feel. "You run as fast as you can as far away from that house as possible. You run to the first house or the first road you come to. You find the first person you can, and you tell him who you are and where you've been. Tell him to take you to the police immediately. The police will get in touch with your father, and he'll come and get you at the police station. Everything will be all right. You'll be safe."

"Mister Driscoll?"

"Yes, Avery?"

"Can you come to the police station too?"

What was I supposed to say to this? It really felt good that he wanted to see me after his ordeal was over. Looks like I finally had him convinced he was at last going to be free. I couldn't tell him the truth. So I lied again.

"You bet. Avery, I wouldn't miss that for the world. I'll probably get there before your dad."

Don't pile it on too thick.

"Then I'll do it," Avery said forcefully.

I knew he meant it. He could do it. I didn't doubt it for a second. Everything was about to work out great. At last, this would all be over.

"Avery, next time I talk to you, it'll be at the police station. Take care. See you soon."

"Thanks for everything, Mister Driscoll. Good-bye."

"Good-bye, Avery."

"Wow, how intense!" exclaimed Theresa.

Beth sat at the table and shook her head. Eddie, too, sat back down, staring into space, screwing up his lips and eyes.

We could do nothing more. He was on his own now, but I had my doubts. As I stood, I said, "We should get to bed. I don't think he'll call anymore tonight. And tomorrow will be a stressful day. I'm just not so sure this escape plan will work. We have to come up with an alternative in case Avery is not successful. I have to go to the nursing home to see Eubbey Litomen again later this morning. I hope that I can get some answers. But he's so weird, I don't know what to expect from him either."

Beth helped me put the dishes in the dishwasher. Theresa and Eddie took off for the living room to retrieve Zachary from the sofa and carry him into the spare bedroom/office.

Beth and I went into my bedroom and closed the door. Of course, Spree had already positioned herself on the floor at the foot of the bed. Immediately, Beth turned to me and kissed me, not the soft, gentle kiss like the one in the kitchen earlier, but urgent, hot and passionate, and long overdue. Our absence from one another had lasted entirely too many months. Our need for each other was so intense we barely made it to the bed, tripping over Spree on the way.

****

Spree woke me up at eight. I had forgotten to let her outside before we had gone to bed. She was whining and softly barking. Beth opened her eyes but rolled over on her side and went back to sleep. I had to get up anyhow if I was going to make it to the nursing home by eleven. Sleepily, I opened the bedroom door, Spree following quickly at my heels.

Eddie was already up, drinking coffee at the kitchen table. I let Spree out the back door, none too soon. Then I got myself a cup of coffee and joined Eddie at the table.

"And how was your night?" asked Eddie with a smirk on his face.

I didn't have to tell him. He knew. After a few

gulps of coffee, I did respond to his presence. "I have to be at the nursing home by eleven this morning. I don't know if I'll learn anything, but I have to give it one more shot. This Litomen guy, it's so strange that he gets so totally out of control with the mention of Avery's name. There's something more to his involvement than what I already know."

Eddie also questioned Litomen's behavior. "Yeah, being a policeman for that many years, you can't tell me he didn't have other cases that were just as traumatic and violent. Why does that one bother him so much?"

"Are you coming with me, Eddie?"

"Are you sure you want me too? Are you okay with me being here?

I put my hand over his. "Eddie, I need you. You don't know how good it feels that you're here. I've got my big brother to help me out again, just like always."

Eddie was truly an asset to both Avery and me.

"Don't get mushy on me," murmured Eddie.

I knew he felt good about my acknowledgement. He may be a self-confident son of a bitch, but even he likes to know that he's needed.

Then Theresa came into the kitchen, holding little Zachary's hand. Spree was scratching at the window of the back door. Zachary, seeing her, ran over to the door all excited. "Mama, Mama, look at the doggie!"

I got up from the table to let Spree in. "I'm not sure how she's going to react to a little kid, Theresa. Maybe you'd better pick up Zachary until Spree gets used to him."

Zachary was so excited. He was not happy when Theresa picked him up. He wanted to get at that dog.

"Mama, lemme down! Lemme down!"

I opened the door for Spree. As usual, she came bounding up to me, licking me, and jumping on me.

"Off, Spree," I commanded.

Then she went over to Theresa and Zachary. First, she started sniffing Theresa, then Zachary's feet. Theresa kept saying, "Nice puppy, nice puppy."

"Here, let me take Zachary. Maybe if Spree sees him with me, it'll be okay."

I reached over and took Zachary out of Theresa's arms. Zachary gave me a very strange look, but said nothing. He was more confused about the situation than Spree was. I was a stranger to him. I hadn't seen him in months, and to a four-year-old, that's a long time.

Spree turned to me and started sniffing Zachary again. I bent down, still holding Zachary, so Spree could get a closer look.

Overcoming the fact I was holding him, Zachary again became very excited over the dog. Spree sniffed Zachary's face, and her cold, wet nose rubbed up against it again. It must have tickled Zachary, for he started giggling. I slowly let him go, still squatting down with him.

It was instant acceptance for both of them. Zachary gave Spree a great big hug. Spree loved it. She licked the boy incessantly and started hopping about.

I turned to Theresa. "The yard is fenced in. Is Zachary too young to be outside by himself?"

"I don't want him out there alone just yet. Maybe after he has had some breakfast, I'll go out with him until he gets used to the place, and we're sure Spree likes him."

I was sure Spree liked him. The dog slobber all

over Zachary's face proved it.

After showing Theresa where the cereal was, I sat down to finish my coffee.

"Should we have a game plan when we talk to this Litomen character?" Eddie asked.

"That will be difficult. He's so unpredictable. He's rational one minute and out of control the next. We need to think of some way to get Avery in the conversation without upsetting him. It'll be wise to keep the attendant in the room with us or very close by. I thought he would hurt himself the way he reacted when I talked to him yesterday."

Beth then came into the kitchen, wearing this soft, silky robe the color of her eyes. She is even beautiful first thing in the morning without any makeup. She got herself a cup of coffee and sat with us at the table.

"What is on the agenda today, Ken?" she asked.

I couldn't just leave these females home while Eddie and I took off to the nursing home. They would be quite bored in a strange town with no wheels, since mine was the only vehicle.

"We have to be at the nursing home at eleven. I thought we'd go to Publix to get whatever groceries we need. I'm sure you don't want peanut butter sandwiches tonight. Besides, we're about out of bread. There's a mall near the nursing home. I can drop you ladies and Zachery off there while we talk to Litomen. Oh! Remind me to call Eric later. He's the guy at work who's coming to the cookout tomorrow. The cookout I completely forgot about until now. Beth, make sure you get whatever food we still need for it. You know, I'm not good at those things."

We had delicious cereal for breakfast. While Eddie,

Beth, and I showered and dressed, Theresa, already dressed, went out in the back with Zachary and Spree. Then we got groceries at Publix before dropping Beth, Theresa, and Zachary off at the mall. We told them we'd meet them at the food court for lunch at one o'clock.

Eddie and I went on to the nursing home. No one was at the reception desk when we entered. Eddie whispered, "This place is kind of shabby. I sure wouldn't want our dad in a place like this."

"Actually, it's a better place than it looks like on the surface."

"If you say so," he said uncertainly.

"Hello? Anybody here?" I called out.

Ms. Morgan came out to the reception desk. "Hello, Mister Driscoll. Mister Litomen is ready for you. I told him he was getting another visitor today. He's a little agitated, but so far he seems rational."

Ms. Morgan had been glancing at Eddie as she talked to me.

"Ms. Morgan, this is my brother, Eddie. I hope it's okay if he comes with me to talk to him. As I told you yesterday, this matter is of utmost importance. I'm really hoping we can get some answers."

"How do you do, Mister Eddie Driscoll? Uhh, I don't see any harm in it. However, perhaps the aide should stay right outside the room in case there's a problem. If you'll go into the waiting room, I'll be sure he is still ready for you."

I sat on the same chair I had sat on yesterday. Eddie looked at the other chairs disgustingly and decided to remain standing. He paced around the room while we waited.

Ms. Morgan returned, "Please follow me. Mister Litomen is anxious to see you."

She led us back to his room. The aide was standing at the open door when we arrived. Mister Litomen sat in his chair with no drool driveling from his mouth. He looked alert and hopefully coherent.

As we entered the open door, his head jerked in our direction. Startled, he said, "Oh, two sonny boys!"

I thought it best to start the visit in a cheerful manner. With buoyancy in my voice and mannerism I said, "Hi, Mister Litomen. How are you today?"

"Ain't so bad. How's yerself? That fella yer brother? Looks just like you. 'Cept he has hair." He chuckled a little with that remark. Eddie and I smiled back at him. So far. So good.

"Do you remember me from yesterday?" I asked.

"Yep." Just s short and simple reply.

"Do you remember my name?" I still kept the conversation light.

"Nope." He wasn't much of a talker.

"I'm Ken Driscoll, and this is my big brother Eddie." I pointed to Eddie as I introduced him.

Litomen's eyes wandered first up and down me, and then he looked at Eddie and did the same. A slight drop of moisture was accumulating at the corner of his mouth. I hoped we weren't in for a downpour. Since the chairs in the waiting room repulsed Eddie, I hated to see his reaction to the slime torrent that could erupt from Litomen's mouth.

"Eddie... Hmmm...Knew a cop named Eddie Dutchcott. Killed by the mob in 1939. Good cop."

Ah ha, an opening! Maybe if I got him talking about his days as a policeman, he'd open up about

Avery.

Eddie must've read my mind. "How long were you a cop?"

"Retired in 1974. Sixty-two," he volunteered.

Good. Everything was still calm and cool. I decided to keep on the 'cop' angle. "Did you ever make detective or captain?"

"Detective. 1942. But joined the army. Germany." He was really opening up to us.

Eddie took over with the questions. "Did you join the police force again when you came back from the war?"

"Yep." Another brief response.

Okay. He was still at ease with us. No major problems. No crazy behavior. I took a shot at it. "What was the most memorable case that you worked on?"

Silence. His eyes began moving from Eddie to me, from me to Eddie. Eddie sensed we were starting to lose him. He quickly changed the nature of the conversation.

"Hey, were you ever married? How'd your wife feel about you being a policeman?"

I noticed him calming down. He didn't answer immediately, but soon he either had regained his composure or had forgotten what the unsettling question had been.

"Nope. Too ugly."

"What do you mean? You were too ugly, or your wife was too ugly?" I asked.

He got a charge out of that question. His face lit up, and his mouth turned up in a big grin. With that nearly toothless grin, the drool coming out of the corner of his mouth, and his skeletal-like face, he didn't have to answer that question.

"Clever, young whippersnapper," he said from his toothless grin.

He seemed to be enjoying the light camaraderie, but we couldn't keep it up forever. We had to get some answers on some tough, disturbing questions. Eddie was thinking the same thing. "When did you first become a policeman?"

"Eighteen," he answered.

"Let's see," Eddie said, thinking aloud. "What year would that be? Hmmm."

"June 18, 1930." Litomen replied before Eddie figured out the answer.

"You must have worked on a lot of cases in your day," continued Eddie.

"Yep."

"Any murders?" I asked.

"Yep." Up to this point Litomen actually seemed to be enjoying our conversation.

"Any kidnappings?" Eddie asked.

Hesitation. The eyes were flickering ever so slightly. Seconds passed. Finally, "Yep."

"Would there be any cases that we might know about?" I asked.

Again hesitation. "Nope," he said without emotion.

I wasn't sure whether we were getting anywhere or not. Should we continue at this slow pace? It seemed to be working. He seemed to be calm, but inevitably, we had to approach the subject of Avery. The problem was how to do it and still keep this guy lucid.

"Did you ever work on any case where a young kid was kidnapped?" Eddie asked.

Oh, shit! Here we go!

His eyes flickered His head moved back and forth. "Piss ant! Piss ant! I told you so! It's too late!"

Damn! How were we going to get anything out of this guy? This wasn't working. Every time we thought we were making headway, he freaked out on us.

"Mister Litomen, what'd you have for breakfast this morning? Heard you had grits and cheese. Hell, I love grits and cheese. All I had was a bowl of corn flakes. Nobody will cook for me. I always have to fix my own breakfast. You're a lucky guy. Grits and cheese. I wish I could have that for breakfast." I rambled on and on, hoping to divert his attention from Eddie's last question.

He was calming down. It was working, but we couldn't keep this up. Time was running out.

"Avery Archer!" Litomen shouted.

Did I hear him correctly? Eddie and I looked at each other with eyes and mouths wide open.

"Avery Archer. Avery Archer. Avery Archer. Avery Archer." He said Avery's name louder and louder each time. He was getting very upset.

The aide stepped in from his station outside the doorway. "We got a problem?"

Litomen looked at the aide, then at Eddie and me. He stopped yelling Avery's name. He was quiet, and he was not jerking or shaking his head.

"Uhh…I don't think we have a problem yet," I said cautiously.

Nobody said anything for several minutes. The aide stood inside the doorway watching the three of us. Eddie and I slowly sat on the chairs that were against the wall facing Litomen, who lowered his head and stared at the floor.

Finally, Litomen mumbled something I couldn't hear. Puzzled, Eddie and I looked at each other again.

"Mister Litomen, did you say something?" I softly asked.

Litomen looked up from the floor and glared at me. He said, "Avery Archer, Independence Day, 1931."

Were we finally going to get some answers? Eddie asked, "Do you remember what happened to Avery Archer, Mister Litomen?"

Silence.

Litomen's eyes were again darting back and forth between Eddie and me, but it was different. He seemed to be in control. He seemed to be actually looking at us, not just using us as pivots for his eye movement. He also didn't have that wild, crazy look he had yesterday or had started to get a short time before.

He answered curtly, "Yep."

"Could you please tell us what happened to Avery?" I asked, anxious to hear his response.

From the look in his eyes and the expression on his face, he was thinking, remembering. "Why you want to know?"

Now that was a very rational question. At last, maybe we would get some answers. He really appeared to be thinking and acting normally.

Litomen spoke again. "You related to Avery Archer?"

It was my turn to answer some questions before I would get any answers from him. I wasn't prepared to tell him the real reason for wanting to know about Avery. There was no way in hell he would be able to comprehend or understand. I didn't think it was necessary for him to know. Actually, I was beginning to think his discussing Avery was going to do him some good. I'm no psychologist, but maybe if somebody talks about his problems they are less apt to consume him. Perhaps this was part of the reason Litomen acted so crazy sometimes. I don't know a whole hell of a lot about Alzheimer's, but it seems to me if he took one big problem off his mind, maybe he could deal better with his other problems.

Thus, even though we were pressed for time, I knew the best thing to do was to take it slowly and answer whatever was required of me, truthful or not. I answered him as I glanced over at Eddie.

"Uhh, yes I am. He was a distant cousin. His Aunt Sophie and Uncle Harold were my great grandparents. I've been trying to find out as much as I can about his tragic, short life."

"Real bad situation. Real bad." Litomen mumbled, but we could understand him.

"Why? What happened?" asked Eddie.

Both Eddie and I moved to the edges of our seat. I even began to sweat a little.

"Too bad. Too bad, it didn't work out. Too bad," Litomen kept repeating.

He again was getting agitated, but I wasn't going to stop him. We seemed so close. "What didn't work out? What happened to Avery?" I asked.

"I tried. I really tried. I didn't want it to go the way it did. It wasn't my fault. I didn't want to hurt the kid." He was shaking his head back and forth.

I was confused. What was he saying? What did he mean he didn't want to hurt him? This was *not* what I expected. I was too bewildered to ask anything else. I looked over at Eddie. He had the same dumb expression on his face that I had.

Litomen then went on. "They told me nobody would get hurt. I was just a kid, too. I didn't know what I was doin'."

He started breathing heavily and shaking. The spittle formed at the corner of his mouth.

Suddenly, more swiftly than I thought he could move, he jumped out of his chair and started pacing in circles. "Piss ant. Piss ant. Shit. Shit. I told 'em. Piss ant. They wouldn't listen. Smarty pants. Thought they knew everything. Piss ant. Damn jerks. That's what. Damn jerks."

His voice kept getting louder. The aide came into the room. "Mister Litomen. Take it easy, sir. It's okay. It's okay. I'm here now."

The aide tried to calm him. Putting his big black arms around Litomen's thin shoulders, he applied an ever so slight pressure; not enough to hurt him, but enough to hinder his movement. Litomen stopped pacing. The aide lightened his hold around Litomen's shoulders. When he was satisfied Litomen was not going to pace anymore, he let go his grip very slowly.

Litomen looked me straight in the eyes. I will never forget that look. It was pure terror. His eyes were nearly bulging out of their sockets. His entire body was shaking. Then as quickly as it started, it was over. A blank stare replaced the look of terror. The shaking completely stopped, and the drool started to flow. The aide went in front of Litomen, took him by the shoulders, and gently guided him into his chair. Litomen slowly sat, saying no more but staring at me with blank eyes and gripping the arms of the chair so hard his knuckles turned white.

Eddie and I witnessed this strange transformation.

The aide broke the silence. "You best get on yer way. No good come of this now." He was trying to get Litomen's grip to relax on the chair by prying his fingers loose.

Eddie and I walked toward the door. I looked at Litomen's face the entire time I was walking. He continued to stare at me, not saying a word, but still trying to grip the chair with all his might. When we were out of the room, I asked Eddie as we walked down the hall, "What did he mean by that? I'm really confused."

"Weird!" Eddie responded. "This thing gets stranger and stranger the deeper I get involved."

"Who could've told Litomen that nobody would get hurt? Why would anybody say that to him? I think he wanted to tell me more. Did you see how he kept staring at me as I walked out the door? Did you see the terror in his face? It was as if he wanted to tell me something so terrible, but he just couldn't do it. What could cause him to go so quickly from sanity to insanity? Is this typical of Alzheimer's?"

"I don't know…" Eddie was as puzzled as I was.

We walked silently toward the exit of the home.

Ms. Morgan was near the reception desk. "Did you get any answers to your questions?"

I said, "Frankly, I have more questions now than I did before. He talked to us more than he did yesterday, but the things he said were confusing and unexpected."

"I'm very sorry he couldn't be more helpful. Perhaps some other day when he has had enough time to calm down."

We continued toward the exit. I turned back to her.

"Some other day will be too late."

We walked out the door, leaving Ms. Morgan standing on her good leg, resting her arm on the desk, staring at us as we departed.

Neither of us spoke until we were well on the way to pick up Beth, Theresa, and Zachary.

"What now, Eddie? What do we do now?"

"I guess we see if Avery calls when we get back to your house. If he doesn't call, then maybe that means he was able to escape."

"Or maybe it means he's dead," I said decisively.

"Ken, don't look at it like that. We still have some time. Today is only the third. Remember, we know he was still alive at least until the night of the fourth. We'll figure something out."

"Unless we've done something to change that—like putting him in so much danger that they kill him on the third instead of the fourth."

"You can't think like that. Just believe that we still have tomorrow." Eddie tried to encourage me to be more positive.

At the mall, the girls showed us what they had purchased. Zachary rode the merry-go-round a few times while we ate lunch. We told the girls of Litomen's surprise revelations. They were not able to offer any enlightenment either.

Theresa and Beth put all the packages and groceries away when we got home. Zachary and Spree went out back to play. Eddie and I sat at the kitchen table, trying to think of alternative plans of actions if Avery's escape didn't work. I wasn't sure whether I wanted Avery to call. If he called, did that mean he was not successful in his escape? Perhaps he would call from the police headquarters. Could he do that? If he didn't call, did that mean he escaped? How would we know? Eddie was thinking too. We didn't participate in Beth or Theresa's conversations while they put things away and planned the next day's activities.

"Ken? Ken? What do you think?" I finally realized Beth was talking to me.

"Huh? I'm sorry. What did you say?"

"I said what about your friend Eric and his girlfriend? Shouldn't you get in touch with him to confirm his coming tomorrow?"

"Damn! I completely forgot about Eric. Yeah, I have to give him a call."

As I was dialing Eric's number, I was still thinking about Avery.

Then I heard in the telephone receiver, "Eric here."

"Uhh. Eric? Is that you?" I asked, confused why Eric was talking.

"Dude, yeah it's me. Who do you think it is? You called *me*."

"Uhh…yeah, sorry, Eric, I'm just not with it today." I was stalling while I tried to remember why I was calling him. "Hey, Eric, you and Melanie still coming over tomorrow for the Fourth of July cookout?"

"Yeah. I was wondering when I'd hear from you. You didn't show up yesterday at work. I didn't know what was going on."

"I wasn't feeling well yesterday. I took the day off."

"So I heard. Nancy said you called in sick. So what's up? Did Beth get in town? Or were you too sick to pick her up?"

I was finally coming around to actually

participating in the conversation. "Hey, my brother Eddie and his wife and kid also flew down with Beth. We'll have a blast tomorrow. We've got plenty of beer so we can party, party, party!" I really wasn't as excited as I sounded.

"Great. What time should we be there?"

I turned to Beth. "Is one o'clock okay for tomorrow? Will that give you enough time to get everything ready?"

Beth looked at me with daggers in her eyes. "What do you mean, for *me* to get things ready? Where will you be?"

Then I realized I was being my old chauvinistic self and looked at her with puppy dog eyes before turning back to talk to Eric.

"Eric, Beth says one o'clock is fine. We'll see you then. Don't forget the brownies."

When I turned toward Beth, she had completely forgotten about my chauvinism when I had mentioned brownies. I think she even loves chocolate better than sex. I'm afraid to ask her that question. I don't want to know the answer.

Then the telephone rang. I thought it was Eric calling back for some reason or another. It was Avery. I could feel my heart go to my feet when I heard his voice.

"Mister Driscoll?" He was crying. He had been unsuccessful. I closed my eyes and turned my face up toward the ceiling. Eddie knew from my expression that it was not good news.

"Avery? Calm down. I know how rotten you feel. I know, I know."

"Mister Driscoll? They…they chained me to the

bed. I only have one arm free. They won't even let me go to the toilet anymore. They said I have to lie in my own pee."

He was sobbing, but it was not the frantic crying like other times. His cries sounded hopeless, like he had given up.

"Avery. Stop crying and tell me what happened." His recapping of his experiences usually helped him to calm down.

"I slept for a while after I talked to you. Then I put my ear up against the door for a long time to make sure the bad men were gone. I did what Mister Eddie told me to do. I took off my shirt and wrapped it around my hand. Then I got one of the soup cans and hit the window real hard to break the glass away. I had to keep hitting it to make enough room to climb through the opening. I only got little cuts on my arm from the glass. Then I took the spoon and knocked out the glass on the edges of the window frame. After I kicked two boards off the window, I climbed through the hole. I really did! I climbed through the hole! It felt so good to be outside on my own. Then I ran until I came to the road. I kept running and running down the road. When I saw a truck coming toward me, I ran toward the truck, but when it got closer, it was the bad men's truck. So I hurried into the woods, hoping they didn't see me but they did. I could hear them slam on the brakes. I ran as fast as I could to get away. I was getting so tired, but I still kept running. Then I tripped and fell on an old branch, and they caught up to me. They were very mad and said all kinds of bad words. They grabbed me and threw me in the back of the truck. I banged my head on the side. I think I fainted or something, 'cause when I woke up they were dragging me into the house. They threw me on the bed. The short man held me there and kept slapping my face. I tried not to cry, but I couldn't help it. Then I heard some banging and clanging coming from the other room. Pretty soon the big man came back carrying a long chain."

Avery started to sob again. "Mister Driscoll, they chained me to the bed. Even my legs. I can hardly move. I don't know how much longer I can stand it."

During all this, Eddie, Beth, and Theresa were staring at me, wondering what Avery was saying. They knew it wasn't good. Eddie came over and motioned for me to give him the phone. Amidst his sobbing, I said to Avery, "Hey, Avery? Eddie's going to talk to you for a minute."

Eddie took the phone. "Hey, pal, it's Eddie. Let me tell you a little story. Did Ken tell you I live in Chicago?"

Silence on Eddie's part, waiting for Avery's response.

"Yeah, it's a big city in Illinois. Anyhow, one day I ran away from home because I got mad at my mom and dad when they wouldn't let me go to my friend's house. I must've been maybe nine or ten years old. You're eleven, right?"

Silence.

"Well, I got on the EL and just started going wherever it was gonna take me."

Silence.

"The EL? It's a train that travels all around the city of Chicago so people don't have to take their cars everywhere. Anyhow, I kept thinkin' how mad I was at my mom and dad and how they would be sorry that they made me so mad. As I was thinkin' and lookin' out the window, I got sleepy and fell asleep. When I woke up it was dark outside. I was really scared, and I wasn't thinkin' straight. I got off at the next stop, which was a big mistake. When I realized that I was in a very bad part of town, I turned around to get back on the EL, but it had already moved on. I didn't know what to do. All I wanted to do was to get home. I wasn't mad at my mom and dad anymore. I was just scared. So I figured I'd call my mom from the pay phone in the train station. I had some money in my pocket, so I walked down the platform into the station. The only person in the place was some drunk woman sleeping in the corner on the floor with an empty whiskey bottle in her hand. I was afraid to wake her up. I saw the pay phone on the opposite wall. I ran over to it and picked up the receiver, but it was dead. Someone had pulled the wires loose. Then I thought I'd go to a store to use their telephone. The clock above the ticket window read that it was five after midnight. I must've been asleep for a long time on the EL because I left my house about six in the evening. I wasn't sure if there would even be any stores open that late.

"I went out of the train station, but I was really scared because I wasn't near any stores or shops or neighborhoods, just a bunch of old, deserted warehouses with all kinds of junk and broken glass lying around. I didn't know what to do, so I went down the train station steps to the street below. I thought if I just started walking, I would come to a telephone somewhere. It was so quiet. Nobody was around. I walked for what seemed like hours. All that I saw were more deserted building. Everything was dark except for a few streetlights that weren't broken.

"Finally, I saw a light flickering in one of the building windows. I ran to it and knocked on the window, yelling, 'Anybody in there?' From above my head I heard a door open, and I looked up. Standing on the fire escape were two guys looking down at me. I couldn't tell what they looked like because it was too dark. One of them said something, but I couldn't understand him. He was talking in some foreign language. They kept talking, getting louder and louder. I had the feeling they were asking me something, but since I couldn't understand them, I didn't know what to say. And they were getting angry with me. Suddenly, they leaped down from this railing that they had been leaning on and grabbed me so quickly before I even had a chance to run away. I started screaming and struggling, trying to break free of their grip, but they were much bigger and stronger than I was. I was not going to give up. Dad had always told me not to fight dirty if I were in a fight, like don't pinch or bite like girls do. But I didn't care about fighting dirty at that time. I opened my mouth so wide and clamped down as hard as I could on the arm of one of the guys and I wouldn't let go. He let out this scream and tried to shake me loose, but I wouldn't let go. The other guy tried to pull me loose, but I grabbed that guy's balls and dug my fingernails in them until he too was screaming. The two of them both released me, and I took that opportunity to run like hell. They weren't out of action for too long. They scrambled to their feet and chased me.

"Maybe Ken told you I was a quarterback on my high school football team, so I could run fast. But these guys were bigger than I was and had longer legs, so I knew eventually that they'd catch up with me. I didn't give up, though, and I kept running. I kept telling myself, 'you can do it; you can do it', and I believed it. I really believed I could outrun them. I didn't have to 'cause as I turned this corner, thank God, there was a police cruiser. It nearly ran me over when I ran out in front of it. When the car stopped, I hurried over to the policeman and started babbling about what was happening. He probably didn't understand a word I said, but he knew I was in trouble. He put his hand on his pistol and looked around the area. Eventually, he saw the two guys chasing me, but they also saw him and curtailed it in the opposite direction. The policeman yelled for them to stop, but they kept running. He didn't chase them any further but came back to me and asked me all kinds of questions. By then I was calm enough to answer him. He took me to the police station where I called my dad to pick me up.

"I know, Avery, my experience is not the same as your situation, but it's something like it. I could've given up and said I couldn't run any more. My side was hurting so bad I thought it would split open. My heart was beating so fast from running that I thought it would jump out of my chest. But I kept running. And that's what you must do. No matter how bad it looks, you have to keep running. You can't give up. You can do it."

Silence.

"Okay, I'm gonna let you talk to Ken now."

I took the phone. "You okay, Avery?"

"Yes, I am. Mister Eddie is right. I can't give up, can I?"

"No, you can't. Remember I promised you that we'll get you out of this. You have to believe that. I know they've hurt you so much, but they haven't broken your spirit. That's what counts, kid. That's what counts. As long as you have the will to survive, you're going to be okay. Do you believe that?"

"Yes, I do, Mister Driscoll."

"I want you to rest now but call me back when you wake up. Eddie and I will talk about what we want you to do next. Get some rest and call back later."

After hanging up, I turned to Eddie. "Man, you're great! You gave him enough courage to go on. Thanks again, big brother."

"Shucks, it was nothing," he modestly replied. I knew he too was proud of himself.

"So what do we do next?" Beth patted the tears from her eyes with a tissue.

"Good question," said Eddie. "Who has a good answer?"

No one spoke.

Then the back door opened, and Zachary entered with Spree. "Mommy, Mommy, two big boys want to play with me. Can they come into my yard?"

I looked out back to see Robby and Matt, leaning on the fence, talking to each other. "Oh, those are Spree's new friends. They've been taking her out to play the past few days. If it's okay with you, I'll let them in the yard."

Theresa wavered, "I suppose so. As long as they stay in the yard, but I don't trust Zachary near the lake. He's not used to being near water."

I went out with Zachary and Spree to unlock the back gate.

"Hey, Robby, Matt. How you doing? Kind of hot today, isn't it? You guys like to come in the yard? This is my nephew, Zachary, from Chicago. He's visiting Spree and me. Would you like to run through the sprinkler if I set it up?"

"Okay! 'Cept I don't have my baving suit on? I don't know if Mommy brung it," said Zachary.

He started running toward the house. "Mommy! Mommy! You have my baving suit?"

Robby said, "My mom doesn't care if I get wet. We always get wet fishin' anyhow."

Spree was so happy to see her old friends, jumping on them and licking their faces. They were just as pleased to see her and patted her head as she licked them. I set up the sprinkler in the middle of the yard. By the time I was finished, Zachary came trotting outside in his Spiderman bathing suit, ready for action.

I said to Spree, "Okay, girl, you watch these boys. Don't let them get into any trouble."

She barked her consent.

In the house, everyone was sitting around the table. Someone had made iced tea and set out four glasses.

As I sat Beth asked, "Did you say that Avery's bed is a metal post bed?"

"Yes. Why?" I questioned.

"Well, it's probably pretty old. Right? Do you think Avery could work any of the metal posts loose and slip the chains off the bed? And did he say they nailed the boards back on the window? Maybe he could try again if he could get the chains loose?"

Eddie didn't agree. "We really don't know exactly where on the bed he is chained or what the bed actually looks like. He has used up most of his strength. Even with my pep talk, it may be physically impossible for him to do too much more exerting activities. The kid has already done much more than expected."

"We have to think of something," Theresa emphatically said, "Any better ideas?"

Nobody could think of anything. There were four of us, and we couldn't come up with an answer. Avery would probably be calling back soon. What would I tell him? Eddie had spent all that time convincing him that hope was not dead. Now we had no answers.

Beth got up from the table and went to the telephone. "I'm going to order some pizza. We need to eat. Maybe that'll trigger some brain cell activity."

I came back to the present. "Uhh…Domino's delivers. Their number is in the little blue book in the drawer."

"Anybody have any preferences?" Beth asked.

No one responded.

"Okay, I'm ordering the works. Maybe the more junk we eat, the more we can think. I know if I have a problem at work that I can't solve I just eat a candy bar. And the answer miraculously comes to me."

Right. A candy bar. Chocolate, of course.

"That sounds good to me," agreed Theresa. "Can you order a small, plain cheese for Zachary? He won't eat all that stuff they put on the supreme pizza."

It was five o'clock on Friday, July third and obviously, the next night was July fourth. Avery would be killed, and we were powerless to stop it.

The pizza arrived. Surprisingly, we actually ate almost all of the two large pizzas. We didn't discuss Avery but talked about our plans for Saturday. Zachary was having too much fun with Robby and Matt that

Theresa put his pizza aside for later.

After eating, Eddie and I took our iced tea into the living room while Beth and Theresa cleaned up the kitchen.

After Eddie sat on the couch, he asked, "So, what are we gonna tell Avery? I can't think of anything."

"This is hard! Nothing that we have ever done in our entire lives has prepared me for this. How in hell are we supposed to know what to do?"

"How could anything prepare you? Would you've ever thought that you'd be in this quandary?" Eddie was as concerned and baffled as I was.

"Not in my wildest dreams. Or nightmares!" I felt like pulling out my hair.

"Let's do some recapping," said Eddie. "We know Avery has only one arm free. We'll have to assume they boarded the window back up. So what are our options? I really think it's impossible for him to get out of the chains no matter how loose the bedposts are. So where does that leave us?"

I raised my hands and shook my head. "I guess we go down to the wire and plan the escape for the actual exchange of the hostage and the money. I don't think we have any choice. They'll be watching his every move, knowing he's tried several times to free himself. How can we be sure they won't do some permanent damage to him before the exchange if he attempts any more escapes? Since his body wasn't actually found, we don't know what shape he was in when they shot him. It's simply too dangerous for him to try anything more at the house. At least if he tries something at the exchange, the law enforcement and his dad will be close by. If he tries anything now, he's completely on his own, and the chances of success over failure are not good."

"I think you're right," agreed Eddie. "He isn't Super-Boy. He's in such a weakened physical and mental state that the best thing for him to do is to spend tomorrow resting, eating whatever they give him, and psyching himself up for the exchange."

"Yeah, which then brings us to the actual event. How can we pull off the escape?" I leaned back on the sofa forcing my mind to think.

We were both quiet for a while, trying to form some plan of action. The women came in the room and joined us.

Eddie got off the couch and paced around the room. "Did you say you made copies of the newspaper articles from 1931? Get them and let me read the events of the evening of July fourth. Maybe something will come to me."

"Good idea. I think I left them on the bed stand. It seems so long ago that I was reading them. So much has happened. I'll get them."

I went into the bedroom in search of the articles. I'd also bring out the copies of the files on Avery that I had made from the records warehouse. Anything might help. I checked the bed stand, but they weren't there. I checked everywhere in the bedroom, but they were nowhere in the room. I went back to the living room.

"I can't find them in the bedroom. I must've put them somewhere else. Let me check the desk in the room Zachary is using."

With horror and disbelief, I stared at the floor in Zachary's room. Apparently, I had laid the papers on top of the desk. At the time, I hadn't expected I'd use that room. The papers were no longer on the desk. They were in bits and pieces, all over the floor. Upon further examination, it appeared that soggy dog teeth marks were on the edges of the pieces. Also, in the middle of the pile of pieces was a pair of scissors and a permanent black marker. The edges that did not have teeth marks had jagged scissor marks on them, and the printing on the paper was obliterated with the permanent black marker. They were completely and utterly unreadable and destroyed. Immediately, I reached the conclusion that the culprits were a pair—one dog and one kid. I picked up several of the pieces and carried them into the living room, holding them out in front of me as if they were contaminated.

"Oh my God!" shrieked Theresa. "What has he done?" She immediately came over and took the pieces from my hands to examine them. Eddie and Beth also came over to see the handiwork of the dog and the kid.

In a monotone voice, I said. "He had an accomplice."

Theresa turned to me. "What do you mean?"

"Look at some of those edges. Feel them. They weren't cut with scissors. They were chewed."

"Oh no!" Beth exclaimed.

Then Eddie raised his hands and shook his head in resignation. "Great! Now what are we going to do? Can we piece them back together? Can we get other copies?"

I knew those tasks were not feasible. "Piecing them back together is impossible with three separate crimes committed on them—chewing, cutting, and permanent black marker. As far as getting other copies, if we had next week to get them, but we don't. We only have until tomorrow night. Tomorrow is the fourth. Nothing will be open. Any information on those papers is long gone down the throat of Spree or in Zachary's artistic endeavors."

"Shit," Eddie and Theresa said simultaneously.

"So now what? Do you remember enough about what was in the newspaper articles?" Beth looked like she was almost going to cry.

I sat back down on the chair and rested my elbow on the armrest. I began to tap my fingers on the side table while my mind pictured the images of the copies I had made.

"I think I do. I read them several times. Let's see. The rendezvous for the exchange was planned for the night of July fourth around ten o'clock. The police were hidden in the shrubs and bushes nearby, but during the exchange, one of the abductors saw them and started shooting."

"Where was Avery all this time?" asked Eddie.

"He was being held by the arm with a gun to his head by one of the abductors. I don't remember if it said which one. It did say they had stockings on their faces so they couldn't be identified. It also mentioned Samuel Avery's car tires were slashed."

"Okay, after the abductors started firing at the police in the bushes, what happened?" Eddie was trying to jog my memory.

Visualizing the article, I said, "Samuel Archer was shot in his left arm. Then either two or three policemen were also shot. Avery was shot in the head and thrown or fell into the lake…"

I stopped abruptly while I was thinking about the details of the article. "Wait! I think it said *apparently* shot in the head. They never found his body... That's it! That's our answer! They never found his body!"

"What do you mean that's our answer? I thought you said that alligators ate him," Eddie queried excitedly.

"That's what they speculate happened. Don't you see? That's what they *think* happened, but maybe it didn't. Maybe Avery wasn't shot either. Maybe he got away."

"Wait a minute. Wait a minute. Slow down. If Avery got away, why is he calling you now to save him? That doesn't make sense." Beth was getting confused.

Holding in my excitement, I said. "It wouldn't make sense if it was absolute. I mean, if for sure he got away or if for sure he was shot to death and then eaten by alligators, but maybe his getting away or his being shot to death depends completely on *our* actions today, not the events of July 4, 1931, that were in the newspaper. Maybe Avery's life depends completely on us, on how we convince him to respond to the events we know are about to happen."

"I think you've got something there," said Eddie, also excited. "I also think it was inevitable that we would be faced with decisions to make for tomorrow night. Everything leading up to it was garbage over which you had no control. Whatever you would've done would not have made any difference. What's most important is we've got to determine the best course of action for Avery tomorrow night. Yep! That's it!"

I felt relieved. Well, maybe "relief" isn't the word I should use, but I now felt that I finally knew the purpose of Avery's calls. Yes, he was shot to death and thrown in Splash Lake on July 4, 1931. And, yes, subsequently, an alligator ate his lifeless body sometime later. But by some freak—call it fate; call it destiny; call it God, I don't know, I have a chance to save him. And with the help of these three people, we were going to do it.

I expressed my thoughts aloud. "The solution is in something Avery has told me in our many telephone conversations. Somewhere in all those bits of knowledge is the key. Something he said…"

I was rehashing everything in my mind that I could remember when the telephone rang. I was sure it was Avery. I picked it up immediately. "Hello, Avery."

"Why do you sound so happy, Mister Driscoll?"

"I am happy, Avery, because I know you're going to survive. I know you're going to see your mother and father again."

"How do you know that?" I heard skepticism in his voice.

"It's hard for me to explain, but believe me, I'm positive you'll be safe in the arms of your parents soon."

Avery sounded very excited now too. "Really?"

"Yes. The only thing is you need to wait until tomorrow night. Can you do that?"

"Yes, I can do that."

"Tomorrow night your kidnappers will take you to exchange you for a large amount of money. Your father will be there." I started to explain about the impending event.

"My father? You aren't funnin' me are you, Mister Driscoll?"

"No, I am very serious. I can't tell you how, but I

know some of the things that will happen tomorrow night. Since I know these things, I have to work out a plan to save you that is foolproof. I know where they're going to take you and who is going to be there. I just have to think about what I want you to do tomorrow night."

"What you want me to do? Are you sure you aren't funnin' me, Mister Driscoll?"

He sounded a little confused.

I could chuckle at that now, and I did. It was great to be able to do so. To know at last why this eleven-year-old kid from 1931 consumed my life for days.

"I'm absolutely positive because what you do tomorrow night will save your life. Tonight and tomorrow, I want you to sleep whenever you can, eat whatever they give you, drink whatever they give you, and do whatever they tell you to do. Don't do anything to upset them. You need to be as strong as possible by tomorrow night. It won't be easy, but you will make it. Do you believe me?"

"I do, Mister Driscoll." Now he too sounded confident.

"Like I told you, I'm not exactly sure of the plan yet. Eddie and I will think about it tonight. After you and I have both had a good night's rest, call me in the morning, and I'll tell you our plan. Don't worry at all tonight. Just remember that tomorrow night you'll see your father again. Can you do that?"

"Yes, I can, Mister Driscoll."

"Okay, then the first chance you get tomorrow, you call me. Good night, Avery."

I lay back against the chair, breathing a huge sigh of relief.

"Sounded good, Ken," said Eddie. "Now what. Did you write anything down from what Avery had told you in your other conversations?"

I looked at him with my eyebrows raised. "Sure did. But Spree and Zachary took care of that."

"Oh, I'm so sorry!" pleaded Theresa.

"It's not your fault." I tried to console her. "I was stupid enough to leave the most important papers in my life lying around where anybody could get them. Who would think it would've been your kid and my dog? So don't blame yourself."

"Well, I should've noticed them on the desk and said something to you. It was stupid of me." Theresa tried to apologize further.

"No, no, really. It's okay."

"I sure hope you're right," Eddie said skeptically. "If that's the case, what is our next move?"

I went back to the desk in Zachary's room and returned with a legal pad and a pen. "I'm going to write down as many facts as I can remember about Avery that could lead to a clue in helping him escape."

I looked up at the ceiling, squinting my eyes in deep thought. "Help me out if you remember anything I might've told any of you."

Everyone started thinking. Beth volunteered what she remembered. "You said he liked baseball. St. Louis."

I wrote that down.

Theresa said, "He reads a lot."

"Yeah." I wrote that down.

"How about any of his relatives?" asked Eddie.

"Well, he had an Uncle Harold and Aunt Sophie. They had a kid name Gerald and a daughter named

251

Margaret. Let me write this down."

"Besides baseball, was there any other sport he said he was interested in?" asked Beth.

I squinted my eyes and screwed my mouth into a weird pucker, at the same time that I was looking at the ceiling. Suddenly, I leaped up from my seat, dropping the pen and pad onto the floor.

"Yes! Yes! He did something, and he did it well!"

"What is it?" they all asked at once.

"He could hold his breath underwater for long periods of time. In fact, he said he held the record at his boarding school."

Again, all at once, we all shouted, "Yes!" They knew what I was thinking.

Avery was an excellent swimmer, especially underwater. That would be the key to his escape.

Eddie began making the new plans. "Okay, we have to first figure out how to keep Avery from being shot in the head. His kidnapper will be gripping tightly on his arm so he can't escape. From past incidents, the guy knows Avery will try it if he gets a chance. However, this abductor will also be so involved in anticipating the exchange he might not be paying complete attention to Avery."

I added, "And we only have Avery to work with. We can't change the actions of the police, nor Avery's father, just Avery, and what effect his actions will consequently have on the others, including the kidnappers. So what do we tell him to do?"

No one spoke for a few seconds.

"Fight dirty." Eddie had the answer.

"Yeah!" I said. "Fight dirty. That's it! The kidnapper will be so absorbed with the activity around him and with holding the gun to Avery's head that he won't be expecting any aggressive action from Avery. He'll expect him to squirm and wiggle to try to get away, but he won't expect him to grab him by the balls. Ha! That's it! Avery will do just as you did when those guys were chasing you at that warehouse. He'll grab the guy's balls with his free hand and bite as hard as he can on the arm holding onto him."

"Then he can jump in the water and swim like hell away from the area," Theresa added excitedly.

"Maybe he can find some plant growth in the lake and hide behind it until the scene calms down." Beth offered her suggestion too.

"I think we've got our plan. Let's just hope and pray that Avery can carry it out, that he's as strong a swimmer as he says he is despite his weakened state," said Eddie, a bit worried.

"I think he can do it. He has to," I said, knowing that Avery would do everything in his power to succeed.

"Oh, my God!" Theresa suddenly jumped up. "I forgot about Zachary." She ran toward the back door. We had been so engrossed in solving Avery's dilemma that we had completely forgotten Zachary was outside for several hours. Theresa bolted through the door to the outside patio. I turned the outside light on before following her. Snuggled next to each other on the chaise lounge was Zachary, still in his bathing suit, and Spree, both sound asleep. Robby and Matt had apparently gone home.

"Maybe we should all get some sleep," said Eddie. "Tomorrow will be a very trying day for all of us."

Theresa gathered Zachary from the chaise lounge. I

tapped Spree on her head. "Come on, girl. In the house."

We retired to our respective bedrooms, although it was several hours before my sweetheart and her guy were able to sleep.

Chapter Ten

Saturday, July 4, 1998

I woke to the sound of the telephone. I wished that Avery had waited until I was more coherent before calling.

"Hello, Avery," I mumbled as plainly as I could.

"Is this Ken Driscoll?"

It wasn't Avery.

"Yes it is. Who is this?"

"This is Amelia Morgan at the Serendipity Oaks Nursing Home. I'm sorry to bother you this morning, but Eubbey Litomen didn't sleep all night. He's been asking to speak to you. He's so agitated, yet he acts different from his normal behavior. I know this is a holiday, but do you think you could come over to talk to him this morning?"

I was wide-awake now. "He's been asking to talk to me?"

"Yes, since about an hour after you left yesterday. I thought it was another of his spells, but as I mentioned, he's acting strangely. He definitely wants to talk to you. I know it's an imposition, but you had mentioned you were trying to get some important information from him. I thought perhaps you would come back to try to quiet him down."

"Sure. I'll be glad to come. How about ten o'clock?

Is that too soon?"

"No, that will be fine. Thank you, Mister Driscoll. Again, I'm so sorry to impose on you like this. He has no one else, you know."

"Who was that?" Beth asked sleepily as I was climbing out of bed to get ready.

"That's the lady from Eubbey Litomen's nursing home. She says he's been asking to talk to me. I'm going over to see what he wants."

"Umm." Beth lay back down and was back to sleep in seconds.

I showered and went into the kitchen for coffee, debating whether to awaken Eddie to go with me. It wasn't necessary, for he was already in the kitchen drinking his coffee and eating toast.

"Where's my doggie?" Zachary came into the kitchen followed by Theresa.

"She's outside taking a shi...err going potty," I answered him.

"After I go potty, can I go outside too, Mommy?"

"You have to eat some breakfast first," said Theresa.

"Okay. I'll have some waffles," he said while on the way to the bathroom.

"Humph! Where does he get that from?" Theresa said indignantly.

"Hey! Not from me," Eddie said defensively. "I fix my own breakfast. You know that."

"I know. I'm teasing. I'm glad he wants to eat something. Anybody else want any waffles?"

"No thanks, I got to go," I told her as I was gulping down my coffee.

"Was that Avery on the phone earlier?" Eddie

motioned for me to refill his coffee.

"No. It was Amelia Morgan from the nursing home."

"What the hell did she want?" Eddie was as surprised as I was at the call.

"It's very strange. She says Litomen didn't sleep last night and has been asking to talk to me."

"What for?"

"I don't know. She said he wasn't acting himself, not that he was going crazy, just different. I told her I'd be there at ten. Care to tag along?"

"I wouldn't miss it. Only thing, what if Avery calls while we're gone?"

"Damn!" How could I have forgotten Avery was going to call? "But this could be very important. It may even change what we want to tell Avery. I think we have to go."

"You're right. Especially if the guy *asked* to talk to you. Something must be on his mind. Let me shower while you have your coffee." He took off for the bathroom.

We were out the door in twenty minutes. I had left word with Theresa that if Avery called to tell him we'd be back shortly. Something very important had come up having to do with his escape plan, and he was to keep calling until we got back.

****

When we entered the nursing home, Ms. Morgan greeted us. "I told Mister Litomen you were coming. He's anxious to see you."

We went down the long hallway to Litomen's room. As we entered, his face brightened up. "Uhh. The two sonny boys. Where you been? Want to talk to you."

257

"We're here now, Mister Litomen? What did you want to tell us?" I asked.

I could tell it was hard for him to form the words he wanted to say. I didn't know if the Alzheimer's or the nature of the topic he wanted to discuss were causing his issue.

He looked down at the floor and said very softly, almost inaudibly, "Avery Archer."

So he *was* going to talk about Avery. That's what had been eating at him all night.

"What about Avery, Mister Litomen?" I asked.

"Didn't have to die. Could of saved him."

"How could you have saved him? He wasn't in the farmhouse when you went to it. He was already dead." My confusion was returning.

"No. Not what I mean."

"What did you mean, then?" Eddie asked.

He looked up at the two of us. "Long story. Don't know if craziness will keep away long enough."

So he knew he had Alzheimer disease. Maybe he didn't know the name of it, but he knew he had bouts of strange, erratic behavior.

"Avery was good kid. Had spunk. Not sissy like most rich brats. Didn't deserve to die. Told them to let him go. But me? Just a kid, too. Nobody listened to me."

"Who did you tell? What are you talking about?" I asked, very confused.

"Lemme finish. Not much time."

He started to hyperventilate. His eyes darted back and forth, but he brought himself under control. He took long, deep breaths, closing his eyes while doing so and holding tightly to the arms of the chair.

He continued with his eyes closed. "Jack Lasery and Mike DeJulio. In the farmhouse. Real bad guys. Me? Too young to mess with them. Not a crooked cop. Only one time. Had to do it. Be killed. Captain Whiting. Crooked. Real bad too. Planned it all. For Gov'ner Windy Appleton. Humph! Win with Windy, he said. Samuel Archer's friend. Humph! Some friend! Wanted to ruin him. Wanted to run him out of Florida. Too much power. Ole Gov wanted power. Couldn't have it with Archer around. Archer knew too much. Would never have won the state. Wanted money. Archer's money. Archer's power. Me? Caught in the middle. Overheard Captain and Gov while takin' a crap. Humph! While takin' a crap! Can you beat it? Never would of thought takin' a crap could get you in trouble."

He stopped for a while and opened his eyes, looking straight ahead. I didn't want to say anything to cause him to revert to his past behavior. Eddie and I both continued to look at Litomen and wait.

He started again. Amazingly, this time he was no longer talking in phrases, but was making perfect sense.

"Gov'ner Windy Appleton wasn't gov'ner in 1931, but he wanted to be in 1932. He knewed Sam and Esther Archer real well. They ran in the same social circles. They both owned lotsa orange groves and had lotsa money. At least everybody thought Ole Windy had lotsa money. But he wasn't runnin' his orange groves too well, and he was losin' money left and right. He owed money to lotsa debtors. So he figgered his good ole friend, Sam Archer, could spare some of his money and thought up the idea of the kidnappin'. With the money, he could bail out his orange groves and put

259

money into his campaign.

"Now Sam Archer knewed the Gov was no good. Sam was a smart man. He knowed Appleton's election would bring disaster to the state, but I doubt if he ever dreamed that the Gov was capable of kidnappin' and killin' his only son.

"But Appleton was desperate. He got his crooked friend, Captain Whiting, my great boss, to help him out. Captain Whiting, you see, figgered he'd stay captain long as Appleton was in office, and Appleton promised him some of the money. The captain planned the whole thing, got Lasery and DeJulio, two gangsters from Tampa, and had them do the actual kidnappin'. Don't knowed if they planned on killin' the boy, but that's how it worked out. But they had the one hundred G's. Hell! They could of asked for five hundred G's or even a million, and Archer would of paid them just to get his kid back. I knowed they were fools, as young as I was. One hundred G's meant nothin' to Archer.

"I was in the crapper one day, mindin' my own business, doin' my daily duty, when I heerd these two voices come in the door. They was kind of whisperin', but I could still heerd them. The whisperin' made me want to listen even more. I reckonized the one voice as Captain Whiting's. I wasn't sure of the other. Then I heerd him keep a clearin' his throat. Only person I knowed to do that was the Gov. I had to guard him lotsa times when he comed to Orlando. And they was plannin' the whole thing. I heerd it all. I would of been okay 'cept I had to fart. Can you believe it? I had to fart. I tried to hold it in, but it just slipped out, loud and smelly. Course, then Captain Whiting and the Gov knowed they wasn't alone. They came over to my stall.

The captain ripped the door open. Strong man. Just ripped it off the hinges. Scared me, it did. When he saw me, sittin' on the crapper with my pants down, he says, 'Get up, boy. Pull up your breeches.' Good thing I had just shit, or I would of shit my pants. 'You heerd nuttin, didn't you?' I said, 'Yes, Sir, I heerd nuttin.' The captain then said, 'You're dead meat if y'all tell anythin' you didn't heerd in that there crapper. Do I make myself clear?' I said 'Yes, sir.' And I hightailed it outta there, still bucklin' my breeches."

He stopped for a few seconds, but we knew he wasn't finished. That was probably the most he had talked in years.

"But that wasn't the end of it. They made me help them. A couple of times I had to go out to the farmhouse when Lasery and DeJulio had to go meet the captain. I didn't go in the kid's room, but I heerd him cryin' in there. Sometimes he pretended somebody was on the teleephone, and he'd talk to them. Sure sounded like he was really talkin' to somebody. When Lasery and DeJulio came back I told them about it, dumb fool that I am. They just laugh and say the kid was nuts.

"After the kidnappin', after the shootin', I had to go to the farmhouse and make sure nothin' incriminatin' was left behind. I had to see the filth that they made that poor boy live in. I saw where he tried to escape. I saw the chains that had shackled him to the bed. Never forget it. Never. Even a dog shouldn't live in those conditions. I was so ashamed for so many years, but I was young. What could I do?

"Archer and his missus left the country for a while after the kid's death. Sam Archer came back a few months later and sold his orchards, lock, stock and barrel. Then he just up and disappeared. Don't know where he went.

"Appleton was elected gov'nor in '32, but he had a heart attack and died after two months. Serves the son of a bitch right. He got his dues. As for Captain Whiting, after Appleton's death there weren't no one supportin' him, so he weren't re-elected. We got a new captain. Damn straight man, too. Heerd tell Captain Whiting drank a lot and was sick for about eight years 'fore he died sometime in the 40s.

"Me? I didn't tell nobody about my part in the kidnappin'. I never got married, too afraid I might tell my wife somethin' I shouldn't. So ashamed. So ashamed that I put my own life afore a l'il kid. Me, an officer of the law. And for nuthin. Poor kid died 'cause of me."

He stopped. The tears gently flowed down his cheeks and absorbed into his large mustache. I went over to him and embraced him. "You did what you had to do to survive. Think of all the good you've done all those years that you were on the force. And those years you were in the army. You're a good man, Eubbey Litomen. And I thank you for telling me about Avery."

I wanted to say more. I wanted to tell him we were going to save Avery. He need not feel the guilt anymore. Maybe some other day. Not today.

Litomen didn't say anything else. He sat there, staring ahead, with the tears flowing down his cheeks, his mouth turned down in a sad frown. I patted his shoulder. "I'll be back." And I meant it.

On our way out, I thanked Ms. Morgan for calling me.

"Did you get the information you wanted?" she

asked.

I wasn't sure whether Litomen gave me the information I expected, but it was definitely information I wanted. It surely would influence our thinking when trying to figure out what Avery should do at Splash Lake. At least I knew why the kidnapping took place and what type of people with whom we were dealing.

In the car, Eddie and I discussed our new knowledge and tried to determine what bearing it had on Avery's situation.

"Eddie, this adds another wrinkle to Avery's escape. What will Avery do after the kidnappers leave the scene? He can't come out of the water while the police are still there. If Captain Whiting is the mastermind of the whole deal, the last thing Avery wants to do is to get into his hands."

"His dad will be there. He won't let anything happen to him," assured Eddie.

"Maybe. Maybe not. What if Avery comes out of the water near Whiting or one of his cronies, but his dad might be looking for him somewhere else along the lake? What's to stop Captain Whiting from killing Avery himself somehow? You know, Whiting would stand to lose big time if the kidnapping didn't go as planned."

"You're right. We have a problem. Also, if his dad was shot, someone might be either treating his wound or even taking him away in an ambulance."

We were silent for quite some time, both thinking of possible scenarios and solutions. It was so difficult to imagine all the possibilities, but it was of vital importance to Avery that we do so. We were dealing with his life.

As I was thinking, I remembered my walk with Spree several days earlier when she and I had ended up at Splash Lake. I remembered the lake had been large, but with very few houses along its shores. More importantly, I remembered the lake had been very near the Kouprianov mansion. Excitedly, I thought of the articles about Ivan Kouprianov in the *Orlando Sun*, mentioning that some member of the Kouprianov family was living in that house in 1931.

I glanced over at Eddie. "I think I've got the answer."

"What?" he said curiously.

"Did you notice that huge house across the lake from me?"

Skeptically, he looked at me and said, "Yeah, what of it?"

"That house was built back in 1890, so it existed in 1931. Also, back in 1931, I doubt if everybody had telephones, but the people in that house were very wealthy. I read some articles about them when I was looking up the stuff on Avery, and wealthy people would have a telephone. Sooo...what if we have him go to that house for help?"

"That's a possibility, but can we be sure they wouldn't call the police? They would've heard about the kidnapping. How could Avery convince them to get in touch with only his father and not the police? He'll come out of that water wet, dirty, and bedraggled. They won't just think he's some neighborhood kid out for an evening swim or stroll."

"You've got a point there, Eddie."

We were silent again, both of us trying to think. At

last, I said, "Wait a minute. In the articles I read, it said that Ivan Kouprianov had left for Russia to bring back some servants. Seems he only had Russian servants and would get new ones every year."

"Sooo?" questioned Eddie, anxious for me to make my point.

"The article also said Ivan's mother, the widow of the Russian guy that built the house, would be staying home that year with the servants."

"Okay. So what?" Eddie didn't catch the drift of my thinking yet.

"Well, it just so happens that according to the newspaper article, Ivan Kouprianov would be in Russia or at least on his way on July 4th of 1931. That would mean his Russian mother and their Russian servants would be home alone. Do you think these Russian-speaking people would follow the local newspaper daily? Seems to me that one of the reasons this Kouprianov dude would bring over Russian servants would be so his mother would be able to converse with them without much difficulty. I really doubt if she would be too fluent in English. After all, she came over as a married woman. And back in those days, did they have the opportunity like we do today to learn English so readily?"

"I think I get what you're driving at," said Eddie.

"So if a kid comes to the door of their house all wet and dirty, and he tells them that he had fallen in the lake, and would they please call his father, don't you think they would do just that? After all, they have no reason to call the police if they didn't know the story behind his being in the lake?"

Eddie added, "He could say he was out in his boat

and the boat capsized."

"That's good. That's good. It might take him a while to get them to understand him, but maybe they will know some English. Somehow he will be able to communicate with them to get in touch with his father."

We felt satisfied that we had at last solved the dilemma of the escape. I then drove as fast as possible. I was beginning to worry we may already have missed Avery's call.

As soon as we entered the house, I asked Theresa if Avery had called.

"Yes, he called about twenty minutes ago. Beth answered the phone."

"Damn!" I was frustrated. I had wanted to be back for the call.

"What did she say? Was he okay? Did she tell him I'd be right back?"

"Take it easy, Ken." Theresa tried to calm me down.

Beth had been outside with Zachary and Spree. She came into the living room just as Theresa was trying to quell my fears.

"It's okay, Ken," Beth said. "He'll call back. We had a nice chat. He's such a young gentleman. It was so weird for me, though. All the time I kept thinking, this isn't possible, him in 1931 and me here today. Now I know what you've been going through. I think he liked talking to me, though. We didn't discuss anything that would make him emotional. Mostly we talked about you and me."

"About us?" I asked, perplexed.

"Yes. He wanted to know about you. How old you are; what you did for a living; that kind of stuff. I guess you never told him much about yourself."

"Uhh…I guess not. I was too busy trying to find out about him." With a smile I said, "I told him about you, though, and how beautiful you are."

Her face turned pink as it always does when she blushes. "Shut up."

I changed the conversation back to Avery. "Did he say when he'd call back?"

"He said he'd keep trying until you returned. I told him you went somewhere that could be very important in helping him. Did you find out anything that'll help?"

I told Theresa and Beth what Litomen had told us and how we had to be sure to keep the police out of our plan. I was telling them our strategy when the telephone rang.

"Avery? Is that you?" I asked excitedly.

"Yes, Mister Driscoll."

"You okay?"

"I had a good night's rest. I didn't wake up all night long."

He mumbled then, "Don't tell your girlfriend that I wet the bed. She'll think I'm a baby. I couldn't help it. They haven't come in my room at all since they chained me up." He started to sob again.

"It's okay. Those guys are just two big, stupid jerks."

He giggled and stopped crying. "Yeah, they're big bumpkins. That's what they are, right Mister Driscoll?"

"You're exactly right," I replied as I heard a smile in his voice.

I wanted to say that wetting the bed was not the worse thing that could happen, but I think he had already experienced those things.

"My dad would call them two buffoons. That's one of his favorite words. He called Buster Keaton one of the funniest buffoons he'd ever seen, but he said he was a good buffoon. He even said Winfield Appleton was a buffoon. I guess he's a funny man too. He told me that sometimes there are bad buffoons. These two big stupid jerks! I bet he'd call them bad buffoons."

I was glad he was able to see some levity in his situation. Sam Archer would've been very proud of his son.

"Avery, it's time to talk about tonight, to plan how you'll finally get free. Are you ready?"

"I'm ready."

"If you have any questions while I'm talking, break right in and ask. It's vitally important that you understand every detail. No matter how insignificant you think the question may seem, ask it anyhow. I want you to be sure of every move you have to make. Everything I tell you will be part of the big plan for your escape. Here is the plan. Sometime this evening those two men will take you to a large lake to trade you for your father's money. When you get out of the truck, they'll be holding on to you the whole time. Your father will be there with the money."

He quickly broke in. "My dad! Oh, goody, goody!"

"Avery, it'll look like your dad is by himself, but many policemen will be in the weeds nearby. You must not let on that you know the police are there. You must stay calm and focused while the bad guy holds you. He'll be gripping you very tightly, so just relax. Don't struggle. He'll take you to the edge of the lake near a large tree. Your father will be by the tree. Don't try to break loose yet. Let the buffoon hold your arm."

I hesitated before telling him about the gun. I had to phrase in it a manner that wouldn't alarm him.

"Here is probably the hardest part of all. The bad guy will have a gun pointed at your head, but if you do just as I say, he'll not be able to harm you. Are you okay so far?"

"I...I...guess so. But what if he shoots me?"

"Like I said, if you do exactly what I tell you, he won't get a chance to shoot you. No way would he even consider shooting you before he gets the money from your dad. And your dad will not give up the money until you are safe. Do you agree with me so far?"

"Yes," he mumbled, still skeptical.

"You'll be near the lake's edge. At this point, everything will be happening very quickly, but you must keep your wits about you. Before your dad exchanges the money, the bad guys will realize that police are in the weeds. I don't know if they see them or if they hear them, but they'll know they are there. They will panic and shoot at the police in the weeds. Here comes the tricky part. Remember the story Eddie told you about those guys trying to beat him up at that warehouse in Chicago?"

"Yes."

"Do you remember what Eddie did?"

"He said he bit one of them."

"That's right. He bit him as hard as he could. What else did he do?"

"He grabbed the other one's private parts."

"That's exactly what he did. That's exactly what you must do. You have to fight real dirty. The bad guy will have you by the arm but also holding a gun to your head. During all the commotion when they notice the police, they'll be so busy trying to figure out what the police are doing that they won't expect you to put up a fight. You have to sense when the bad guy who's holding you is getting nervous. You won't have much time to react, so you have to be very aware. His grip on you will feel more agitated. He may even be moving the gun slightly. This is when you must act. You have to surprise him so he can't react by shooting you. You quickly lower your head to the man's arm that is holding you, and you *bite* him as hard as you can. Biting him will catch him off guard, but remember he still has a gun. Now that you have lowered your head, you'll be briefly out of the gun's line of fire. Then quickly reach your free hand over his body. Grab his private parts and squeeze them as hard as you can. I know it sounds gross, but believe me, this will disable him. He'll definitely double over in pain. That's when you dive into the lake as quickly as possible. You'll hear shots very near you, but if you dive underwater immediately, they'll miss you completely.

"Do you have any questions so far?" I wanted to give him time to think about what I had told him.

"He's going to shoot at me?"

"Yes. I'm afraid he is, but as I told you, you're going to give yourself several seconds by disabling him with the biting and the squeezing of his balls. That's all you need, Avery, is a couple of seconds."

I knew he wasn't completely confident.

"With all the brave things you've done this past week, I know you can do it. Remember I told you that you were the bravest person I've ever known? I mean bravest person, not just kid. And I have no doubt at all that you'll be able to do this one last act of bravery before finally being with your mom and dad.

"I'll continue because there's more.

"After you jump in the water, dive underwater immediately. Even if the buffoon is shooting at you, the water will slow the force of the bullets. Now it's my turn to remember, and I remember you told me you were the best swimmer at your school. You were especially good at swimming underwater. Isn't that what you told me?"

"Yes, I did." He sounded a little surer of himself.

"You will get the chance to test those skills because you must swim away from those men as fast and as furiously as you can. Underwater. I want you to swim away from everybody. I want…"

"Wait!" he broke in. "What do you mean, everybody? What about my dad? Can't I swim to him?"

"Avery, in all the confusion, it won't be safe to go to your dad. The police and the bad guys will be firing their guns. I don't want you caught in the middle. You'll be with your dad. You'll just have to wait a little longer."

"Then where am I supposed to swim if I can't go to my dad?"

"Good question. The lake that you'll be in— somewhere on its shore is this great big house. Actually, you can see the same house across the lake from where you are now. You see the back of it, but the front of it faces the lake where they'll take you. I'm not sure exactly where it'll be, but you'll recognize it. You have to swim to that house without *anybody* seeing you, not the bad guys, not the police, not anybody. You'll be on your own. You must swim underwater as much as possible. Swim into the grass or weeds in the water to rest, but be sure no one sees you. Pay no attention to the confusion and the shooting. Just keep swimming toward that big house no matter what."

"Mister Driscoll, you said not to let the police find me either. Wouldn't I want them to find me so they could take me to my dad?"

"I've found out that some of those policemen are bad men, too. Since we aren't sure who the bad guys are, we have to stay away from all of them."

"But how am I going to get home?"

"You first swim to that house. That lake is big, but not impossible to swim. Besides, you can go into the weeds whenever you want to rest. It doesn't matter if it takes you a half-hour, an hour or more. You just have to get to the house. Once you get there, go directly to the front door. A servant will most likely answer the door. An elderly lady also lives there. Ask the servant if you could use their telephone to call your father. The servant and the woman of the house are Russian. They won't speak English very well, but you must make them understand you somehow. Tell the servant you were fishing, and your boat capsized. Tell him you want to call your dad to come after you. I know it's not right to lie, but in this case if you tell them the truth, they'll immediately contact the police. Since we don't know the good police from the bad, we don't want them called. Your dad will be so relieved to hear from you that he'll immediately pick you up."

"That'll take him a long time to drive. Do you think they will let me wait in the house until he gets there?"

"I can't be positive, but I would think so. Nobody would want to send a soaking wet kid out onto the streets that late at night. They'll probably give you a blanket or towel. Then all you have to do is wait for your dad. How does that sound?"

"Okay. I guess."

"What do you mean, you guess?"

"It's just that how come you know so much, but you won't be there to help me? Can't you be there maybe with a boat so I don't have to swim so far?"

Even as mature as Avery appeared, he was still just a kid. If adults like Eddie, Beth, Theresa, and me have such a difficult time with the concept, no way could an eleven-year-old comprehend his predicament. So I didn't really lie to him. I just held back some of the truth.

"Believe me, if I could be there, no one would keep me away. But it's just impossible."

"Is something wrong with your legs?" I guess he thought that was a good reason for not helping him at the lake.

"No, it's not my legs."

"Then what is it? Are you too busy?" His voice sounded disappointed.

"Oh, no! It's not that at all. Helping you has occupied all of my time and my mind these past few days. I would give anything in the world to be with you tonight, but I just can't."

"Are you in jail?" That surely would keep me away.

"Well I guess you could say I'm in a sort of jail because I definitely can't get to you. Someday you'll understand."

"You mean you won't even be at my house after my father takes me home?"

Maybe I should let him think I'd meet him at his house. By then, he'll be so happy to be home that it won't matter as much that I failed to show up.

"I'll try, Avery. I'll really try."

I wanted to be sure he understood everything. "Now, why don't we go over again the plan for tonight? Remember, you can't forget anything I have told you."

Avery repeated all the details of the plan perfectly. He would be extremely afraid, but I had confidence he could pull it off. He seemed convinced that he could do it.

I suspected this would probably be the last phone call I would receive from him. I had very mixed emotions. I wanted it to be all over, but I was so consumed in his quest for freedom that I knew there would be a void when I no longer heard from him. Whether good or bad, life would return to normal. I would just be another accountant juggling numbers for a living, going to work every day, fighting traffic and road rage, carrying on all the mundane tasks of life. But for Avery's sake, I was very happy it would be over. At that moment, I knew I had to say good-bye to Avery for the last time. I didn't want to lose this link, but I had no choice.

"Well, Avery, I guess this is it. You know what you have to do. It has been the greatest pleasure in my life to have known you."

Avery interrupted, "But, Mister Driscoll, I'm going to see you at my house."

"Of course you are. I just meant we probably won't be having these long conversations anymore. You'll finally be able to get back to your normal life again with your family."

274

"I feel like you are part of my family. I couldn't get through this if it wasn't for you. You are the best friend I've ever had."

That kid was something else. I probably will cherish those words more than any other words. Even Beth's "I love you" or "I do." Of course, I'll never tell her that. Avery and I had developed a unique relationship over the past few days. We were confidants; we were schemers; and we were partners. We laughed and cried together. As Avery said, we became best friends. He, an eleven-year-old, a fine young gentleman, and me, a twenty-seven-year-old, who had been so absorbed in his own life that there was no room for anybody else. Avery showed me how to care. He showed me that no matter how insurmountable an obstacle might seem, I could always get through it.

I gained my composure, my eyes tearing. "Avery, you're my best friend too. And I'm so very proud to be your friend."

"Thank you, Mister Driscoll, for everything. Please come to my house tonight. My father and mother will be very anxious to meet you."

"I will try my best. Thanks again for being such a great friend. See you tonight. Good-bye."

I felt empty. I had come to look forward to talking to him regardless of the stress and turmoil. I also felt extreme disappointment. After countless hours working for his freedom, after numerous dead ends, I didn't know whether I'd ever learn of the success or failure of our plan.

After I hung up, no one said a word. I sat on the couch, putting my arm around Beth. Eddie also put his arm around Theresa. Beth and Theresa were both softly crying. We probably would've stayed like that for the rest of the day except Zachary came bursting in from the backyard.

"Mommy, Mommy, can Matt and Robby come to our picnic? Please. Please."

Theresa turned to Zachary. "What? Oh, I don't know, Zachary. They're probably going to do something with their own families."

"No. They said their dads have to work at Dizzey World today. Can we go to Dizzey World, too, Mom?"

"Wait a minute. Wait a minute. One thing at a time." Theresa tried to calm Zachary at the same time she was trying to shift from a very emotional state to the mother in charge personality.

"Let me talk to them." She went into the back yard.

Beth turned to me. "We should get ready for the picnic. Your friends will be here soon. It's almost twelve-thirty."

"Jeez! You're right. I completely forgot about it. We'd better get on the ball. Eddie? Do you want to help me with the grill? You're better at that than I am."

"Sure," answered Eddie. "I hope you got us some good steaks."

"Well, I got steaks. Whether they're good enough or not, we'll soon find out."

We went about the preparations for the picnic. None of us spoke any more about Avery, though he was in the back of my mind the entire time.

Eric and Melanie arrived about one-fifteen. I made all the introductions. Melanie joined the ladies in the kitchen preparing the food. The three of them seemed to hit it off well. As promised, Melanie had brought a huge tray of brownies. Beth's eyes lit up at the sight of them. I wondered to myself how many of them would be gone by the time the meat was cooked.

Eric joined Eddie and me outside at the grill. We participated in some small talk, though bouts of silence existed when my mind strayed back to Avery. When I was not in one of those bouts, I noticed Eddie, too, would at times be in deep thought.

Finally, Eric, realizing that we were not giving him much attention, confronted us. "Okay, Ken, what's going on? You're off in some cloud somewhere. You did invite us over for a party, am I right?"

He was right. We were supposed to be enjoying ourselves, not acting melancholy over something that we no longer had any control.

"You're right. I apologize. I've had something on my mind lately."

"I'd say that's putting it rather mildly," Eric said, reproachfully. "What's going on?

"It's about Avery."

"Shit! Not that again!" protested Eric.

"What do you know about Avery, Eric?" Eddie was unaware of how much information I had told Eric.

"I know Ken claims he's been talking to this dead kid, but I thought he finally realized some smart ass was playing some sick joke."

"It's not a joke. I talked to Avery too. So did Beth. As hard as it is to believe, it's for real." Eddie definitely could vouch for Avery's authenticity.

"You're all crazy." Eric seemed annoyed with us.

Eddie proceeded to fill Eric in on all the details, focusing on Avery and Eubbey Litomen. Eric listened attentively.

When Eddie had finished, Eric backed away from

us. His face showed his disbelief. "Come on! You guys are pulling my leg, aren't you?"

"It's all true. Why do you think I've been a basket case lately?" I tried to make him understand.

"You have been acting rather strange lately. I attributed it to having second thoughts about your wedding," Eric agreed.

"I'm actually looking forward to the wedding, especially after seeing Beth again. It's this Avery thing. And not knowing if he's going to live or die."

"You guys are serious, aren't you?" Eric shook his head back and forth.

"We sure as hell are, but I can see how somebody else would be very skeptical." exclaimed Eddie

"This is incredible! You guys are really pulling my leg, right?" Eric seemed unable to accept our explanations.

"I wish we were, but it's true. That's all." I gave up trying to convince him.

"That's all?" Just like at the luncheon with our co-workers, Eric didn't want to let it go.

"That's all," I said. Was Eric purposefully trying to badger me?

"No speculation?" he nagged.

"Nope." At this point, there was no use trying to convince him of anything.

"Well, what are you going to do now?" Eric asked in a mocking manner.

"What do you mean?" I think my frustration was getting the best of me.

"I mean, what happens now? Will the newspaper articles just magically change to say you saved this kid's life? How about people's memories? Like my mother, for instance. She told me about it years ago. Will she just conveniently forget it?"

"How the hell do I know?" I was getting very irritated. "First of all, I don't know and I may never know if his life will be saved. Second, I have no idea what'll happen to the newspapers or to people's memories. Hell, I never in my wildest dreams thought anything like this could happen. So no way can I predict anything. It's all so crazy."

"You're right about that," Eric agreed. "So do you plan to find out what happened to him?"

Everything was starting to take its toll on my nerves, and I reacted to Eric's questioning unfairly. I was annoyed with myself for not knowing the answers.

"How the hell am I ever going to find out what happened to him? Give me a clue!" I raised my voice as I spoke.

Eddie tried to calm me down. "Take it easy, Ken. He's just trying to get some answers, just like the rest of us. Don't bite his head off."

Eddie was right. I had no business taking my frustration, my weariness, out on Eric.

"I'm sorry, Eric. It's just that things have been overwhelming lately. I know it's not your fault. Sorry."

"Hey, man, we all have our days. You've just had a few of them lately."

I thought it would be wise to explain to Eric my feeling about what might happen to Avery. I owed him that after the way I snapped at him.

"Seriously, Eric, I want so much for Avery to be safe, but I probably will never know one way or another."

I again was getting very emotional. I put the fork

down I was using to turn the steaks and slowly walked toward the lake. I felt like my mind was going to explode. I had to get hold of myself. I walked to the weeping willow tree and sat against its wide trunk, looking across at the Kouprianov house, which also reminded me of my last conversation with Avery.

Apparently, Theresa had allowed Zachary to play with Robby, Matt, and Spree, for I saw them in the completely renovated gazebo, running back and forth on the dock. I hadn't even noticed Spree was gone. The four of them looked like they were having a great time. Did Avery get to have fun again? Was he ever able to play baseball again or go to the movies with his mother? Or maybe see that football game with his dad? I didn't know how I was going to cope with not knowing.

"Ken?"

I looked up at the call of my name to see Beth standing there. "Hey, guy, let's walk around the lake. I think I've devoured too much chocolate."

She grabbed my hand to help pull me up. Then we began walking, hand in hand.

"Do you want to talk about it?" Beth asked.

"No. I'm just so confused right now." I couldn't even put my feelings into words for Beth.

"Hey, let's walk over to that big house." She was looking at the Kouprianov house.

That somewhat got me out of my melancholy mood. "Uhh…that's not such a good idea."

"Why not?" I had never told her about my introduction to the police officer.

"It's a long story, but let's just say I mistakenly did that once and was warned not to do it again." I was a little embarrassed about the encounter and wanted to pick a better time to explain.

"Uhh…okay Was this something you conveniently neglected to tell me about?"

I really hadn't planned to keep it a secret. "I guess so. It wasn't intentional. I'll explain it to you someday."

We slowly strolled along the water, not speaking anymore, but still holding hands. Every so often, she would give my hand a gentle squeeze. We stopped briefly at the dock of the Kouprianov house while Beth told Zachary, Robby, and Matt that we would be eating soon. We followed behind them as they meandered back to my house.

Melanie and Theresa were taking the food out to the screened porch when we got back. When we entered the house, Theresa said, "Sure, Beth, you eat all the brownies, then walk out, leaving us to do all the work. What did you do? Go down to the lake and barf them all up?"

"Did you barf in the lake, Aunt Beth?" asked Zachary.

"Oh, gross," Robby and Matt exclaimed simultaneously.

Defensively, I said, "No, no. She didn't barf. She's a girl who handles her chocolate well."

We were now ready for an afternoon of fun and camaraderie. I tried my best to keep my mind off Avery. We ate our delicious steaks. At least I had bought decent cuts of meat (pure luck) even if I didn't help much with the grilling. The ladies had worked wonders with the side dishes. A few brownies were even left over. Actually, that was before the boys got to them. Of course, they had to fight with Beth for the last one.

The females cleaned up after the meal while we superior males sat on the porch drinking beer, talking about the Bulls, the Magic, the Predators, and various other important sports topics. The boys and Spree played some kind of game using sticks and cans. The women joined us after they had cleared the food away. They weren't happy with the sports topics. They changed the conversation to such educational topics as Ally McBeal's love life next season on her television series. The day was very enjoyable, and with the help of these good friends and family, I was able to put Avery out of my mind—temporarily.

About five o'clock, Robby asked, "Would y'all like to play baseball?"

We adults looked at each other. I thought to myself, "Is this kid nuts?"

Then Eddie said, "Sure, kid."

Eddie probably hadn't played baseball since high school. How he expected to play now was anybody's guess.

"Let's go, everybody," Eddie said as he followed Robby out the door. Foolishly, we followed him too.

Robby led us to a large, vacant lot cleared of debris and plant growth. Apparently, kids used it often for a baseball field. A few boys were playing catch and having batting practice when we arrived. Eddie asked the boys, "You guys want to play a game of softball with us?"

"All right!" someone responded.

We picked teams. Robby was captain of one team and Matt was captain of the other. Robby chose Eddie on his first pick. Matt chose Eric. Robby chose me on his second pick. Matt chose Jason, one of the kids already at the field. The women appeared impatient, waiting their selection. Next Robby chose Davey, another kid at the field. Then Matt chose Gavin, another of the kids; and Robby chose Kyle, the last of those kids.

Ah, ha! Now down to the women and children. If this were a Titanic situation, they would have been first, but alas, we are talking about a man's sport. It takes strength. It takes power. It takes guts. It takes having testicles to scratch while standing on base. Do women have these things? Maybe power. Sometimes guts. But strength? Testicles? I don't think so. Therefore, I can only assume that Matt next picked Zachary, a little boy, because he had the most important attribute to play the game. Need I say more?

They were down to the three women. As pretty and as sweet as Beth is, she has one major fault. She is probably one of the most uncoordinated, klutzy women on earth. Sure, she can run fast, but catching or batting a ball? She just doesn't have the "balls."

Then there was Theresa. Don't get me wrong. Theresa is okay, but I've never seen her do any type of physical activity other than playing with Zachary. She is also slightly overweight, which would also hinder her baseball aptitude.

Lastly, there was Melanie. I only knew what Eric had told me about her, and he had never mentioned anything about any sports prowess.

I told Robby to choose Beth. I didn't care if she could play ball or not. I always wanted to be on her team. Instead, Robby chose Theresa. I guess he thought if she was a little bigger than the other two women were, she might be tougher.

That left Beth and Melanie. I saw Eric whisper something in Matt's ear. Sure enough, Matt chose Melanie. Since Robby was first to select his team, he got the last player, Beth.

Matt's team, the Dashing Denizens, went to bat first. As our team, the Sunny Sluggers, were selecting our gloves, Eric said to me, "We're gonna beat your ass."

"Yeah, sure. You and who else?" I childishly replied.

"Well, Melanie, actually," he said.

"Melanie?" I raised my eyebrows. "Yeah, right."

"No, I'm serious. She almost made the women's Olympic Softball Team," he informed me.

"You're joking, of course," I skeptically said.

"No, I'm not." He smugly turned away and walked up to bat.

I thought nothing more of that exaggeration, and we proceeded to play the game. Robby was pitching for our team. Eric had two strikes and three fouls when Robby hit him with a wild pitch, so he walked to first base. Matt was up next. He hit the ball out to left field, my position. The sun was in my eyes, so I missed the ball. I picked it up and threw it to Eddie on first base, but Matt was safe on first, and Eric had made it to second.

Jason was up next. He hit a double out to left field. Because the sun was in my eyes again, I missed the catch. I picked up the ball and threw it to Beth at second base. By the time she picked it off the ground, Jason was safe on second, Eric had made it home, and Matt was on third base.

Gavin stepped up to bat next. He hit a grounder right to Robby, but Robby didn't get the ball over to Eddie on first base fast enough. Eddie then threw it into home too late, for Matt had slid into home plate before Kyle, the catcher, caught the ball. Jason had made it to third base and Gavin had made it to second.

Zachary was up next. He wasn't too bad for a little kid. He nailed the first pitch, but it went foul. The second pitch was a strike also. He hit the third pitch with a lot of power, but it went straight into Robby's hand. Robby threw it to Theresa, who was playing third base. She caught it and stopped Jason from progressing to home.

So Jason was still on third base and Gavin was on second base when Melanie stepped up to bat.

Teasingly, I yelled from left field, "Easy out. Easy out."

Melanie looked in my direction as if she wanted to kill me. Then she loosened and tightened her grip on the bat several times and wiggled her tiny butt while she was getting ready to bat.

Big deal. So what if she looks like she knows what she's doing. She is only maybe five feet two or three. She can't weigh more than one hundred ten. What could she do?

Robby threw the ball. Strike one. She sure swung that bat fast. Oh well, maybe she was a better than average girl player. Robby threw the next ball. I couldn't believe my eyes. Melanie hit that ball so hard that it landed probably twenty-five yards behind me in the thick growth of weeds. I just stood there, amazed.

Eddie yelled, "Get the ball, Ken. Wake up out there."

I got the ball and threw it to Robby. With such amazing speed, Melanie had already made it safe at home plate preceded by Jason and Gavin.

The rest of the first half of the first inning was uneventful. Eric got to first base, but both Matt and Jason struck out.

They had six runs and three outs. It was our turn up to bat.

It was a disaster. Robby made it to first base. Eddie made it to first base, putting Robby on second. I struck out. Davey fouled out, and Kyle hit a fly ball out to right field, where Melanie caught the ball.

Actually, the entire game was a disaster. They slaughtered us. The boys on our team were irritated that Eddie and I couldn't play as well as Eric and Melanie. The final score was a whopping twenty-five to three. Even Zachary got a run, which was one more than both Eddie and I got.

It was going on eight o'clock when the game of shame was over. The kids who had joined us for the game walked off, arguing with one another. Dejected, the remainder of our team walked back to the house. Those on Matt's team kept throwing their victory in our faces all the way home.

"Uncle Ken," Zachary said when we got back on the porch. "The losers should treat the winners to ice cream."

"That's a great idea," volunteered Melanie. "We deserve it."

Everyone piled in my Hyundai and Eric's Explorer, and we went to the local Tastee Cone. The cones were very refreshing and just what we needed to celebrate our victory or mourn our defeat.

We returned to my house about nine o'clock. We adults were tired and flopped on the living room furniture. Matt and Robby went home. Theresa gave Zachary a bath and put an exhausted, little kid to bed. In the living room, I turned on the television. I was flipping channels when I came to a local news station. The pretty, blonde anchorwoman was talking about a local kidnapping.

Damn! I had pushed Avery to the back of my mind until that damn female reminded me. Now all my anxieties were returning with the same intensity as previously. It was a different type of kidnapping on the television, a divorced father taking his daughter from her daycare. However, it still made the tension return.

Beth reached over and quickly took the remote from my hands. She switched the station to a rerun of *Early Edition*, but by then it was too late. My mind was already back to my concerns for Avery. I even felt guilty about having enjoyed myself all day. Everybody seemed to notice the drastic change in my disposition.

Theresa tried to console me. "I think we should talk about it, Ken."

"What's there to talk about?" I responded, rather curtly. Then I realized I shouldn't be taking my emotional state out on the others.

"I'm sorry, Theresa. I didn't mean to be rude, but if it's all the same to you, I'd really rather not talk about it."

"I know you think you don't want to discuss it, but it would probably be the best thing for you," she reminded me.

"That's a bunch of hogwash. Do you know some of those therapy groups often make their members more

287

depressed? Can you imagine if you were raped and every time in one of those sessions on rape therapy, you had to relive your rape as well as the rapes of every other participant? How would that make you get over your problems? How would that make you accept it any better? Seems to me it would just be a constant reminder of the traumatic experience, which I'm sure you would want to forget."

"You have a point there," she agreed. "But there has to be something that'll shake you out of it. There is absolutely nothing you can do about anything now."

"It's just going to take him some time. Our being here has helped him tremendously. He was able to put it to the back of his mind during all the activities today. That's at least something," explained Beth.

"You will have constant reminders, like you had just now with the news, but eventually, it won't hurt so much. I'm not saying you'll forget. You'll never forget. Nor will any of us. I'm not saying it's going to be easy or quick either, but time eases a lot of pain. Remember when Grandpa died? We both thought we'd never get over it, but eventually, the hurt and anger subsided, and we had the memories of him to help us through that time. It's like that with Avery. You'll remember all the conversations you had with him and what a good kid he was." Eddie tried his attempt to bring me out of my melancholy.

"I suppose you're right. I'm just sorry I had to spoil your visit. You came expecting to have fun and enjoy the weather. Then I subjected you to my problem." I felt guilty for depriving them of what their vacation should've been.

"Hey, little brother, what are big brothers for?"

interjected Eddie. "We knew before we came that you were dealing with some issues. We probably wouldn't be here had Beth not told us you were so wrapped up with this thing. We thought we might be able to help you out."

"You helped me not only with your conversations with Avery, but also just being my support. I couldn't have handled these last few days without you."

"Wait a minute," Eric cut in. He had been watching television while we were boring him with our sentimental gibbering. "Isn't this the show where the guy gets the newspaper the day before it actually comes out in print?"

"I've never seen it before," said Melanie.

"It's about this guy, Gary, who gets a newspaper every morning delivered by an orange cat, and the newspaper is always tomorrow's news." Theresa had seen the series before.

"That's weird. So what does he do about this newspaper?" Melanie seemed curious.

Theresa explained the storyline to us. "He tries to change the events before they happen. For instance, if he knows there's going to be an accident at a certain time and a certain place, he'll go there and do something to prevent it from happening."

I was unfamiliar with the show, but Theresa's description caught my attention. I began watching it intensely. The premise was unique, and I wanted to see how this Gary guy handled the problems invoked by the newspaper. The episode we were watching dealt with a kid in an abandoned building. According to the newspaper, workers found the boy dead after the building was demolished. Gary's task was to get the kid out of the building before its destruction. How ironic that Gary's situation was very similar to mine. Of course, Gary was able to save the kid just in time, and everybody lived happily ever after. That's television. Avery was reality. If I could call talking to somebody from sixty-seven years ago, a reality. I wish it could've been as easy as Gary made it seem.

The show demonstrated that this Gary was not able to take care of everything in the newspaper. He had to be selective, using his own discretion as to what situations he would pursue. In a way, his dilemma could've been a lot worse than mine was. Several events in the paper could have required attention at the same time. He had to decide which was the most important, which needed acted upon first, and which needed no pursuit at all.

After the episode ended, Eric and Melanie went home, saying they were looking forward to Beth's permanent residency in Florida. The others continued to watch television, half interested in the summer reruns, but dozing from the exertion and heat of the day. I could no longer concentrate on television. My thoughts inevitably turned to Avery. My utmost concern at that time of the night was that it was probably the very same time in 1931 that Avery was in the midst of the actions that would mean life or death to him. It was as if his attempt to escape was happening at that very moment, not sixty-seven years ago, but right now at this location, and I was powerless to help him or to change or stop the chain of events. As I sat gazing at the television but not seeing it, my mind formed scenes involving Avery and his kidnappers. I could see what they were doing to him. I could see the fear on his face, the terror in his mannerism.

Suddenly, I got to my feet. "I have to go to the lake. I have to be there for him. I know he won't see me, but I have to be there."

"Let me come with you," Beth said.

"I'm coming too," said Eddie.

"Oh…I have to stay here with Zachary," said Theresa, disappointedly. "You guys be careful."

"Be careful of what?" Eddie asked, confused as to what she meant.

"Oh, I don't know. Just be careful," Theresa answered as they rushed out the front door.

We got in the Hyundai. I didn't want to waste time walking. Something was telling me to get there as quickly as possible. I drove around to the front of the Kouprianov house, quickly parking the car at the walkway leading to Splash Lake. Beth and Eddie followed me as I swiftly jogged down to the lake.

The night had turned misty and foggy, and the lake was deserted. An eerie calm surrounding us. I felt compelled to walk around the lake. Eddie and Beth followed without speaking. The only sounds were our footsteps in the brush beneath our feet.

After about fifteen minutes, we suddenly came upon a clearing. Near the edge of the lake straight ahead was a huge oak tree with its massive trunk almost as thick as a grain silo. Its limbs stretched about thirty or forty feet on each side of the trunk, extending over the lake. I knew that this was the spot.

"This is it," I said not necessarily talking to Beth or Eddie, but more to myself aloud.

We had reached the location where Avery was at that very moment sixty-seven years ago in his attempt to escape. I ran to the edge of the lake. I closed my eyes and could actually see the exchange occurring at that moment. I sensed the tension. I sensed the police hidden in the brush all around. I looked in the direction where they hid and saw shadows. I sensed Avery's father and the turmoil he experienced, knowing that one false move would mean the death of his son. And I sensed Avery standing in the exact spot where I was standing.

How or why, I don't know, but with my own body, I did exactly as I had told Avery to do. I jerked my head down and bit an imaginary arm that had been holding my left arm. I actually felt the piercing of my teeth on the flesh and tasted the salty blood in my mouth. Then with my right hand, I lunged and grabbed the imaginary genitals of my captor, squeezing as hard as I could, drawing blood from my own palm. Then I jumped into the lake, losing one of my shoes in the process. Somewhere in my distant mind, I could hear Beth scream and Eddie yell out my name, but the layers and layers of fog in the atmosphere shrouded all sounds from my ears.

I swam as fast as I could, first underwater, and then when I needed to come up for air, I swam on the top of the water. I kept swimming for what seemed like an eternity, yet my body and my energy remained strong. Only when I knew I had reached the shoreline in front of the Kouprianov house, did I stop. Only then, did I come out of the water. I walked up the walkway leading to the street, breathing heavily. Still in a trance, I walked across the street and up the cobblestone walk toward the Kouprianov house. I mounted the steps of the front porch and knocked on the front door with the ornate brass knocker. The house was still empty, but somewhere in my subconscious mind, I expected the Russian servant of sixty-seven years ago to come to the door. I kept knocking repeatedly, not realizing the passage of time.

Suddenly, Beth and Eddie were beside me. They each gently grabbed my shoulders. "Let's go home, Ken," Beth said. "Come on. Let's go home."

I stopped knocking but could not let go of the brass knocker. Finally, Eddie pried my fingers loose. He turned me around, and the two of them led me down the stairs to my car. They put me in the back seat. Beth sat beside me, clutching my wet body. Eddie found the keys in the ignition and drove us home.

As we entered the house, Theresa immediately came to the door. "What happened? Ken, you're all wet; you look awful. You ripped your shirt. Where's your shoe? Oh my God!"

Eddie turned to Theresa. "Shh. It's okay. He just had a little swim. We'll explain later. We've got to get him to bed."

Beth was leading me to the shower. I was still in a daze, not really knowing if it were 1998 or 1931, not really knowing if I were Ken or Avery. I obeyed Beth's every command like a programmed robot. She stripped me naked and turned the cold water on full force.

Reality hit me, and I came back to the present. I let the cold water flow over my body while I stood there, shivering. The pounding of its force and the temperature of the water helped me gain my sense of reality. Finally, after a few minutes Beth turned the water to warm letting it seep into every pore of my body, then she turned it off.

"Okay, Ken. That's enough. Come on."

She led me out of the shower and draped a large towel around me. I sat on the bed, still somewhat confused and lost in time. Naked, I lay back on the bed and closed my eyes. In my mind, I had actually *been* Avery. I had escaped for him. I had swum to safety for him. I knew he could do it, for I had been Avery for that brief period. I fell asleep, satisfied that I physically helped Avery save his own life.

Chapter Eleven

Sunday, July 5, 1998

I awoke at eight the next morning. Somehow, I was lying in the correct position on the bed. Beth was asleep beside me. I sat upright on the edge of the bed. My mind was more at peace than it had ever been before. I no longer doubted whether Avery was able to pull off his escape. I knew he had. I had been there.

I put on a T-shirt, some underwear, and a pair of shorts and went into the kitchen. As usual, Eddie was at the table already drinking his coffee.

"You okay?" he asked.

"Yes I am," I said, satisfied.

"You scared us last night, you know."

"I'm sorry for that, but Eddie, I know Avery is okay now. It's weird. I don't know how to explain it, but for a brief time last night, I became Avery. I was in his body, doing the things he had to do. And I did them, just like I know Avery did them also."

"With all the other strange things that have happened these last few days, that isn't any stranger. Maybe you were Avery. Maybe not. I'm just glad your mind has finally accepted whatever has happened. You started to worry me."

"Hey, what are big brothers for? They're supposed to worry about little brothers." I patted him on the back.

"Yeah, you're right." He got off his chair to give me a big bear hug.

We were standing like that when Theresa and Zachary walked into the kitchen.

"Daddy? Uncle Ken? What are you doing?"

Eddie let loose of his bear hug. "Oh, one brother is telling another brother how much he loves him, son."

"That sure is funny." Zachary giggled as he went to find Spree.

Cautiously, Theresa had a questioning look on her face. "I guess everything is okay now?"

"Yes, sis, everything is fine. The world is a great place in which to live. I have the best brother and sister-in-law in the world. I have the best girl in the world."

"I'm sure glad to hear those happy phrases. By the way, you know our plane leaves at one this afternoon." Theresa reminded me.

I had completely forgotten that they were scheduled to fly back to Chicago that day. "Damn! I did forget. I mean I guess I just don't want you to leave. I'd better wake up Beth."

I needed time to say good-bye properly to Beth. I wouldn't see her again for a couple of months. That in itself was hard enough, but if I didn't spend some quality time with her before she left, I'd never forgive myself. After passing out last night, she probably called me all kinds of rotten names.

In the bedroom, I knelt beside her sleeping body. I softly kissed her forehead, her nose, her eyelids, and her lips. Believe me. You have to love somebody to kiss them on the lips after they've been asleep for eight hours. Her body started to stir. So did mine. I crawled back into bed with her to give her my final good-bye.

Afterwards, there was the hustle and bustle of packing. Zachary kept whining that he didn't want to go home. Why couldn't he live in Florida too? Why couldn't he take Spree back with him? Theresa was stressed out trying to gather up everybody's clothing, toiletries, etc.

"Eddie, I could use some help here, you know."

Eddie, who had been gazing out the back door, sprang into action. "Sure, what do you want me to do?"

"You can at least pack your own stuff," she ordered while picking up Zachary's toys.

"Sure, honey, sorry. I'll get right on it."

In the kitchen alone, sipping my coffee, I played back in my mind all the events since their arrival. What a hectic, yet fulfilling couple of days. And unforgettable for everyone. Even little Zachary.

Beth came into the kitchen looking radiant. Probably my good-byes helped that out. "I'm hungry. Is there any food left over from yesterday?"

"I know there are no brownies, sweetheart."

"Stop that! I didn't eat all of them. I had a little help, you know."

"I know. I know. I just like to tease you. You're so cute when you get angry."

She soberly turned to me. "I'm not angry. I don't think I'll ever get angry at you again."

I put my arms around her. "Sure you say that now, but wait until you have to put up with me every day of your life."

"I'm looking forward to a lifetime with you." She gently bit my ear.

"Okay, love birds, that's enough. We have a plane to catch." Eddie came back into the kitchen. "Is there any food left around here? You can't let your guests go away hungry. We won't come back again."

Beth searched the refrigerator for some food. Theresa and Zachary came to feast on the leftovers also.

By then it was nearly eleven o'clock. We wanted to leave for the airport about that time. The women started cleaning up the food. I was getting up to replenish my iced tea when I heard a knock at the door. It was Robby and Matt.

"Hey, guys, sorry, Zachary has to go home today. I have to take him to the airport now."

Robby kept looking at his shoes. I looked down at them too. They were somewhat worn, but I saw nothing else wrong with them.

"Uhh…We didn't come to play with Zachary. He already told us he had to go home today," Robby said.

"Spree can't come out until I get back, and I won't be home for several hours."

"We didn't come to play with Spree either," said Matt.

"Well, what's the situation here, guys?"

"We have something to tell you. Is it okay if we come in for a minute?" Robby asked as he furtively looked around in both directions.

"Like I say, we've got to get to the airport," I told them hurriedly and somewhat impatiently.

"We'll make it fast," said Matt.

They were beginning to intrigue me.

"Okay. Come on in." I closed the door behind them. "What is it?"

In a hushed tone, Robby began to explain. "We was over at that big house across the lake this morning, and this man kept walkin' up and down the street. He kept lookin' at us and lookin' at your house. Then we forgot about him and started playin' with our Frisbee. Then we were gonna come over to say good-bye to Zach. Well, when we came around to your house, this same man was standin' in front of your house, starin' at it, like somethin' was wrong. When he saw us, he walked away, but he kept lookin' back at your house."

I wondered who would be looking at my house on a Sunday morning. Beth, Theresa, and Eddie gathered in the living room while Robby was talking to me.

"What did the man look like?" I asked.

Still in a hushed voice, Matt described the man. "He was old like a grandpa, but he had nice clothes on. He didn't look like a homeless guy like the ones that ask for money."

"Who could it be?" asked Beth.

"I have no idea," I answered. "I'm going outside to have a quick look around."

In the front, I looked up and down the street but saw no one. I went around to the back of the house and still saw no one. I looked across the lake at the Kouprianov house and couldn't see anyone walking on that property either. I knew it was getting late, and I couldn't spend any more time searching. We had to go to the airport.

As I walked back around to the front of the house, an old man stood staring at my front door. As the boys said, he didn't look like a bum. His face was clean-shaven, and his full, white hair was trimmed short. He was dressed in a white, long sleeved shirt with a medium blue printed tie. His expensive looking, navy blue trousers were neatly pressed. The expression on his face looked bewildered and confused, but definitely not threatening. I startled him as I approached my front door.

"Can I help you, sir? You look like you could use some assistance. What address are you looking for?"

He didn't say anything at first. He just stared at me with his mouth slightly open and his jaw dropped.

I repeated, "Sir, can I help you?"

He said something then, but it was so soft that I couldn't hear him. He also had some type of accent. We were probably about five or six yards from each other.

"Sir? Sorry, I didn't hear you. What did you say?"

The man looked very muddled. He looked up and down the street. Then he spoke again. I had walked closer to him so I heard him this time.

"I said I'm looking for a house."

It was a British accent. No wonder I couldn't understand him. I never could understand the British English. "What's the address?"

"I…I…don't know." By then he was staring at me rather than looking around.

I was beginning to think this was another guy with Alzheimer's like Eubbey Litomen. "Can I help you in any way?" I was getting impatient. We had to leave for the airport.

"Uhh. There was a house…right here," he hesitated, looked directly at me and continued. "Your voice sounds so familiar, so familiar. The farmhouse was right here, across from that strange house on the other side of the lake. I remember."

I just about jumped out of my skin! He said farmhouse. My heart was racing a mile a minute. I walked up to him. I was standing just a few feet away. I could hardly talk. I knew my answer even before I asked. "Are...are...you Avery?"

In a daze, he said, "Yes...I am." *Hesitation.* "Are you... Is it possible?"

I literally could not speak. I finally gained my composure enough to say my name in a guttural voice. "Ken Driscoll."

His head jerked upright. His eyes opened wide. "Mister Driscoll?"

I cannot describe the emotions I felt at that moment. The world was at a standstill. This old man and I were the only ones on this earth. Nothing else was around us. Nothing else existed. Nothing else mattered. Only he and I. I looked at him. He looked at me. We knew. We had at last, after all these years, after all these days, come face to face with one another.

Epilogue

My family did not make their flight that afternoon. After the realization that Avery Archer was standing at my doorstep, all hell broke loose. Eddie had been looking out the living room window. When he saw Avery and me embracing, I think he also knew the identity of this stranger. He yelled to Beth and Theresa that Avery was in the front yard. They all came running out, tears streaming down their cheeks. It was an unbelievable sight. Five grown people sobbing and embracing while a little four-year-old and a big brown dog stared at them as if they were completely mad. Even lawnmower man next door, who had just finished mowing his lawn, stared at us in disbelief.

After the hugging, the crying, the kissing had subsided, we went in the house. Beth and Theresa got us lemonade, and we gathered in the living room to find out what had transpired in Avery's life these past sixty-seven years.

"I can't believe it. I can't believe it. 'Tis too good to be true. My Mister Driscoll at last." Avery was still choked up with emotion.

Eddie finally asked, "Avery what happened to you that night back in 1931?"

Avery stared ahead, visualizing the events that had taken place.

"You were correct about almost everything, Mister

Driscoll, you and Mister Eddie. After I had my last conversation with you, I was very despondent, but I knew you had faith in me. I had to make you worthy of that trust. I fell asleep shortly after we had ended our conversation. When I awakened, it was very dark and still, and I was frightened. Soon I heard the men returning to the house. Then I became more frightened, for it would soon be time to go. I sat on the bed, waiting. The more I waited the more frightened I became. Then my waiting was over. The short man came into the room. He unlocked the chains from my arm and leg. Then he dragged me from the bed. I went stumbling after him through the house and out the door to the truck. When we were in the truck, they put the stockings over their faces. I knew then we were about to meet my father. This was the night I had both anticipated and dreaded.

"We were only in the truck for a short time before we reached our destination. The short man dragged me out of the truck, holding my arm very tightly. I saw my father's automobile parked along the roadside. I was so elated, for I would at last see him. The large man pulled out a knife from his dirty overalls and slashed all the tires on my father's automobile. Then the short one pulled out his gun and dragged me down an embankment to an area near the lake. The large man had his gun scanning the weeds nearby. They looked around in all directions.

"Up ahead I saw a lantern glowing and the silhouette of a large tree. I saw a man standing near the tree, but we were too far away to know if it was my father. The large man went ahead of us, poking a stick into the weeds as he walked. We went toward the glow of the lantern. As we drew nearer, I recognized that the man standing near the tree was indeed my father. The large man pointed his gun directly ahead of us. With his right hand, the short man tightened his grip on my left arm. His left hand held the pistol to my temple. When we were several yards from my father, he called out to me, 'Avery? Son? Is that you? Are you all right?'

"I answered him, 'Yes, Father, I'm fine.' Of course, I wasn't fine, but I didn't want him to worry any more than he already had. Just as you said, the large tree was very near the lake, and the short man and I stood right next to the lake. Several times, I furtively glanced toward the water to determine the distance I would have to jump to get into it. I was afraid that perhaps the water was too shallow near the edge. I had many other fears, but I tried not to think about them."

"The large man called out to my father, 'Archer, throw the money bag out in front of you.' My father replied, 'Let my son go first.' This angered the large man. He said to my father, 'I'm calling the shots here, Archer.' My father eventually threw down the money bag. I could feel the tension in the man holding my arm. The pistol was shaking against my temple. I knew that I would have to act soon.

"Suddenly, the short man said, 'Jack, there's coppers all around us.' I saw my father lunge forward toward us. That's when I made my move. I quickly lowered my head and bit the arm of my captor as hard as I could. I tasted his salty blood in my mouth. Then I reached over and grabbed his privates, digging my nails as deep as I could into the soft flesh of his genitals. He let out a scream, his arm released me, and the pistol pointed toward the sky. With all my strength, I jumped the few steps to the lake and dove in the water, going underwater immediately. I swam and swam with all my might.

"Mister Driscoll, I had the strangest feeling that you were swimming with me. Not exactly beside me, but as if your strength was my strength, as if you were part of me. I actually heard you say to me in my head, 'You can do it, Avery. I know you can.'

"And I did do it. I heard gunshots behind me, but I kept on swimming. I knew I couldn't swim aimlessly, so I went behind some tall weeds to look around the lake for the mansion you had described. I noticed a few dim lights off in the distance. I knew that had to be my destination. I continued onward, constantly aware that you were helping me, that I was never alone.

"At last I made it to the shore before the mansion. I was very weak, but you helped me up the long path and the many stairs leading to the door. You raised my arm to lift the brass knocker, and I banged it up and down with all my strength.

"Soon a servant came to the door. He spoke to me in a strange language. I believe you had told me he was Russian. He gave me a rather odd look when he saw my wet clothing and the bruises and scratches on my body. I asked if I could use his telephone to call my father. He didn't understand me but invited me into the house, as disheveled as I was. He went away for a moment. When he returned, a very tall, old woman wearing many items of jewelry preceded him. She too spoke to me in Russian. I repeated my request to her to use her telephone. I made hand gestures as if I were dialing the telephone. She finally understood what I was saying and told her servant to show me to the telephone. He motioned for me to follow him. There before me was the telephone. I nearly knocked a lamp over trying to get to it. My hands were shaking uncontrollably, but I heard your voice tell me, 'It's almost over. Soon you'll be with your father.' I dialed my father's number, the same number I dialed to talk to you, Mister Driscoll, countless times before."

Avery stopped his narration and looked at me. I knew he was thinking of our many conversations just as I was also thinking of them. I knew also by the way he looked that somehow, someway he now realized he was held captive in 1931 in a farmhouse that occupied the very spot where I lived now.

"Isabel answered the call to my father's house. She screamed when I told her it was I. She must have dropped the telephone, for Homer, the butler, picked it up. He also did not believe that it was I, for he informed me I was dead, that I was shot in the head. I told him I was very much alive and wanted desperately to speak to my father. Father was not home, but Homer asked where I was so he could send Clayton, our chauffeur, to get me. I was very upset that I couldn't speak to my father, for I had been waiting so long to hear his voice and to see him once again. It took me quite some time to determine the address of the house from the tall, old woman, but I eventually was able to get her to understand me. I told Homer the address. He said he would immediately get in touch with my father, and Clayton would be there as soon as possible.

"The foreign woman gave me a large Turkish towel with which to dry my body. Then she had her servant get me a clean shirt and a pair of trousers into which I changed. She also had the servant give me a cup of cocoa to warm me while I sat in her study impatiently awaiting Clayton's arrival. I was so anxious to see my father and to finally meet you, for I was so sure that you would be at my house when I got there.

"When Clayton arrived, the servant immediately showed him into the study. I was so glad to see him that I nearly spilled what remained of the cocoa. I thanked the foreign lady and her servant for their gracious hospitality. I walked out of the house to a strange automobile in front of the mansion. I asked Clayton where Father was and why he was driving the strange automobile. Clayton said my father would explain as soon as he arrived.

"Apparently, upon hanging up from our conversation, Homer had somehow contacted my father. Father had arranged for Clayton to drive me to a secluded house of a dear friend of his on the coast. We drove some distance to the house. Isabel was there to greet me, but my father had not yet arrived. I was so bewildered. A strange automobile; a strange house; no father or mother; and you weren't there, Mister Driscoll. After days of trauma that I had endured, I was so distraught. Isabel tried to console me, but I would not listen.

"Finally, after several hours, my father arrived. When I saw him standing before me, I couldn't hold back the tears. I was so happy and so relieved to be in his arms at last. When we broke our embrace, I noticed my father had his left arm in a sling. He told me he was wounded, but it was not serious. Later, I learned of the forces behind my kidnapping, of which I know you are now aware. I also learned my father had to disguise himself when he came to meet me. He wanted no one to know I was still alive. That secret was the reason for the strange automobile Clayton had driven and the reason he did not drive me to my home.

"Father told me of the involvement of Captain Whiting and Governor Appleton in my abduction. He told me it was imperative everyone assumed I was shot to death. They were going to search for my body in the lake the next day. I would be staying at the private residence of his friend, where Isabel would be looking after me until he had arranged for my departure overseas. I regretted not being able to see my mother that evening, but it was for the best. I remained at this house for several days. Most of the time I slept. When I wasn't sleeping, I was eating. I believe I gained ten pounds in one week. My father came every night to see me. Thus, I didn't have much time to get lonely, for I was so busy recuperating from my ordeal. However, I thought about you often, Mister Driscoll, and I was so disappointed that you never came to see me."

"Then Isabel took me on a train ride to Miami, where we boarded a large ship bound for England. I didn't know until we left the harbor that my mother and father were also on board the ship. Even then, we met secretly at night. Father did not trust anyone. Finally, when we arrived in England and situated in our new home, we were once again a family. Father said he would have to return to America in a few weeks, but he would be back to stay after that.

"And that is where I spent most of my life. I married a lovely lady and raised a fine family, but I never forgot you, Mister Driscoll. I continually asked my father if he had heard from you. He would simply tell me he had not. I later learned he thought you were my imaginary friend who I had invented to cope with my traumatic circumstances. You see, he knew the telephone in the farmhouse was not connected, just as my abductors had known. Later in my life when I became aware of this, I had a very difficult time understanding what had happened back in the farmhouse. I knew with all my heart and mind I had not imagined our conversations. Yet I was unable to relate the reality of the disconnected telephone to the reality of my conversations with you. I was angry with you for not coming to me. Surely, if you were the friend that you said you were, you would not forget me. You had promised to be there for me. Over the years I finally realized that something unique had taken place in that farmhouse in 1931. I remembered the many excuses you gave me for not saving me yourself. I remembered you knew of events before they would actually happen. In time as my understanding of the world increased, so did my understanding of our relationship. Then one day during the war while I was lying on the hard, cold ground, like a light exploding in my head, I realized you never could physically save me. Nor could you have a boat for me on the lake so I wouldn't have to swim. You were unable to meet me at the house of my father's friend. You couldn't come to me because you just weren't around. I was very saddened by this recognition. I thought I might never see you, meet you face to face, to thank you for what you had done for me. However, I was also elated that you had not abandoned me. I knew then that you would have been there if you could."

There was not a dry eye in the house. I reached across the room and clutched Avery's hand. "You must now know the frustration I felt because I couldn't physically be there. I felt so inadequate, leaving a frightened boy alone to fend for himself against people much more powerful than we were."

"But I wasn't by myself, Mister Driscoll. You *were* with me. I cannot explain it, but you were with me when I bit my abductor on the arm. You were with me with every stroke of my arms in the water and with every step up that path to the mansion. I needed you, and you were there. I was not alone. Can you believe that?"

"Yes, Avery, I do."

I too was thinking of the events last night, how I was nearly out of my mind reenacting what I had wanted Avery to do. Perhaps it wasn't a reenactment at all. Perhaps it was real for both of us.

Eddie, who had been listening to us, asked Avery, "Why did you come here now? Why didn't you come ten years ago, or twenty years ago? How did you know to come now?"

Avery folded his hands. He looked up at the ceiling and closed his eyes. When he opened them, he looked directly at Eddie. "It took me a long time to figure out when Mister Driscoll would *be* here. I mean, here, in the place where I had been that terrible week. I tried to remember all the personal things he had told me about himself, anything that might give me some hint as to when he would be alive. I remembered talking to Beth."

Avery turned toward Beth, smiling affectionately. Then he looked at me. "And by the way, Mister Driscoll, she is as lovely as you always told me she was."

I looked over at Beth. She was blushing in that cute

little way of hers.

Avery looked back at Eddie and continued. "The one thing we both had in common was that we liked sports. I was a big baseball fan, and I remembered that Mister Driscoll was a big basketball fan. The Chicago Bulls, in fact. At the time, I knew little about basketball, but I remembered what he had told me about the team. He had said that they had won the championship six years out of eight, and that they had just beat the Utah Jazz two years in a row for the championship. In order to find out when this actually occurred, I had to become a Chicago Bulls fan. Thank you, Mister Driscoll. That became a joy to me. I kept watching them through the years."

"In the late fifties and early sixties, the Boston Celtics dominated the sport. I knew the time wasn't right yet. In the eighties, the Los Angeles Lakers were the dominant team, but I started hearing about this great player, Michael Jordan. That's when I really became an avid fan. Then in 1991 when the Bulls took the championship with Jordan at the helm, my hopes started to rise. I watched them each year after that. In 1997 when they beat the Utah Jazz, I was elated, for I knew 1998 was the year. I had also vaguely recalled that during one of our telephone conversations when Mister Driscoll had been angry with me and did not believe that I had truly been in danger, he had said something to the effect that my father hadn't lived in the house on Scruffsdale for over sixty years. Thus, remembering that remark and remembering his fondness for the Chicago Bulls, I had no doubt that 1998 was the exact year. I was so excited, but I didn't quite know what to do.

"My wife had passed away three years before, and my children were grown with families of their own, so there was nothing to keep me from coming to the United States. Money also was no obstacle. You knew how wealthy my father was. Even though he sold his orange groves in Florida, he invested his money wisely in England. Thus, being the only son, I inherited all that wealth.

"I knew I had to find you, for you would not know if I had survived or not. In fact, according to the media, I was dead. As you now know, my father wanted it that way. He wanted Captain Whiting and Winfield Appleton to think that too. He was afraid my life would constantly be in danger by them or someone else in the police force or Appleton's entourage. For that reason, we relocated to England.

"I scheduled a flight to Orlando a few days ago. My memory of places in the area is not too vivid. I knew I had been held in Nawinah, but I wasn't sure where. I went to the library to look up articles on my case. I learned from the librarian that someone else had also been interested in the case several days before. Naturally, I was elated. I knew I had the right year. I knew it had been you at the library trying to get any information you could to save me. From the articles, I was able to get details as far as locations were concerned. Then I rented a car and searched the area. When I saw the big mansion across the lake, I knew I had found the right place. I walked the neighborhood several times until I realized your house must be located on the very location as the farmhouse I had occupied. So here I am. Back in the same place after sixty-seven years. It has been a very long time for me. I wasn't sure whether my health would hold up over the years. I was so afraid I might die without thanking you for saving my life. As you know I am not a young boy of eleven anymore. But with God's grace, I was able to weather the many years since 1931 and be here today."

I could see the tears forming again in his eyes. He was not alone. We all had tears welling up.

Then Avery arose from his seat. "Would you mind if I look out the back window for a spell?"

"No. Not at all," I said while staring at him, still not being able to comprehend that Avery Archer was finally standing before me.

I led him into my bedroom. The others stayed seated while we were gone. Avery went over to the window. I opened the blind so he could see the yard and the lake.

"Amazing. After all these years, this scene is still so vivid in my mind. The mansion almost looks the same. It hasn't aged at all. Perhaps it has been painted a different color."

I interjected, "They're doing some major renovations on it these past few months."

"Ah, that explains it. It looks so like it did back in 1931. And that willow tree. It has truly grown."

He moved his head closer to the glass, craning his neck to look at the sides of the house. "Of course, there were no other houses around the farmhouse then."

He straightened up and turned away from the window. I had been standing behind him off to his left. He put his left hand on my right shoulder. "Mister Driscoll, how can I ever thank you? You gave me back my life."

"Your being here, knowing you escaped, is all the

313

thanks I will ever need."

We again embraced each other. I will never be able to describe the feeling of joy I felt.

When we returned to the living room, Eddie asked, "Avery, how long are you planning to stay around Orlando?"

"I really hadn't thought about it since I hadn't known what I would find once I got here."

Then Eddie turned to me. "What about Eubbey Litomen? Do you think we should take Avery over to see him?"

"Eddie, that's a brilliant idea! That may be just what Litomen needs."

Avery then asked, "Wasn't Eubbey Litomen one of the policemen on my case?"

We then told Avery about Litomen and his involvement in the kidnapping. We told him how guilt over not saving Avery when he had the chance consumed Litomen,

"Ahh. There is no need for a man to waste his life on a guilt he does not deserve. I would very much like to see Mister Litomen."

Beth and Theresa stayed behind. Since they had undoubtedly missed their flight, they were going to make different travel arrangements for the next day.

On the way to the nursing home, Avery told Eddie and me about his life in England. He had three children, seven grandchildren, and two great grandchildren. It was very strange listening to him say these things, for to me he was an eleven-year-old to whom I had just talked the day before. He was the scared kid. I was the father figure. Overnight the roles had been reversed. Yet every time he talked to me or about me, he referred to me as Mister Driscoll and I would call him Avery. So even though we were aware that he was now a seventy-eight-year-old man and I was twenty-seven, our minds could not forget the closeness, the dependence we had felt as the boy and the young man. We continued to think of each other in that manner regardless of the sixty-seven years Avery had experienced while I, in a sense, had only lived through a few days of my life.

We had not called the nursing home before we left the house. I was almost certain Ms. Morgan would permit us to see Litomen once she knew who our companion was.

This time a receptionist was at the front desk. I asked if we could see Litomen. I said it was very important. She called someone in the building. When she hung up she said, "An aide will be out to take you to Mister Litomen's room."

The aide was a Hispanic woman about forty-five years old. "Please follow me, *senors*." She led us to Litomen's room. "If you need someting, just ring the bell."

When we entered the room, Litomen was dozing in his chair with the back of his neck resting on the top of the chair, his face looking upward and his mouth wide open. Avery stayed behind Eddie and me.

"Mister Litomen? It's Ken and Eddie Driscoll." I called out, loud enough to awaken him without startling him too much.

Litomen closed his mouth and opened his eyes without bringing his head to an upright position. When he did bring it forward, his eyes darted from side to side. Soon he was calm and looked at Eddie and me, but said nothing.

"Remember what we talked about yesterday? Remember you told us about Avery Archer?" I asked.

His eyes started quivering and moving rapidly again. I thought it best to continue before he got too upset.

"We've brought someone with us who I think you would like to meet."

"Don't need no more company," he grumbled.

"I'm sure that you'll be very glad to meet this person."

He was trying to look around Eddie and me to see who was behind us. I moved aside; Eddie moved aside; and Avery stepped forward.

Avery spoke before I got a chance. "Mister Eubbey Litomen, my name is Avery Archer."

Litomen turned white as a ghost. I hadn't expected that. "No! No! You're dead! They shot you at Splash Lake. You're dead. You're a ghost. Go away!"

Avery broke in before Litomen could get more excited. "No, the shot missed me and was fired into the air. I jumped into the lake and swam away before they could fire any more shots at me."

With his eyes as big as walnuts and his mouth open wide, Litomen stared at Avery. "No. It can't be."

"But it is. I escaped and called my father who took me to England immediately. I know about Captain Whiting and Winfield Appleton. Father did not want them to know that I was alive."

"Then you didn't die? I'm not responsible for your death? You're here?" I could actually see the pain lifting away from Litomen face.

"Yes, I'm here. And I have had a very good life in England, so there is no need for you to feel guilt or remorse any longer."

With that revelation, Eubbey Litomen covered his face with his hands and sobbed so hard his shoulders began to shake. I started forward to put my hand on his shoulders, but Avery beat me to it. "'Tis quite all right, old man. 'Tis quite all right. Your burden has been lifted."

They stayed like that for several minutes, Avery patting his shoulder until the sobbing subsided. Litomen took his hands away from his face, looked up at Avery while covering Avery's hand with his own, and simply said, "Thank you."

Eddie and I also felt the heightened emotional level in the room. Eddie put his hand on my shoulder.

"I'm very tired, but I will be at peace for the first time in sixty-seven years. Please help me into my bed," Litomen asked as he looked toward the two *sonny boys*.

Eddie and I went forward and gently grabbed Litomen's arms as he arose from the chair. We assisted him into the bed. We could hear him say "thank you, thank you" repeatedly as he closed his eyes and fell asleep. The three of us quietly left the room.

On the ride home, I also thanked Avery for that gesture of kindness. I then asked what his plans were. He told us he had planned to stay only a few days in Orlando before going back to England for his grandson's wedding next weekend. He didn't want to miss the wedding, but he knew he had to be here on July 5, 1998. As long as he was alive, nothing would have stopped him.

At the mention of the word "wedding," I had a brilliant idea. We were driving on West Colonial, going toward Nawinah. I pulled into a small shopping strip. I stopped the car. Avery and Eddie both looked confused. I turned to Avery.

"Avery, you probably remember that I will be getting married in October. My brother is going to be my best man. I love him dearly, but I'm going against all protocol or wedding etiquette, whatever it's called. I'd like to have two best men at my wedding. Would you do me the honor of being one of my best men?"

Avery simply stated, "It would be my privilege, Mister Driscoll."

A word from the author...

I am a mature woman living in unincorporated Orange County, Florida, with my daughter, her family, four dogs, eleven chickens, five Nigerian Dwarf goats, and 40,000 Italian honey bees. Graduating summa cum laude from Youngstown University (when it was still Youngstown College), I was an art teacher for several years and now am a part-time staff accountant for a CPA firm, working primarily from home. My daughter, Wendelin Saunders, collaborated with me in the writing of *Let Freedom Ring*. Wendy passed away from cancer in 2009. She graduated from Illinois Benedictine College with a major in mathematics. Before her death, she and I ran a forever animal shelter home, which included forty dogs, twenty-two cats, and four rabbits.